Jennie Spallone

FATAL REACTION

A Mitzy Maven/Maggie O'Connor Mystery

D1455972

Published and printed in U.S.A
www.Create Space.com

ISBN:1495364615
ISBN-13:9781495364617

DEDICATION

I dedicate this book to my husband, children, and doggies who over the years have supported me with their unconditional love and encouragement. May this book acknowledge the parents, guardians, and teachers who wrestle with their own inner challenges to daily provide emotional sustenance to children with special needs.

ACKNOWLEDGMENTS

A heartfelt thanks to Diane Piron-Gelman for her great copy and developmental editing, Gin Kiser for an amazing book cover, Dr. Larry Tornquist, ED.D, for insights into organic brain disorders, former Kildeer Illinois Police Chief Jay Mills for providing clarification on procedure, and Indian Trails Library Writing Critique Group for helping me birth *Fatal Reaction* into reality! I also want to thank the following Raffle winners who created names, physical descriptions, or careers of characters in *Fatal Reaction*.

Danielle Elovzen, Temple Chai winner, chose Robert Elovzen (in loving memory) for the school union attorney.

Kim Lane, Princess Cruises winner, chose Joseph for the name of Ellie's father.

Ellen Cooperson, Writers Digest Conference winner, chose Sammy Cooper for the boy bullied by Ellie.

Marcia Cowing, Anshe Shalom winner, chose Norman for the name of Mitzy's special education colleague.

Bradley Boker, Romance Writers Convention winner, for using his own name as that of the English teacher's lover.

Eric Eligator, Temple Emanuel winner, chose his own first name for the detective.

Richard Herbstman, Printers Row winner, picked Ed Gimmel, the perfect name for a geometry teacher.

Marion Diamond chose her own name as that of Shirley Maven's long-time friend.

-Continued-

Michael Cloud, Love is Murder winner, conjured up Dexter James Stacey, the perfect name for a bank president.

Roxe Anne Peacock, Rockford Barnes & Noble winner, chose Camie Walker, for the young school social worker!

Phillip Frydendall tossed Kristin Fry onto the lapel of a corporate financial advisor.

Linda Lurvey chose Edna Jerguson for a health teacher.

Carol Modlin picked the perfect profession for Lynette LaFleur.

Janey Gottsman chose a great description of our English teacher. "Tall, brown hair, shy, determined to be a leader."

Chapter 1

Sammy peered into the bathroom mirror, watching helplessly as red blotches spread like connect-the-dots across his face. Intent on creating a safe distance from the eighth-grader shaking down the younger kids for lunch money, he'd scampered away from the bully. Once outside the lunchroom, he shoved his sandwich down his gut without checking its contents. *Big mistake!*

Crumpling the bag with the remains of the offensive sandwich, he slam-dunked it into the garbage can, which was already overflowing with used paper towels. He paced back and forth anxiously. *No way can I go to math now.* Focusing on how to extricate himself from his unfortunate dilemma, he failed to notice the entrance of a girl with purple-streaked hair and piercing blue eyes.

"Hey," came a mocking voice.

Sammy whirled around, his heart pounding. "What are you doing in the boys' bathroom?"

"Escorting you to math."

He shivered so hard, his teeth chattered. "Someone's going to see you and you'll be in big trouble."

"I don't think so."

Sirens went off in Sammy's head. He instinctively inched backwards. "What do you want?"

The girl eyed the urinals. Then she spat on the tiled floor. "You guys actually pee in these stinky things?"

A loud noise split the air.

"It's the bell. We're going to be late," Sammy said, suddenly eager to get to math class.

The girl flicked a blotch on his cheek. "You can run from the lunchroom, but you can't hide."

Sammy stepped backwards, puke clogging his throat.

"Think you're big shit, dissing me in class? You've got learning disabilities and you're only in seventh grade. You're not supposed to do better than me."

"I don't diss you."

"You calling me a liar?" Ellie asked, advancing on him. "You need to be taught a lesson."

A girl was beating him up. "Just let me get to math and I'll make more mistakes from now on," he pleaded.

"And get even more attention from Mr. Gimmel and Ms. Maven?"

"You make them hate you," Sammy mumbled.

"Excuse me?"

A wild daring took hold of him, and he kept going. "You act crazy in class."

She grabbed him and pushed him through the stall door. "I've had enough of your backtalk. Get in that stall and face the toilet."

Sammy froze, his feet heavy on the floor tiles. "What?"

"Do it!"

The next thing Sammy knew, he was on his knees, his face being smashed into cold clean water, then lifted. Sputtering through the waterfall, he looked up from his kneeling position in time to see Ellie slam past Tremayne, who'd just entered the bathroom.

"You okay, man?" Tremayne asked, helping Sammy to his feet.

Sammy stood there, tears flowing down his cheeks.

"Shit! A girl done that to you? Let's get her ass booted out of here."

"No, don't say anything," Sammy begged. "You'll only make it worse."

"I ain't afraid of nobody. You comin' to the principal or do I go myself?"

Sammy's eyes fell to the front of his shirt. "I'm dripping wet."

"You in or out?"

Sammy meekly followed the older boy out the bathroom door. He cast his eyes down as he drifted past the school custodian and his mop bucket.

Chapter 2

Only twenty minutes until first-period! Mitzy Maven yanked open the door to Room 206 and plopped her briefcase on the battered wooden desk. Then she slid into the ergonomically-correct computer chair and checked her staff email. Dozens of emails for Norman Stein, the behavior disorders teacher. Only a handful for "action lady." Not surprising. After all, she was the new kid on the block. For all the other teachers knew, the stylishly dressed learning disabilities specialist who inclined her head as she passed them in the hallway each morning could be harboring a Saturday Night Special in her rose-colored Prada.

Mitzy sighed as she scrolled through her messages. If only she could breathe in Norman's repertoire of disapproving body gestures. Nicknamed "Lion Man" by his cubs, the whiskered teacher who shared her classroom dealt with his behavior problem kids in a low-key manner that elicited respect from students and colleagues alike. At thirty years old, she possessed more real-life experience than Norman. Yet she remained clueless on how and when to exert her role as disciplinarian and imparter of all that was wise and true.

Teaching was Mitzy's second career. In her first vocational incarnation, she'd spent six years writing investigative reports on topics ranging from gang-bangers to disgruntled employees. She'd luxuriated in her news editor's grudging approval of a story and the resulting high-fives from colleagues. Even more affirming were the hundreds of emails "action lady" received from the public, praising her "hound dog ability to ferret out the truth."

There were also those intangibles so soothing to one's soul. Like zooming off to the nation's capital to interview a bigwig in Congress, then dining out on sushi or shrimp and charging it to her expense account.

Then the Enron and Tyco Toys scandals occurred, an endless barrage of corporate malfeasance that sent her cynicism barometer crashing through its glass ceiling. But as long as those monthly bills on her silver Nissan 350 Z kept rolling in, she'd felt chained to her job.

Her "earth to Mitzy" moment occurred while researching a feature story entitled, "Is Your School Really Providing Your Special Needs Child With Services Guaranteed By Law?" One out of every seven kids had learning disabilities or attention deficit disorder. When these students shuffled off the bus on the first day of school, they expected the new academic year to turn out exactly like those in the past years: failing grades, verbal put-downs, and negative self-talk. Their average to above-average IQ was a curse, for they recognized their inability to meet the expectations of parents and teachers.

Humbled by the courage of these students, Mitzy delved deeper. Apparently, Albert Einstein, Thomas Edison, Charles Darwin, Sir Isaac Newton, Galileo, Leonardo DaVinci, Michelangelo, Ronald Reagan, Tom Cruise, and Cher all had learning or attention problems. Even George W. Bush had a word-retrieval problem; yet he'd been re-elected president.

As a journalist, Mitzy had showered her interviewees with fake compassion. This time, however, tiny molecules of empathy for the families she was interviewing seeped into her consciousness. That, plus a traumatic Christmas Eve hostage incident, forced her to examine public service options previously undetected on her personal radar screen.

After stuffing her oversized duffel bag with the hundreds of printed-out emails she'd received following publication of her special education article, Mitzy submitted her resignation to the *Chicago Tribune*. Then she'd waved good-bye to her peers, tearfully traded in her Nissan for a Celica, and enrolled in National Louis University's eighteen-month Teaching Certificate Program.

Mitzy's gaze fell to the bottom subject line of an email from Roz Cohen, the learning disabilities supervisor at White Oaks Middle School. The email read: *Ellie Barge is scheduled to return to school on Wednesday. Her multidisciplinary parent-teacher conference will convene on Friday, 8:30 a.m.*

Mitzy smiled ruefully. Her two-week hiatus would soon be a blissful memory, like her ex-lover's caress.

"Hey."

Mitzy swiveled around in her chair. "I didn't hear you come in."

"Sorry. Didn't mean to interrupt your email reverie," said Norman Stein, the short, muscular special education teacher. He snapped open his briefcase and extracted a cascade of papers. "Say, what's happening with Ellie? Rumor has it she's coming back this week."

"Rumor's right. She's due back in school tomorrow."

"Bet you're excited."

"More like ambivalent," Mitzy confided. "Even though it's hell cajoling her to write an expository essay, I know where I stand with her. When she says 'I hate you,' I tell her she's stuck with me until she completes the goals in her individualized education plan. Besides, I'm fascinated by the insights she shares in her writing."

"Screw IEP goals! No way could I put up with her rude behavior."

Mitzy shrugged. "I've only got Ellie in the mornings so it's not so bad. Sammy's the real challenge. He talks in monosyllables and refuses to look me in the eye."

Norman laughed. "That behavior describes three-fourths of my students."

"I'm more concerned about Ellie's father ranting about the teachers persecuting his daughter," Mitzy said.

"Influential bank executive inflicts psychological horror on school staff," Norman joked. "Sounds like one of the investigative reports you used to write."

Mitzy flushed. "You read my stuff in the Tribune?"

"Well, yeah! You were kind of a household name, you know."

Mitzy struggled to mask the pleasurable warmth of recognition. "Too bad Ellie's dad vetoed placing her in a self-contained class for kids with behavior disorders. You'd work wonders with her."

"No thanks. I'm already on 'saving souls' overload with the kids I have," Norman said, plucking out materials from a tightly packed bookshelf. "Speaking of saving souls, weren't you doing more of that through the exposés you wrote?"

"I thought so," Mitzy said, "but after a bullet whizzed by me on Christmas Eve 2003, I decided there might be a safer way to save the world."

Norman whistled softly.

"Disgruntled postal worker cuffed my throat, dragging me backwards, while he's screaming, 'Christmas is the season for sharing. Everybody down on the ground!'"

"You must have been scared shitless."

"Next thing I know, the police are shouting for him to release me. He grabs me tighter, cutting off my air passage. 'You come any closer, she's dead!' My vision's blurry and I'm starting to black out. Then I hear 'boom, boom, boom'. People around me start screaming. His eyes are dazed. He loosens his grip. I fall to the floor. Then a final 'boom' and he's collapsed in a pool of blood. Dead."

"Whoa," Norman said. "You've been through a lot."

Mitzy shook herself from the nightmare.

"Understatement of the year."

A ruddy-faced student shuffled into the classroom and tossed a sweater-sized box on the desk. "Hey, Mr. Stein. Got a present for you."

"Thanks, Jimmy," Norman said. Expectation filled the air. "Lots of tape on there, huh?" Mitzy watched as Norman slid his finger around the box and removed the top, then waded through several pages of newspaper cartoons. "Great wrapping, Jim." Then he reached in and pulled out … a dead goldfish.

Mitzy gasped.

"Ringo died last night," Jimmy said. "He was my favorite pet. I was going to put him in my scrap book, but I thought you'd like to have him."

"Jim, what would I do with a dead goldfish?" Norman asked, his voice rising slightly.

Jimmy turned bright red. Tears welled up in his eyes and started streaming down his cheeks. "You're my favorite teacher. He was my favorite pet. You hate Ringo," he screamed, running for the door.

Mitzy shook her head and swiveled back to her computer screen. "Looks like you'd better shake a leg."

"Be gentle with yourself," Norman tossed over his shoulder as he lumbered into the resource center after Jimmy.

Chapter 3

Clutching her math packet, Mitzy hurried down the hall to Mr. Gimmel's geometry class. Ellie Barge's imminent return permeated her thoughts. The girl's father was a prime example of the vocal minority who voraciously complained about White Oaks Middle School not meeting their children's needs.

Joseph Barge was absent when his thirteen-year-old daughter acted the buffoon, refusing to do the work assigned by her classroom teachers. He'd been absent when Ellie dunked Sammy's head in the toilet bowl during lunch recess. But he was always present to berate his daughter's teachers for "turning her into a maniac."

Ellie had thwarted every behavior plan her teachers had attempted to implement. It didn't take a genius to figure out she required alternative high school placement in the fall, but White Oaks Middle School was in for an uphill battle. In earlier confrontations, he'd vehemently protested residential school placement for his daughter, but the alternative would be even more distasteful. Mitzy sighed. Everything would come to a head at Friday's IEP meeting.

~

Roz Cohen's hand trembled as she plucked Sammy Cooper and Ellie Barge's folders from the student files. "I've been their case manager since sixth grade, scheduling their classes, monitoring their IEP goals, and setting up annual reviews. It's been a real lifesaver having a professional writer onboard to assist."

"Glad to lift some of the burden," Mitzy said. "I have one concern I'd like to run by you."

"Shoot."

"When Ellie comes back, do we act like nothing happened?"

Roz shrugged out of her cardigan sweater. "I don't know why Mr. Ramiros keeps it so hot in here. The social worker's already talked to your kids about bullying, right?"

Mitzy nodded.

"Did she mention these kids went through the D.A.R.E. Program in fifth grade?"

"Yes, but she said the program focused on smoking, alcohol, and drug prevention."

"They also do a unit on bullying; how to not be a victim, how to report it, that sort of thing," Roz said.

"Would it be appropriate for Ellie to apologize to Sammy for instilling a fear factor?"

"While it's exciting to watch a reality show in which people confront their fears, that's expecting way too much of a junior high school kid."

"They have to learn that lesson somewhere," Mitzy protested.

"Unfortunately, utopia has no address in the classroom."

"Not even to acknowledge and apologize for hurting someone? We do that on Yom Kippur so G-d will inscribe us in the Book of Life."

"Admirable sentiment, but temples, churches, mosques, home, that's where those values need to be instilled."

"So an apology is out of the question?"

"You certainly can't orchestrate one."

"That reminds me of a feature story I wrote on character education in the Arlington Heights school system. Each week their schools teach a different value."

Roz winced as she massaged the side of her head. "Are you always this intense?"

Mitzy smiled demurely. No used alarming her supervisor.

Chapter 4

Ellie tossed her hair straightener into her backpack, along with her toothbrush. Her watch read 3:56 p.m. Her father would be here in four minutes to sign her out. He'd expect her to be prompt: no excuse that she'd been in the hospital for the last two weeks. She was happy to do his bidding. She couldn't wait to get home, slip into her pajamas, and curl up beneath her down comforter. Read all her poetry there. Dream all her dreams there. So unlike the Mr. Hyde personality her teachers criticized and her classmates feared. If they could only see the bruised puppy she really was.

At least she could confide in Aunt Fay, thanks to email. And the yellow flowered journal Ms. Maven had given her last Christmas was a real lifesaver. There she could express her feelings, which switched from red-hot to arctic freeze in milliseconds.

It had been so peaceful lying beneath the starched hospital sheets, light years from the screaming matches she regularly engaged in with her father. With Anya, her housekeeper, she could be really nice, but her father made her crazy with all his expectations. So much easier to immerse herself in Grand Theft Auto or practice her karate.

Ellie had started taking martial arts back in fifth grade, after some kids in her class called her the Pillsbury Doughboy. Her pediatrician called it baby fat, predicting it would fade with exercise, but her dad, a former army colonel, hadn't bought that explanation. He'd confined her to nine hundred calories a day, a strict regimen for a ten-year-old kid. She'd focused on turning her body into an indestructible weapon. After three years of working out, she was a muscular black belt.

Her formal karate lessons ended in seventh grade. Bristling from a particularly obnoxious encounter with another student, Ellie had asked her science teacher for a drinking pass. Moments before, the boy had asked to go to the bathroom. Ellie dawdled by the water fountain, biding her time. When he emerged from the bathroom, she'd spun around, spit a stream of water in his direction, and delivered a high kick to his nose. As she observed the scene that followed, Ellie felt separated from her physical body, everything happening in slow motion. Blood everywhere. The boy's cries muffled, as though emerging from the bottom of the ocean.

A few minutes later, Ellie felt her mind and body reconnect. No longer the butt of someone's smartass joke, her emotional fire extinguished, she'd calmly turned and walked back to the classroom. She was dissecting a frog when the principal burst through the door.

~

Sipping from a frosty mug of V8 Splash, Mitzy flung her Abercrombie shirt and jeans on the granite bathroom counter and slipped into the steamy bubble bath. Her eyelids fluttered shut and she breathed in deeply. Orange essence tantalized her senses, her fatigue slowly succumbing to the succulent array of rainbow-colored bubbles simmering atop her tummy. *Mmm. Delicious.*

As she splashed warm soap waves across her flat belly, Mitzy reveled in peace and contentment. Opening her eyes, she lazily observed the reflection of the sunset casting orange shadows across the freshly painted ceiling. How she loved the multihued colors that cascaded through the windows of her tiny studio apartment. So different from the spacious downtown loft she'd shared with her ex-lover, another investigative reporter. Though she'd only moved to the North Shore eight months ago, the life she'd shared with Juron was already oozing away at a rate more befitting a one-night stand than a long-term relationship.

Her former live-in arrangement was one secret Ellie's mother had failed to pry loose from her wandering tongue. Left with nothing of dire consequence to worry about, Shirley Maven had sunk her teeth into her newest passion: her daughter's physical safety. "Kickboxing emotionally disturbed kids won't work, you know."

"Mom, I told you. My caseload's mainly students with learning disabilities."

"How are you going to teach kids who can't learn?"

Mitzy shuffled the deck of cards and dealt a hand of gin rummy. "LD kids are as smart as you and me, but there's a big discrepancy between what they're capable of achieving and what they actually achieve in school."

"In plain English, please?"

"These kids function at one-and-a-half or more years below grade level in one or more subject areas."

"So a seventh-grade student could be working at grade level for everything except math."

"You've got it!" Mitzy leaned across the card table and gave her mom a squeeze.

"Darling, what you're doing is very altruistic, but how are you going to pay off your loft in the South Loop?" her mom asked as she perused her cards.

"I signed a lease on a studio apartment in downtown Evanston."

"Why are parents always the last to know?"

"I'm over twenty-one, Mom. I don't share every itsy-bit of information with you."

"I wouldn't define moving into a new apartment in a new

area as 'itsy-bitsy,' but that's just me. Janie must be pretty upset about having to move out, huh?"

"Jur—I mean Janie just got promoted to assistant editor. She'll be able to afford the loft on her own."

Mitzy glanced at her mother, but Shirley Maven was dealing another hand of gin rummy and didn't seem to have caught her slip of the tongue. "Making an impact on kids' lives is a lot more important than buying expensive clothes and hanging out at fancy nightclubs," Mitzy continued.

Eyeing her daughter's torn jeans, Shirley chortled. "I still can't get over you being into high fashion."

Mitzy put one hand on her hip. "That is so mean to say."

Her mother was conciliatory. "Sorry, sweetie, but you used to be such a tomboy."

"That was then, this is now."

Her mother's fiancé sauntered into the den. "Are my girls fighting again?"

Shirley was focusing on her cards. "We were talking loud, not arguing."

"Speak for yourself," Mitzy said wryly.

"Should I deal you in?"

"I'll just watch."

"Sometimes I feel like I'm playing solitaire, a game Mitzy's father loved, by the way."

Mitzy glanced up from her cards in time to see Harry's eyes flicker.

"Good going, Mom. Now you've made Uncle Harry feel bad about Dad."

"Your mother was just making conversation," Harry said, easing himself into a card table chair.

Shirley gathered all the cards. Then she reshuffled the deck and dealt herself and Mitzy a new hand. "Arnie's been gone twenty-three years this month," she said, a slight tremor in her voice.

"Can we not go there?" Mitzy pleaded, drawing a new card. She didn't need to become embroiled in one of her mother's flashbacks.

"Let's talk about something else, then." Shirley eyed

with interest the queen of hearts she'd drawn from the stack.

"How 'bout a joke," Harry said.

Mitzy's mother rolled her eyes. "Everything with this man is a joke."

"Lighten up, will you Shirl? Saw this one on You Tube. It's after hours and this guy craves a beer but the liquor store's closed. So he lifts a cinder block and heaves it at the store window. The cinder block bounces back, knocking him unconscious. Doofus didn't know the window was made of Plexi-Glass."

Mitzy giggled. "That guy for real?"

"Yep. Out in Arkansas."

Shirley tossed a jack of spades onto the table. "You two have a warped sense of humor, laughing at a guy who suffered a concussion."

Mitzy and Harry looked at each other and broke out in guffaws.

"Aw Shirl, you got no sense of humor," Harry kidded.

"Here I am, trying to keep my daughter from making a career disaster and all you want to do is joke around," Shirley said. She extracted an ace of hearts from the card deck, then threw out a jack of clubs. "Remember the time Mitzy wanted to join that cult after she got out of college? She was going to save the world."

"Um, I'm sitting right in front of you, Mom, you can speak to me in the first person. And that wasn't a cult, that was the Peace Corps!" Mitzy added the jack to her hand and threw out a six of diamonds.

Harry chuckled. "You nixed that idea when you found out there was no indoor plumbing where you were going."

Mitzy glanced at him. Had it really been that long since the confirmed bachelor had entered their lives, beaming hope and humor into their tedious existence? Distracting Shirley from shining the spotlight on her daughter's every move? Harry's unexpected negativity really stung.

"Thanks for the emotional support," she said, bopping her left knee up and down beneath the table. She did that when she felt stressed.

Shirley shook out a cigarette from her Marlboro Light package, then lit up. She inhaled deeply and blew smoke rings into the air. "We're not trying to put you down, darling. But be realistic. How can you help these kids most effectively? As an inexperienced new teacher or as a seasoned investigative reporter rooting out injustice?"

Mitzy threw her cards down on the table. "Gin! Writing about problems is not the same as being there, Mom, it just isn't. Decisions sometimes materialize by themselves, and this is one of them. At least I won't be in any life-threatening situations as a teacher."

"Oh yeah? How about the nanny in Winnetka who shot the teacher and a little kid?"

"That happened twenty years ago! Why can't you be happy for me?"

"I am happy for you," her mother had said, reshuffling the cards. "Another hand?"

Mitzy jumped to her feet. "I don't think so." She angrily marched out the door.

Back in her Evanston apartment, Mitzy stepped out of the cooled bath water and turban-wrapped a purple striped bath towel around her dripping hair. She slipped into an oversized tee shirt and sweatpants and hoisted herself onto the bathroom vanity counter. Then she took three deep breaths and assumed the cross-legged posture. Meditation to clear her mind.

Chapter 5

Joseph Barge glanced at himself in the hall mirror as he hunched over to adjust his gray pinstriped tie. At six foot four, he always seemed to be bending over, whether sliding into his Ferrari or laughing at his boss's asinine jokes. Yep, good old Joe was always around to pick up the pieces. Sometimes he wondered if that was the only reason he was still at Town Center Bank. Couldn't be the clients he'd been signing up lately.

With the economy creeping back to life, and miniscule interest given on savings and CD accounts, customers with big bucks had pulled their funds from TCB, investing them instead in middle to high-risk mutual funds. Many times he had urged his boss to consult with Paramount Financial about adding new services and products. But Dexter James Stacey was old school; pristine customer service would ensure their survival in the marketplace.

On the sly, the bank sales manager had run the teaming concept past Paramount's chief financial adviser. Kristen Fry had responded coldly at first. "When it comes to offering clients a varied portfolio, Town Center Bank is a dinosaur." Joe had grabbed his raincoat and started for the door. But the

CFA's next words had surprised him. "However, we would be interested in exploring various career options with you."

"Excuse me?"

"Word on the street is you're a genius when it comes to Internet sales. How does vice-president of Internet Marketing sound?"

"First you tear down my bank, and then you offer me a job? I don't think so."

"Would doubling your salary sweeten the pie, Mr. Barge?"

Joe's eyes widened.

"My partners and I have been watching you for some time. We're impressed by the quality service you offer your clients, as well as your technological know-how."

"I appreciate the offer."

"Good. Give it some thought and get back to me by Monday."

Joe nodded and sauntered out the door. Once outside, he whooped for joy. Doubling his salary? Vice-president of Internet Marketing. He felt like Michael Jordan dunking the winning basket. No more kowtowing to a boss from the Stone Age. Wait until he told Lani. Then his face paled. *She'll never know*, he thought mournfully. Since his wife's car crash five years ago, he couldn't drive past a McDonald's restaurant without pulling over to the curb, an excruciating pain attacking his gut.

Joe wondered if it would be kinder to take his comatose wife off life-support and place her in hospice. The cost of maintaining her at Glen Tree Nursing Home plus paying off the mortgage on their Lake Forest estate was staggering. Recently, he'd been flirting with the idea of driving off a bluff; his wife and daughter would receive the million-dollar life insurance policy. But now there was no need to take such drastic action. Paramount's job offer would flood his pocketbook.

Fortunately, his wife would remain unaware of Ellie's descent from loving child to abusive adolescent. That personality change was brought on by the accident. She'd never know the school planned to exile their daughter to a high school for kids with emotional disorders.

Joe hated what it would do to his reputation to have his kid placed in an alternative school. Rumors in their small town flowed like slime into every nook and cranny. Like the snake tattoo he'd gotten when he was young and thoughtless, gossip couldn't be erased. Paramount would rescind their offer if they got wind of it.

He massaged his throbbing forehead, recalling the verbal barbs he and Ellie had hurled at each other last night. Their encounter had started out calmly enough. His daughter had asked how his day at work was. He grunted a response and poured himself a Scotch.

She'd shyly lifted her bare arms to hug him. "I'm glad I'm home," she said in a little girl voice he'd not heard in five years.

"Uh huh," he'd said, giving her arms a quick pat. Then he saw the newly healed barbed-wire scars around her wrists. The knife slits she'd so carefully drawn made his own wrists burn, a constant reminder of their mutual grief.

He flung Ellie's arms from his neck and smashed the whiskey glass in the fireplace. "Next time you try to kill yourself, finish the job!"

His daughter crumpled in a heap at his feet. "Sometimes living hurts too much."

Compassion flitted through him like a gust of air. Then it was gone. "Don't talk to me about pain, little girl. You weren't so greedy for a fuckin' hamburger, your mother would be here now."

She started to sob uncontrollably. "I never meant to hurt her!"

"Well, you did a damn good job of it."

"I want to die!"

A familiar fear surged through Joe's chest. "You cold-hearted little bitch! Leave me alone without you or your mother?"

Ellie jumped to her feet and started pulling at her hair. "Nothing I do is ever right with you," she screamed. "I try so hard to be your little girl and you treat me like crap."

The sight of his only child struggling in the hell he'd rained down upon her extinguished his rage. His expression softened as he cupped her tear-drenched face in his hands and looked into her eyes. "The school wants me to sign off on your alternative placement papers tomorrow."

"You're going to tell them 'no' like usual, right?" she sniffled.

He scowled. "They're pretty steamed you pushed that kid's head in the toilet!"

Defiantly, she swiped the tears from her eyes. "He deserved it."

"You need help, honey."

"But the doctor says...."

Joe raised his hands. "Enough!"

Ellie pulled at his arm. "Please, Daddy, I'll be good," she screamed.

"Save it for Anya." He'd shaken her off and walked out the door.

Joe finished straightening his tie. Last night's confrontation had been over the top. He and Ellie were two islands set adrift. The harsh truth was that her incessant pestering had distracted his wife from the road that horror-filled night. But berating his daughter would not rouse Lana from her coma.

Wincing at the familiar burning in his gut, Joe fished out a third roll of Tums and downed the pack. He was turning into a goddamn asshole, rage his constant tour guide. It was time for him to take a stand. Go on prescription meds instead of self-medicating on booze. Get Ellie enrolled in a high school that would help her grow up and deal with life as it was. For once, he looked forward to the school meeting.

~

Mitzy eyed the clock as she helped Roz Cohen dole out teaching certificate renewal packets along the rectangular lunch table in the teachers' lounge. Fifteen minutes until first period lunch.

"My kids' parents have been awesome so far," Mitzy said.

"You're on honeymoon time, sweet cakes," Roz said. "White Oaks Middle School parents ferociously advocate for their children. Then there's the parents who advocate for their own self-interest."

Mitzy raised her eyebrows. "How so?"

"Ellie's a prime example of why severely disabled students require alternative academic settings from the get-go; both they and their regular education peers need to learn without constant disruption. But Joseph Barge refuses a more structured setting for his daughter."

"What's in it for him?"

"He maintains he'd be demoted or fired if his employer learned his daughter was crazy."

"That's crazy," Mitzy protested.

The LD supervisor leaned across the lunch table and stared into Mitzy's eyes. "You know what makes me crazy? That Barge's paranoia results in Ellie being taught by regular ed teachers with meager training in special education. That's why we're so glad you're here to provide resource room assistance, as well as team teach."

"I've been here eight months, and Ed and Lynette are still the only regular ed teachers receptive to me team teaching in their classrooms," Mitzy confided.

Roz snorted. "They still view you as the enemy."

Mitzy's eyes widened. "Because I teach using a multi-sensory approach so that all students can benefit?"

Roz patted her arm. "Veteran teachers are wary of yet another new program. They need your guidance in educating a wide spectrum of children with special needs. And those kids need you to safely guide them from a self-contained classroom like Norman's into the world of regular education."

Mitzy blanched. "I'm still a newbie here."

"Trust me. By next year, all those teachers will trust you with their cherished lesson plans and answer keys."

Mitzy slapped the last certificate on the table. "I really appreciate your encouragement."

Roz slammed her fist on the lunch table. "If they don't, I'll kill them!" The lunch bell rang. She marched out the door.

Mitzy's mouth flew open. What was up with Roz Cohen, the consummate professional? This was the wrong time to ponder such a strange utterance. Right now, Mitzy needed to prepare for tomorrow morning's parent-teacher conference with Joseph Barge and his daughter. Although she'd never been the object of his wrath, she trembled at the consequences of advocating for Ellie's alternative placement. Sometimes in life you just had to do the right thing. No way could a kid as socially impaired as Ellie Barge make it in a mainstream high school setting. Her student's fate would soon be sealed.

Chapter 6

Sammy buried his head under the red and black Bulls comforter, pretending to be asleep, but his mother's insistent voice invaded his thoughts.

"Come on, sweetie," Theresa Cooper wheedled. "We want to be on time for your IEP meeting."

"I'm not going to no special ed meeting," the boy murmured groggily.

"But honey, now that you're going into eighth grade, you have a say-so in your academic future."

Sammy groaned. "Why should I believe you when you tried to poison me with that stupid sandwich? My face was so blotchy, I looked like a clown."

"That was an accident. Today of all days, let's not fight." She tossed an outfit in his direction. "I bought you a new basketball jersey and khakis for the occasion."

Sammy angrily sat up in bed and threw the clothes back at his mother. "What part don't you understand? I'm not going."

"You should be happy. Come September, no more LD resource room for you. Mrs. Cohen says you'll be included in all regular ed classes."

"So?"

"The other kids won't look at you as 'special ed' anymore."

"What planet are you on?" Sammy sneered, picking at his big toenail. "Losing the label means shit. When was the last time one of those kids invited me to a party? The only reason they're moving me into the regular classroom is because the other special ed kids are a lot worse than me."

"Honey, you're exaggerating."

"Oh yeah? Allie repeats her words. Ms. Maven has to help Brandon complete every assignment. And Odalis argues with everybody."

Theresa sighed. "I don't want to argue with you. Just get dressed." She turned and left, quietly closing the door behind her.

Sammy hung his head. He hated making his mom so sad, but nothing ever turned out the way she promised. This year he'd been so excited to be mainstreamed into the regular classroom for algebra, his favorite subject in the universe. Two weeks later it was a whole different picture. The kids were nice enough. But by the time he was on problem four, the rest of the class had already finished the whole page.

From there, it only got worse. In science lab, his table partner had to read the steps to each experiment aloud. In social studies, Ms. Maven took notes for him because the teacher talked too fast. And in language arts, he was the only kid still having trouble writing a three-paragraph essay. Then one day after lunch, Ellie Barge had pushed his head in the toilet bowl! Even the custodian had given him a sorrowful look as he'd swished the long stringy mop around the toilet stall. How much humiliation could one kid take?

Sure, it would be cool to ditch all these freaks. But what if he couldn't handle being in regular classes all day? Was it worth the effort to try? What if he wound up back where he started? His parents and teachers would really be bent out of shape.

Sammy jerked to attention and checked the clock on his

dresser. His heart pounded. Ellie's conference! Only thirty minutes to change his life! Tossing his comforter to the floor, he quickly dressed and hurried downstairs.

~

Ellie swung open the double doors to WOMS and staggered down the empty hallway towards the conference room. From the corner of her eye, she noticed a lanky figure pushing a mop bucket at the other end of the hallway. The new custodian, who probably didn't speak a fucking word of English. She turned her back on him, dissing his wave. Then she checked her watch. Ten minutes until the bell rang. Had Sammy chickened out? If he didn't get here soon, she'd have to carry out the plan herself. It was all her father's fault.

The traitor had made his decision. Now she was making hers. She felt for the Nardil capsules in her jeans pocket. Though she pretended to sleep during Ms. LaFleur's language arts class, she'd paid close attention when they studied *Romeo and Juliet*. Unfortunately, there was no hottie involved in her plan.

Panic flooded her insides and a wave of dizziness volleyed her breathing back and forth. Not again! Since her mother's accident, she'd lost control over her mind and body. Stumbling down the empty hallway, she attempted to focus—breathe in, breathe out. Just like they taught in karate. She opened the office door and staggered past the front desk towards the conference rooms.

"Hey Ellie? What are you doing in the office so early?" A smiling face framed by brassy red hair peeked out from the Xerox room.

"Hey, Ms. Maven," Ellie said, smiling wanly. "Mr. Stein asked me to get him some blue computer paper from the work room."

"You look kind of shaky. Are you all right?"

"I'm fine. Just a little dizzy."

"No way are you fine." Motioning to a chair outside the nurse's office, Ms. Maven said, "Stay right here. The nurse should be coming in any minute now."

"But Mr. Stein's paper."

Her teacher smiled reassuringly at her. "Not a problem. I'll give it to him on my way back to the resource room."

Mumbling thanks, Ellie settled into the brown folding chair in the hallway. As soon as her special ed teacher disappeared back into the Xerox room, Ellie streaked out of the nurse's office.

~

Mitzy flicked on the conference room lights and settled comfortably into one of the eight steel-gray leather chairs that skirted a mammoth round table. A quick glance at her Tiffany watch indicated that in exactly five minutes, parents, staff members, and Ellie's psychologist would begin to arrive. Time was an ally; it provided structure. She'd often won high school swim meet trophies and medals by a tenth of a second. An assortment of gold, silver, and bronze trophies still sat huddled atop the old thirty-two-inch television in her mom's living room.

Time had likewise worked for her as a newspaper journalist. Whether her interviewee was a fleeing politician or an alimony-delinquent father, her final zinger question often resulted in a home run.

Now here she was, five minutes early, sitting in an empty, sterile, overlit conference room waiting for yet another student's academic future to be determined. Restless, she drummed her French-manicured nails on the table, then slid a tapered fingernail along the crevice of a Krispy Krème Donuts box.

The door squeaked open. "Goodies at a parent-teacher conference. That's a surprise," joked Lynette LaFleur, the eighth-grade English teacher, as she set down her can of Dr. Pepper across from Mitzy.

"There's a donut shop down the block from my house. Thought we might placate Ellie's dad with some of these." Mitzy grinned as she settled back into her maroon leather chair. "Gotta save one for Mr. Ramiros. One of my kids vomited after lunch yesterday. He was right on it."

"You're so lucky to have good custodians here. I used to teach at this day school on the North Shore. The custodians acted as elitist as the parents!"

Mitzy laughed. "Speaking of elitist, bet you can't wait to face Mr. Barge this morning."

Lynette grimaced. "That man gives me panic attacks. No wonder Ellie's so messed up."

"What did you think of Jerry's pep rally yesterday?" Mitzy asked.

"He's right. When Mr. Barge comes in, we all need to be on the same page. Ellie's emotional needs will better be served at an alternative school."

"This morning she was so helpful, coming into the office early to get paper for Norman."

The English teacher frowned. "Norman knows students aren't allowed in the office until the first bell rings."

The door swung open once more. Mitzy smiled as her mentor breezed into the room. "Good morning, scouts." Roz dropped several stapled packets on the table. "Here's copies of Ellie's current IEP. Take one."

The LD supervisor had indeed regained her geniality. For that, Mitzy was grateful. Half-heartedly flipping through the annual academic and behavioral achievement goals, whose contents she'd written, Mitzy watched Principal Jerry Fillmore, the social worker, and Ellie's psychologist all file into the room. They nonchalantly greeted the rest of the staff members as they picked up their packets and took their seats around the table.

Ellie's father sauntered into the conference room a few minutes later, a Starbucks cup in hand, sporting a broad grin instead of his usual cold dark glare. If Ellie hadn't once mentioned her father's strict aversion to prescription and non-prescription drugs, Mitzy would have attributed his expression to a cocaine high. Maybe he was just hopped up on coffee.

"Welcome, everyone," Jerry Fillmore said. "Today we're here to review Ellie's IEP goals and determine high school placement for the fall." He paused, waiting for a confrontational response from Mr. Barge, but today the man was quietly reviewing the written academic and behavioral goals for his daughter.

His expression wary, the principal continued. "Ms. LaFleur will share Ellie's progress in language arts."

The deafening bong of the fire alarm cut him off.

"Everyone follow me," Fillmore said, with a startled look. A shuffle of chairs and a quick exit ensued. Suddenly Fillmore made a U-turn. "Ms. Cohen, I left something in the conference room. Can you get everybody out?"

Roz nodded. "No problem."

~

Jerry Fillmore briskly re-entered the conference room. "There you are," he mumbled, grabbing the Barge folder. Then he noticed the Starbucks coffee cup.

~

The sun was turning the last frost to mush and little green buds were pushing through their pods on the willow tree overlooking the playground. He'd really done it, Ellie rejoiced, swinging her legs up to the sky and back down again. Sammy Cooper had actually pulled the fire alarm, just like she told him to. For once, something went the way she planned. She laughed aloud, remembering when her dad used to push her on the swings, the wind dancing beneath her dress. "Reach for the stars," her dad would shout as she swung her little legs up, up into the atmosphere. He'd be right behind her, laughing at her squeals of delight, like he hadn't a care in the world. They'd come home to her mom's welcoming embrace and the smell of corned beef and cabbage.

Ellie dragged her feet against the gravel stones to slow her velocity. The day her mother was wheeled into Glen Tree Nursing Home was the day the sun vanished from the Barge family's solar system. She'd been in third grade when a semi-trailer totaled her mother's BMW. Five years later, her energetic, fun-loving mother remained hooked up to life support. Ellie wondered how her mother could have left them even though her body was lying in the bed, her chest moving up and down in machine rhythm.

At first, Ellie and her dad visited her mom two nights a week. But once she figured out Lani Barge had chosen to punish her by neither opening her eyes nor speaking to her, Ellie locked herself in her room on those nights. Her dad screamed at her to go with him, but she refused to give in.

On the nights he didn't visit her mom, Ellie's dad staggered home late from work, smelling like cigarettes and beer. He'd hired a Russian nanny, Anya, to look after her. In that time span, Ellie morphed from an exuberant little kid into a cynical teenager who had the kind of fun her father and teachers criticized.

Even when her father totally lost it, he never played the alternative high school card. But last night he'd shattered her soul. In her grief, a crystal of hope had flashed, like an angel, before her eyes. She'd seized that crystal like a parachute jumper whose chute opens at the last second. Tonight she'd talk to her father in a clear, calm voice. Make him realize she didn't need an alternative school. Convince him she could be the good little girl he craved.

A little while later, Ellie left the playground. She sauntered up the circular driveway and reentered the school, a smile on her face.

A small group of teachers and the school social worker huddled outside the principal's office, solemnly watching her.

Principal Fillmore broke the silence. "Where have you been, Ellie?"

"Fire drill."

"That was forty-five minutes ago."

"It was such a nice day, I went to the playground."

"You left the school without permission."

Ellie felt her neck muscles relax. This was familiar territory. "Sorry."

"We need to talk," Mr. Fillmore said. He ushered Ms. Walker and her through the small crowd and into his office. Then he shut the door.

Ellie thrust her hands in her jeans pockets. She wondered why the social worker was joining them.

"I'm suspended for leaving the premises, right?" she asked, sensing something amiss.

"We'll place that on the back burner for now," the principal said.

"Huh?" Ellie felt nervous. The social worker was moving in close.

"Ellie, I regret to tell you something has happened to your father," Mr. Fillmore said.

Ellie's heart pounded in her ears. "What are you talking about?"

"You were supposed to attend your IEP meeting," Ms. Walker said.

"I overslept," she lied. Back in fifth grade D.A.R.E. class, a police officer had taught Ellie and her classmates about cold pricklies. Her father's rage-soaked words had echoed inside her brain many a time. But the cold prickles of fear popping up on her arms now were a million times more scary. "Where's my dad?"

The principal's expression was grim. "Your father was at the meeting when the fire alarm went off."

The social worker spoke. "Shortly after we returned to the conference room, your father keeled over."

"What does that mean?" Ellie asked frantically.

"He stopped breathing, Ellie." Ms. Walker reached out to hug her. "The paramedics attempted to resuscitate him."

Ellie slid away from the social worker's arms. "He's dead?" she shrieked.

The principal silently nodded.

Ellie felt the room spinning as she fell to the floor.

~

Ellie awoke to the bright lights of the nurse's office. Ms. Walker sat by the door, wearing a concerned expression. "Welcome back, honey," she said.

The nurse handed Ellie a paper cup of water. "This will make you feel better." Ellie drank thirstily.

"We pulled your contact card," the nurse said. "Your Aunt Fay is on her way."

"Would you like to talk?" the social worker asked.

Ellie attempted to process what was going on, but her brain was operating on slow.

"Ellie?"

Feeling the sweet pull of unconsciousness, Ellie shut her eyes and sank into oblivion.

Chapter 7

Mitzy grunted while she did her 50-lb. leg lifts. "Her father's sitting across from me, poised to sign off on the alternative high school forms, when the fire alarm goes off. When we return to the conference room, he keels over, dead."

Detective Maggie O'Connor rhythmically puffed in and out as she lifted 100-lb. barbells in an up-down pattern. "Your school liason officer radio in for a detective?"

"Yep. They were all busy protecting a US senator who was in town, so Officer Franco ended up questioning all the staff members who'd attended the IEP meeting. He attempted to talk to Ellie after they revived her, but she refused to speak." It felt good to talk to Maggie about it. Who would have expected her hostage rescuer to become her best friend?

"This the girl whose mom's in a nursing home?"

"Uh, huh," Mitzy said, gritting her teeth as she lifted her legs one last time.

"Tough break. Who's watching the kid?"

"Her aunt came up from Chicago."

"Considering the circumstances, she should be placed on suicide watch."

Mitzy jerked upright. "Why?"

"You've complained this kid's behavioral outbursts have escalated since the fall, yet her father, whom you've described as antagonistic towards the teaching staff, refuses to send her to an alternative high school. Suddenly Dad comes to the IEP meeting, all smiles, eager to sign the appropriate forms. Why'd he change his mind?"

"What's that have to do with his death?"

"Think about what this girl's endured. Comatose mother in nursing home. Nanny who speaks little English. Father who's a tyrant. Did Ellie want to attend an alternative high school? Up until now, Dad was her ally, protecting her from going. But something or someone caused him to have a change of heart."

"She thought her actions forced his hand," Mitzy said.

"And if she got Daddy really mad the night before the conference, she subconsciously thinks she killed him. She's quiet now because she's numb, but she should be watched so she doesn't cut herself."

"You should have been a psychologist instead of a detective. She does have a history of cutting."

"Okay, then." Maggie wiped the sweat from her brow and then checked her sports watch. "Gotta go. I'm on night shift."

Waving goodbye to her friend, Mitzy leaned back into the weights. She'd be seeing her student soon enough, at her father's wake.

~

Ellie stared at the daffodils and violets outside her lilac-curtained bedroom window and felt her body melt into her red bean bag chair, like something from *Wicked!*. A trickle of laughter welled up inside as she visualized Ms. Maven acting out the evil witch's demise. Then shame rushed through her, hot and painful. How obscene to be happy, even for a moment, when her father lay at the morgue. She deserved to melt away. Her laughter swirled down the toilet.

It's not my fault he's dead, she screamed inside her head. *I didn't mean to kill him!*

Her face wet from tears, Ellie hugged the child-sized circus bear her father had won for her in a carnival shooting game. After her mom's accident, she'd poked the bear's eyes out. But she still clung to him at night, when the darkness threatened to swallow her up. Now her father had disappeared into that darkness.

She glanced at the yellow-flowered journal lying on the computer, a Christmas gift from Ms. Maven. During the last five months, she'd confided her anguish and joys onto those lined pages as an extension of the emails she shared with her aunt. But the argument with her dad the night before his death had shocked her to the core and she'd vowed that frenzied night of journal writing would be her last; her heart had become a cadaver. In her mind, she saw Ms. Maven give her a thumbs-up on the analogy.

Frowning, she pinched herself.

You don't get to have happy memories.

She would write no more.

Silently, she continued to stare out her bedroom window.

Chapter 8

The early morning sun reflected through the sparkling window panes in the teachers' lounge. "We're in damage control mode right now," Principal Fillmore was warning the eighth grade team. Along with Mitzy and Roz Cohen, the team included Lynette LaFleur, Bill Haisley the science teacher, Ed Gimmel who taught math, Edna Jurgenson the health teacher, and the PE teacher. "If the media attempts to interview any of you, immediately refer them to Robert Elovsin, our attorney."

Mitzy frowned as she twisted the top off her Fruitopia. As a former newspaper reporter, that "us against them" attitude set her blood boiling. What secrets were they hiding, she'd wonder, then get busy ferreting out the truth. An institution or company that laid its cards down at the start seldom had to worry about her hound-dog research.

"Don't be intimidated by police presence in the building," Fillmore went on. "If an officer questions you, give the same line you give the media."

Mitzy sipped from her bottle. "Do we actually know what caused Mr. Barge's death?"

"Rumor is gas fumes from an unlit pilot light on the

kitchen stove leaked into the conference room," Bill Haisley said.

"At this point, all we know is that an autopsy was performed," the principal answered.

"Shit," mumbled Roz Cohen. "This damn laptop's down again."

Mitzy furtively glanced around the room. Everybody was too caught up in the discussion to notice Roz's faux pas.

"At least we don't have to worry about asbestos in the walls," the health teacher observed. "This building's only twenty years old."

"Several of my students didn't show up today," Lynette said.

"Ellie looked like a statue at the wake." That remark came from the young gym teacher the kids nicknamed Mr. C. "Really freaked out the kids."

"For all those reasons, we need to keep the lid on," Fillmore said. "Any more questions or comments? Okay, then. Hang in there and try to have a good morning. Ms. Walker will run a traumatic stress group first through fifth periods in the library. Now would be a good time to sign your class up for an open spot. That's all." He turned to leave.

Mitzy fell into step with Roz as they headed back to class. "We're scheduled for first period."

Roz nodded.

"Sounds like things are going to get pretty fishbowl around here?"

"You ain't seen nothing yet, kiddo."

"How bad does it get?"

"Mr. Barge to the tenth power. When President Bush first signed the No Child Left Behind Act, teachers and parents really bought into the idea of one-hundred percent of students achieving ten-percent growth per year. All hell broke loose when the majority of English as a Second Language and special education students failed to reach that goal. It was like Armageddon around here, with parent advocates, lawsuits, and media accusations. That's why Jerry is extra cautious this time around."

"A father suffers a heart attack at his daughter's parent-teacher conference. Isn't that a pretty open and shut case?"

Roz stopped and stared at her. "Like Jerry said, the autopsy isn't back yet."

The first period bell rang. The LD supervisor disappeared into her office.

~

Hector Ramiros secured the main door of the school. Then he sauntered towards his Dodge Durango, shaking off the image he'd carried with him since the fire drill this morning. Better not to think about it. After all, he wasn't absolutely sure who he'd seen entering the conference room after it had emptied. Even if he could identify that person from the opposite end of the hall, the consequences could only bring grief to him and his family. That was why he'd left Mexico in the first place, so they wouldn't have to deal with corrupt police pounding on their door.

A purple-pink horizon greeted him as he left the school, but he had no worries about the reception he'd receive when he finally arrived home. His wife and children, they appreciated his hard work. He was proud to provide for his family, to set an example of the blessed life that they, through hard work, could earn in the United States. The perfume of flowering bushes would have smelled as sweet in the country of his origin, yet Hector had no regrets about leaving Mexico for the promise of a financially stable existence for his children, as well as a better education for their inquisitive minds.

Hector fired the ignition. The Dodge Durango grunted in response. He could put it off no longer. This weekend he'd have to replace the battery. An expense they did not need, yet necessary to support the one wage earner in the family. Not that being a custodian was a hardship. He enjoyed keeping the school clean. He did not mind lending an ear to students having a hard time of it with their families, teachers, or kids at school.

He shrugged off his thin jacket, rolled down the windows and slowly drove past the ornate mansions of Lake Forest. The scenery changed drastically as he entered the humbler town of Highwood, with its smaller ranch-style houses. Back in Mexico, they had a saying that money did not make the man. Rich or poor, all children needed love, attention, and respect to blossom into the souls they were meant to be. And rich or poor, no parent had all the answers on how to bring about that result. His heart went out to the girl whose father had died. A girl with curses on her lips. An unhappy child.

Enough sadness! The cool air on his bare arms made his skin tingle. Hector envisioned a half-dozen tortillas on his plate, with an extra helping of beans and rice when he arrived home. His wife Maria's tortilla, flauta, and quesadilla fillings were always a surprise. When he worked overtime for several days in a row, Maria rolled in seasoned steak and cheese. On nights when money had been spent on clothing or household goods, chopped corn and butter or mustard was the filling of the day. One night his fifteen year-old son made a ketchup milk shake for dinner. A strange dish, but Hector took pride in his family's resourcefulness.

Twelve minutes later, Hector pulled into the long driveway of a green ranch house with a well-manicured front yard. No sooner did he emerge from the car than his three younger children ran toward him across the grass and threw their little arms around his legs. Who'd have thought that at his age, he'd have six-year-old triplets? "Papa, papa!"

Then his wife came outside, their one-year-old Chihuahua attempting to leap from her arms. She gave him a quick peck on his cheek. "Hungry?"

Hector kissed her lips. "*Si.*"

They went inside. Maria put the dog down and removed the covers from several pots on the stove. Then she set his tortillas and a bottle of beer before him. "The kids couldn't wait any longer. I had to feed them."

"Come sit, come sit," he said, and tore into the food.

"José," she called to their teenage son, "go take the little ones to the playground."

"*Sì, mama.*" Two minutes later they heard the back door slam.

Hector was impressed. Usually his son put up all kinds of excuses for not taking care of his siblings. But tonight he didn't want to get caught in a discussion about the kids, for something else was on his mind.

Chapter 9

Mitzy discreetly maneuvered her chair into the student circle, between Anita and Tremayne. "How many of you have attended a wake or funeral?" Camie Walker, the social worker, asked.

Four out of seven hands shot up, a fifth hand wavering halfway. Camie glanced at Enrique, a tall, thin boy in red Nikes. "I got there just as they were carting out the body," he said.

Mitzy shuddered.

"Whose body was that?" Camie asked.

"My uncle. He was sliced up pretty bad."

A collective "Ewww!" rose from the gathered students.

"His gang killed him 'cause he tried to break free."

"That must have been awful for you."

"Hell, it was a lot worse for my four little cousins."

"Anyone else?"

"When I was in fourth grade, my hamster died," Sammy said. "Me and my neighbor, Petey, had a funeral service. Then we buried it in my backyard."

"How did your hamster's death make you feel?"

"Bad."

"Anyone else?"

Anita, a cocoa-skinned girl with corn-rowed hair, raised her hand. "My granddaddy's funeral."

"How old were you?"

"Eleven."

"How did that make you feel?"

"Kind of sad, kind of not sad."

"Sounds like you had mixed feelings about your granddad."

She nodded. "Sometimes he be real nice, but he be real strange when he do his drugs."

"Anyone else?"

Shana raised her hand. "I went to my mom's friend's funeral when she died of breast cancer. That was so sad."

"Was your mom close to her?"

"They were best friends since high school."

Camie looked around the circle. "What feelings do you experience when a loved one dies?"

"You feel like crap," Enrique said. Mitzy gave him a warning glance.

"Like your arm's been cut off," Anita said.

"You want to be cuddled like a kitten," Shana said.

"Like the sky's turned black and it's only breakfast," Sammy said.

Mitzy stifled a powerful urge to share how she'd felt when her father died: like she'd been buried alive. She didn't want to display her vulnerability. The purpose of this group session was to help her students work through their feelings about the death of Ellie's father.

Camie went on. "You've described some powerful visual images of what it's like to lose a loved one."

"What's a visual image?" Enrique asked.

Mitzy groaned. How many times had they gone over that in class?

"A visual image is a picture you form in your mind that reminds you of a word or event," Camie explained. "How many of you are going to Ellie's dad's wake tonight?"

A few hands tentatively went up.

"Do you think Ellie might be experiencing some of the feelings you just described?"

A couple of kids nodded.

"How would you feel if only a few friends came to support you when your loved one died?"

"We're not talkin' friends here, Miss Walker," Tremayne said.

"Oh?"

"Ellie bosses kids around," Shana said.

"In social studies, she acts like a fool," Enrique said.

Mitzy smiled to herself. Definitely a case of calling the kettle black.

Tony spoke up. "Ellie's not that bad. She plays a great game of chess."

"Remember what she did to you, Sammy?" Anita asked, turning towards the only seventh grader in the class.

Sammy nodded, his eyes focused on a pencil scratch on his desk. Mitzy guessed he was wishing they'd all forget about the toilet bowl incident.

"What I'm hearing you say is that if someone does not act in a socially acceptable way, she doesn't deserve to be supported in her time of need," Camie said.

"Right!" Tremayne said.

"Is that how all of you feel?"

Five out of seven heads nodded.

"How would you feel if you were Ellie and everyone deserted you?"

"Inside, I'd know I deserved it," Anita said.

"Did you ever hear of the word 'compassion'?"

"Something to do with caring?" Jordan asked.

Camie nodded. "Does every human being deserve compassion?"

"My dad says we should care more for the people who get hurt and less for the people who do the hurting," Shana said.

"But Ellie's our classmate," Tony said. "We have to care about her."

"Then you all can go to the wake. I ain't going. She be

nothing but a bitch to me," Anita said.

"Maybe she never learned how to be nice to people," Jordan said.

Enrique shrugged. "That's not my problem."

"Maybe she can't see how she comes across to other people because she's so into her own problems," Shana said.

"I'm going to Ellie's dad's wake because it's the right thing to do," Sammy said softly.

All eyes turned to him in surprise.

Tony broke the long silence. "Anyone need a ride tonight?"

The hands of seven students went up.

Mitzy and Camie Walker exchanged jubilant glances.

~

From the far side of the room, Mitzy watched as a few dozen people trickled into the funeral parlor to pay their last respects to Joseph Barge.

"Not too popular, huh?" Maggie O'Connor said.

"This is the second night," Mitzy said. "My students stopped by earlier."

"His daughter seems really out of it."

Mitzy's heart went out to the slight figure slumped in her armchair, her aunt's arm encircling her. She flashed back to a similar moment of being consoled while her own father lay in an oak casket. At the time he was killed, she'd been much younger than her student.

In Jewish tradition, a funeral took place within twenty-four hours of death, its time frame elongated only by an intervening holiday or out-of-town family members unable to book a flight. Her father's funeral had been the very next day, an open casket immediately preceding the service.

Recently introduced then to Fashion Barbie, Mitzy had been unable to understand why she had to wear a plain black dress instead of her new pink-flowered dress. Even more weird was that her mother, aunt, and grandma were all dressed in black, with snips of black ribbon pinned to their clothing.

She hadn't understood the Hebrew words that flowed like gibberish from the rabbi's mouth as he led the mourners in prayer. Why were her uncle and cousin, along with a few of her parents' friends, coming up to the microphone to talk about her daddy? She'd tugged on her mommy's arm, whispering that she wanted to go up there and sing daddy's favorite song, "When You're Happy, the Whole World Smiles With You". Shirley Maven had broken into tears at her request. Alarmed by her mother's outburst, Mitzy had started crying, too. Then Florence, her Aunt Joanie's mom, had enfolded Mitzy and her mother in a loving embrace, just as Ellie's aunt was doing right now. A lone tear fell on Mitzy's cheek.

"You all right, Mitz?" Maggie asked, concerned.

"Just some unbeckoned memories."

"Reflecting on your own dad's funeral?"

Mitzy glanced up at her friend. "How'd you know?"

"You shut down and turned pale. I'm an expert at body language."

Mitzy clutched the rhinestone keychain in her coat pocket. "When did I ever mention the death of my father to you?"

"Your memory's like a sieve, you know that?" her friend joked.

Mitzy frowned back. Those were the exact words she used on her mom all the time.

"Field Museum. King Tut exhibit."

Mitzy heaved a sigh of relief. She let go of the keychain, letting it escape to a hidden cranny in the dark pocket. "Oh my gosh. I remember. I was going nutso investigating a serial killer story. We met for lunch at Subway. It was the last day of the King Tut exhibit. I gave some kind of lame excuse to my editor. Then you and I high-tailed it over to the museum."

"Bingo," Maggie said.

"When I was in pre-school, we did this fun project on mummies. My dad came to school and demonstrated the procedure by wrapping me up in a sheet."

"We didn't study mummies until fifth grade."

"I was in a progressive school," Mitzy joked.

"Your father was a pharmacist and a mummy expert?" Maggie teased.

"He was intrigued by the special compounds they used to keep the bodies from decaying. I can still smell the fresh spring scent of that newly cleaned sheet being draped around my body."

"Listen, we've been here a half-hour. You ready to split for dinner?"

"Sure," Mitzy said. Glancing back one more time at the open casket, she noticed a bearded gentleman, accompanied by a younger man, kneeling and making the sign of the Cross. Despite the warm spring night, both men wore wool suits and ties. Recognition crossed her face.

"Why are you stopping?" Maggie asked impatiently.

"Those two men are from the bank Ellie's father worked at. I saw the older guy at a tsunami relief fund-raiser our middle school hosted. He's the bank president."

"How 'bout the younger guy?"

"He's one of the personal bankers," Mitzy said. "Helped me open a checking account."

"They need to be interviewed as character witnesses for Barge," Maggie said.

"Ellie's father could have died of natural causes, you know."

"I'm betting someone did him in, be it a business colleague or his daughter," Maggie said.

"Why would Ellie harm her own father?" Mitzy scoffed.

"Only time will tell," Maggie said, ominously rattling her car keys.

Chapter 10

Mitzy turned away from the white board. "A helping verb is the main verb's best buddy."

A chorus of snickers rang out among the seven students. Mitzy ignored it. "Sometimes you and your best friend are inseparable, right?

"What's that mean?" Anita asked, fiddling with one of her cornrowed braids.

Mitzy turned back to the white board and wrote inseparable. She circled the in. "Remember what this prefix means?"

"'Not'," Tony called out.

"Correct." Mitzy smiled. "Now what does 'separable' mean?"

"Hell, you s'posed to know that, Ms. Maven!" Enrique said.

"First warning on swears, Enrique. If we take off the – able suffix, we have 'separ', as in sep—"

"Separate," Tony yelled.

Mitzy gave a thumbs-up. "So inseparable means—"

"Not separate." Anita's answer was quick and confident.

Mitzy felt the flash of excitement that always came when

one of her students "got" it. "Yes! You and your best friend are inseparable; you go everywhere together," she said. "The helping verb and main verb are usually inseparable, too; first we see the helping verb in the sentence, then the main verb. But sometimes the helping verb and the main verb don't sit side by side in a sentence. Can you think of a time when you and your best friend went somewhere together but didn't stay next to each other once you arrived?"

"When Gina and I went to Walgreens yesterday after school, she looked in one row for vinegar and salt potato chips and I looked in another row for ring pops," Shana said.

"So you and your friend were in the same store at the same time but searched different aisles," Mitzy said.

Shana nodded.

"In the same way, the helping verb and main verb can be in the same sentence but separated."

"Just like Ellie and her dad," came Jordan's voice from the back of the room.

"That don't make sense," Tremayne said, swiveling around in his chair, "'cause they're not in the same place at the same time."

"Does 'inseparable' only refer to a place you can see?" Mitzy asked.

"There you go again," Enrique said, "askin' questions you already know the answer to."

Mitzy stared back at him solemnly.

He shrugged. "Okay, okay, just sayin'—"

"If your mom is working and you're in school, you could be inseparable from her in your mind," Jordan said.

"No you can't, dummy, 'cause you're not in the same place," Enrique said.

"That's two, Enrique," Mitzy said.

"You can love your mom and think of her anytime you want," Anita said.

"That's what I mean," Jordan called. "Ellie's inseparable from her dad because she thinks about him all the time, even though he's up in Heaven."

"Or Hell," Enrique quipped.

"That's three," Mitzy told him. "Indoor lunch today."

"Aw, man!"

"And she's not talking to anybody because she's hurting inside," Jordan finished.

The lunch bell rang and the students streamed out the door. Mitzy shook her head. These kids' insights were amazing.

Chapter 11

Mitzy cut the ignition on her silver Celica and headed towards the Barges' white brick house. Only in a future incarnation could she afford one of the mansions she'd just driven past. Many Lake Forest mansions existed within cut-back forests. However, the Barges' long winding driveway was unusually barren of trees, giving the grand structure beyond a look of vulnerability. A lone pick-up truck stood parked outside the three-car garage. The twittering of birds flying high overhead briefly punctured the silence. *What an isolated place for a kid to grow up*, Mitzy thought as she rapped on the front door.

The door swung open. "I help you?" asked a tall young woman with friendly eyes.

Mitzy held out a hand. "I'm Mitzy Maven, Ellie's teacher. Just wanted to see how she's doing."

The woman's handclasp was firm. "I am Anya, her nanny. Ellie talk about you so much. Please, come in," she said, ushering Mitzy into a large foyer. "I tell her you here."

While she waited, Mitzy silently marveled at the potpourri of colorful Chinese vases that graced the expansive room, each one propped on a Plexi-Glass pedestal of varied height. With this kind of lifestyle to maintain, it wasn't surprising Mr. Barge wanted to protect his executive position at the bank. His sudden attitude shift in sending Ellie to an alternative high school made no sense.

The nanny reappeared. "I am sorry, but Ellie see no one today."

Mitzy's eyes widened.

"Since funeral, Ellie not speak. She hardly move or eat. I thought you coming make her happy, but she still not speak."

"May I try talking to her?"

Anya looked doubtful. "Okay, but only for short time. Her aunt be home soon. She not want anyone to see Ellie like this."

Mitzy nodded. "Lead the way."

~

Mitzy stifled a gasp at the sight of Ellie. The girl sat staring out her bedroom window, a vacant look in her eyes, rocking slightly. Her purple-streaked hair was stringy and matted.

"Hey, sweetie," Mitzy said, laying her palm on the huddled figure's shoulder. Ellie shrank from her touch. Mitzy fished something from her pocket. "Here's a new wristband for your collection," she said, placing a pink breast cancer awareness band in the girl's lap. "Your health teacher says she's going to be doing the three-day walk. Isn't that sweet? Where's all your other bands?"

No response. The gift lay untouched.

"Well, I just came to tell you we all miss you. It's too quiet around school without you! I know you must feel awful about your dad's death. But you have to get better so you can come back soon. Enrique's got nobody to keep him in line."

Ellie stared out the window, rocking to and fro.

Mitzy noticed the yellow-flowered journal she'd bought Ellie for Christmas. "Shall I hand you your journal?" No response. On impulse, she picked up the diary and ruffled quickly through it. The first third or so was filled with Ellie's handwriting, right up to a few days before her father's death. After that, the pages were blank. Mitzy frowned, wondering why Ellie had stopped writing then. Not that it was her business, she reminded herself. Even troubled kids like Ellie needed a private life. She put the diary down and patted Ellie's arm. "Okay, I'll see you real soon."

As she turned to leave, Mitzy saw three prescription drug bottles sticking out from beneath the girl's bed. Listening for the nanny's footsteps, Mitzy knelt to read the name on the labels. *Elizabeth Barge*.

Ellie said her father flushed her meds down the toilet after a few weeks so she wouldn't get addicted. The results had been a roller coaster of brighter, more alert days coupled with duller, head-in-arms hours. Could Ellie's catatonic state be caused by an adverse reaction to her most recent prescription, Mitzy wondered. She'd check out drug interactions online.

~

The voice on the other end of Detective Eric Whelan's phone was his old friend and colleague, Maggie O'Connor. "How is it we graduate from the Police Academy and I end up with gang-bangers while you end up with the rich and famous in Lake Forest?"

"Great to hear your voice, too, Magpie," Whelan said, balancing the phone on his shoulder as he used his free hand to enter computer data on a recent mugging. "From what I've been reading, sounds like south State Street's undergone a transformation since I last saw you."

"Oh yeah. Cabrini Green's been cleaned up and turned into a senior citizen building. Chinatown's alive again, with young middle and upper-class Asians moving back into the city. Lots of new townhouse construction going on just west of State Street. And Arne Duncan contracted out another elementary school to be turned into a privately run charter school."

"Pacific Gardens Mission still there?" Eric asked.

"Nope. Jones Magnet High School was busting at the seams; needed to house their students there. Another neighborhood finally accepted the Mission."

"Bet that went over real big with the neighbors."

"Way big. Listen, I need a favor," Maggie said.

"Hang on. I got to lay you down for one sec."

"Ooh! Sounds exciting!"

"Still the kidder." Eric chuckled as he rummaged around for a notepad, then picked up the telephone again. "Go for it."

"I got a friend named Mitzy Maven. She's a special education teacher up in your neck of the woods. The father of one of her eighth-grade students was about to sign his daughter into an alternative high school for emotionally disturbed kids when he suddenly kicked the bucket. You familiar with the case?"

"You struck pay dirt. I'm the detective assigned."

"No shit! Cause of death?"

"Coroner should be receiving the tox report in a couple of weeks."

"You guys suspect foul play?" Maggie asked.

"Why the sudden interest?"

"How'd the autopsy play out?"

She hadn't answered his question. He decided to give her a little of what she wanted, see what was up. "The vic was a six-foot-four, two hundred twenty-five pound, forty-year-old white male presenting with an enlarged heart and damaged liver."

"How about the urine screening?"

"Evidence of drugs and alcohol in his system. Too soon to tell whether or not the drugs were self-administered."

"Interviewed any suspects yet?"

"Stopped by the house to interview the nanny about the father's physical and mental condition before his death. She doesn't speak English too well, so that was a bust."

"Bringing in a translator?"

"I'm going to give it one more shot first."

"How 'bout the daughter?"

"She's been in a catatonic state since her father died."

"Mitzy mentioned the kid was totally unresponsive when she visited," Maggie said. "How about the mother's sister?" The detective whistled. "You do have all the particulars, don't you? Talked to Fay Shimmer on the telephone. She only visits the daughter at Christmas. Brother-in-law got verbally abusive when he'd been drinking, and he'd been drinking a lot since his wife's accident."

"If that toxicology report comes back conclusive, would you be willing to bring Mitzy in on the investigation?"

"Hang on. Wasn't she the reporter who wrote exposés for the Trib? No way do I want a civilian, a journalist, in on anything."

"Thought you'd want to talk to the girl's teacher, gain some insights. That's what Mitzy does now. She's a teacher."

He thought about it a minute. Normally, he wouldn't even consider Maggie's proposal. But Maggie was a good cop, with well-honed people instincts. That she trusted this Mitzy Maven meant something, and a little extra information never hurt. "Fine. But there better be no leaks to jeopardize the investigation."

"Hey, it's your call. I'll arrange a meeting. And next time you get downtown, give me a ring. I'll give you a private tour of Millenium Park."

"Sweet."

Chapter 12

"This pizza's a beast," Mitzy said, licking her lips as she lifted her third slice from the serving dish.

"Oh, yeah." Maggie O'Connor raised her mug of root beer.

"The owner reserves this back room for uniforms, so we get a lot done without interruption," Detective Whelan said.

"So how can I be of service to the Lake Forest Police Department, Detective?" Mitzy asked, munching on the crisp crust with gusto while she stared into his aquamarine eyes. That really was the only word for them. "Blue" didn't cut it. Mitzy shook herself. She was here in her professional capacity, not to scope out good-looking guys.

"Maggie suggested I bring you in on consult. As Ellie Barge's special education teacher, you might be able to offer the police some insights on the girl."

"You always invite your consults out for pizza?"

"You've got me to thank for that," Maggie said. "I told Eric that when you worked for the Tribune, you dug up some impressive information that helped me close the files on a couple of cases that just wouldn't go away."

"That's a fact, though I never divulged my sources,"

Mitzy said proudly.

"You're no longer bound by those ties, right?" Eric asked.

Mitzy paused, half-eaten pizza slice in her hand. "Detective, I went into teaching because I wanted to make a difference in the lives of children who are misunderstood by society. I'll be glad to share with you what I know about Ellie, but I should tell you now that I won't be your mole."

"Then it wouldn't interest you to know that the toxicology report pointed to a cocktail of drugs as Joseph Barge's cause of death," the detective said.

"Prescription drugs?"

"Come on, I'm giving you as much as I can."

"Self-administered?"

"Can't say right now."

Mitzy recalled the bottles of prescription drugs sticking out from beneath Ellie's bed, yet her voice remained neutral. "Mr. Barge was a volatile character. He stormed into the English teacher's class on several occasions, demanding she step out into the hall to discuss his daughter's most recent 'F'. He'd go ballistic at Ellie and her nanny after visiting his comatose wife in the nursing home. Then he'd down several rolls of Tums. He was also being considered for a plush job at one of his bank's competitors. Could have overdosed due to stress."

"Barge's most recent physical occurred a year ago. At that time, he was diagnosed with hypertension but refused high blood pressure meds."

"What did the autopsy reveal?" Mitzy asked.

Whelan gave her a warning look. "If you leak any of this to the press, I will deny this conversation took place."

Mitzy grabbed a crumpled napkin and swiped at her greasy lips. "Look, Detective, I'm doing you a favor here, not the other way around. You either you want me in or out."

Whelan paused for a moment, as if in internal debate. Finally he continued. "The forensic pathologist's report indicated Barge suffered from a hidden history of coronary artery disease; his constant heartburn fits that profile. He was also a heavy drinker, exemplified by a yellow tint to his eyes, yellowish purple bruising, and a liver gone kaput. A significant amount of drugs remained in his bloodstream because his liver couldn't filter it out. How would you describe his behavior the morning of the meeting?"

"At peace with the world!" Mitzy said, with a flippant edge.

Whelan caught it. "Atypical of his usual conduct at school?"

"Definitely."

"I'm guessing Barge was already sloshed by the time he arrived at the meeting," Maggie said. "The drinking and drugs produced a fatal reaction."

"The coroner's report indicated Barge consumed the drugs sometime that morning," Whelan said.

"You think somebody slipped them to him?" Mitzy said, with a sense of unease.

"It's plausible."

She shook off the thought that came to her then. "That's crazy."

Whelan shrugged. "I need you to keep your eyes and ears open at school. You said you visited the girl at her house. If you get her to open up, contact me ASAP."

"Will do." Mitzy reached into her purse for some cash. Detective Whelan grabbed the check. "Pizza's on me."

"Big spender," Maggie teased, grabbing her jacket.

~

Detective Whelan leaned forward on the paisley living room couch. "Thanks for talking to me again, Anya," he said. "I'm sorry to tell you your employer died of a drug overdose."

Anya looked briefly confused. "What this mean?"

"He swallowed too many pills. Did he take drugs of any kind?"

She frowned and shook her head. "*Nyet*. Mr. Barge, he say drugs bad."

"Even prescription drugs?"

Anya nodded.

"Does his daughter take prescription medication?"

She looked at him warily. "Sometimes yes, sometimes no."

"What kind?"

Anya shrugged. "With mother in nursing home, she depressed."

"Was she taking antidepressants?"

"Doctor prescribe, but father not want her get hooked."

"How would you describe Ellie's behavior at home?"

"Around me, Ellie good girl. Around father, always fight. No fight with fists, fight with words."

"What did Ellie and her father argue about?"

"Ellie tell father medicine make her not so angry and sad. Concentrate better at school. Father say she too lazy to control herself, not need drugs. Sometimes he get so mad and dump pills down toilet."

"They argue about anything else?"

Anya leaned forward. "School want Ellie to go to high school for bad girls. Father not want her to go. Bad if people at his work find out. But her behavior get so bad, he change his mind."

"Did Ellie and her father argue the night before the school meeting?"

Anya wrung her hands. "They scream so loud, I hear what they say. Ellie just come home from hospital. Father mad because she cut herself on wrist again. Tell her next time do better job."

"How did Ellie react?"

"She scream and cry."

"Then what happened?"

"Her father say he send her to school where she get help. She beg him: 'Please, I be good.' He say discussion is over, leave room."

"Then what happened?"

"Ellie start kicking tables, punching walls. Then run to her room. Slam door. Not come out until morning."

The detective stood, extending his hand. "Thank you for talking to me again."

"Any way I help, I help," Anya said, walking him to the front porch.

~

After the policeman's car pulled away from the curb, Anya backtracked into the house and headed for Ellie's bedroom. The door was open. Ellie was curled up in a furry red blanket, watching the sun descend into the trees. "Ellie?" Anya said, placing her hands on the girl's shoulders. The child did not respond. "Policeman say your papa die of taking too much pills." Still no response. "No worry. They find out who did this and put them in jail." Silence. "Your aunt be home soon. I go make lamb chops and mashed potatoes."

As Anya turned to leave, she saw three prescription bottles sticking out from beneath Ellie's bed. She opened the bottles and peered inside. A thin layer of colored pills lay at the bottom of each container.

Anya gawked at Ellie. Swiping tears from her eyes, she flushed the remaining pills down the toilet. Back in Ellie's room, she grabbed a permanent marking pen from Ellie's computer desk, blackened all three prescription labels, and stuffed the bottles in her pants pockets. "No worry. Garbage man come tomorrow," she reassured Ellie. "You be safe."

Anya glanced at the yellow-flowered diary on the computer desk. Ellie moved, almost imperceptibly. Anya opened the diary. Her tears blurred the pages as she read. She flipped to the two pages preceding the morning conference. Only a clean tear returned her gaze.

Chapter 13

Mitzy reclined on a green striped patio chair and sipped iced tea from one of her mother's china cups. A warm spring breeze flowed in from the lake, canceling out the hullabaloo of mid-day traffic fourteen stories below. She peered down at Lake Shore Drive. "The Edgewater area's a great location."

A pair of reading glasses perched low on her nose, Shirley Maven reclined on a white chaise lounge, jotting notes in a journal. "So you say every time you visit."

"Serving tea in china cups is real cute, too."

"Hey, if it's good enough for the English, it's good enough for me."

"I don't think they drink iced tea in teacups," Mitzy said, chuckling.

"If they can't take a joke, the hell with them," Shirley said, inserting numbered bookmarks into various pages of an oversized book.

Lifting the delicate cup again, Mitzy noted its detailed decoration. "You buy this tea set at an antique shop?"

Shirley looked up from what she was doing. "Actually, this was Grandma Rose's. She gave it to me right before she moved to Arizona to live with Joanie and your cousins."

"How come I never saw it before?"

"It was stuffed in one of our unopened boxes in the storage room."

"It's gotta be fifteen years since we moved from West Rogers Park, Mom."

"Unpacking trinkets doesn't rank high on my list of priorities."

"Why unpack the tea set after all these years?"

"Afternoon tea."

Her mother never did anything without an ulterior motive. "Just like that?"

"What, I can't be spontaneous?" Shirley inquired, her eyes open wide. "Remember the time I went parachute jumping with Harry?"

"You changed your mind at the last minute," Mitzy said.

"Did I?"

"Now look who's blanking. So what gives about the tea set?"

Shirley laid her book on the patio table, then curled up on the chaise lounge. "Your Grandma Rose's husband, Nathan, died before you were born. He was an M.P. stationed in China during World War II."

"M.P.?"

"Military Police. He was decorated by the army for uncovering a major drug smuggling operation. Several of his army buddies died in that bust."

"Interesting, but what's that have to do with the tea set?"

"While they were stationed in China, lots of army servicemen traded cigarettes and gold coins for mementos. Your grandfather brought Grandma Rose this tea set, a gold-plated vase, and a peacock decorated fruit plate."

"You still have the vase and plate?"

Shirley shook her head. "Grandma Rose gave those to Joanie's family." She paused. "Aren't you the least bit curious about what I've been working on today?"

"Not really. I'm just enjoying the day and trying not to think about all the homework I need to grade when I get home."

Shirley squinted through the sun at her. "Glad you changed careers midstream?"

Mitzy shot her a guarded look. Shirley enveloped herself in so many social causes, she seldom dug into her daughter's daily scores and defeats. "I'm glad I went into teaching. I just didn't realize writing lesson plans would prove so time-consuming. It's a challenge to design and measure academic and behavioral goals for each special ed kid."

"The first year in a new career's a big *tsimmes*," Shirley said. "I remember when I first started downtown at Morris B. Sachs after your father died. All the other sales ladies had worked in retail for years. Me, I had to bluff my way with customers until I got the hang of it. Standing on my feet all day was no great shakes, either."

"How'd you get along with the other sales staff?" Mitzy asked.

"Most of the women had married kids. They worked part-time for extra spending money or because they were bored; they had their husbands' salaries to live on. I was a widow who worked full-time with a young child at home to support."

"It's tricky striking up a relationship with these teachers, even after all these months," Mitzy mumbled.

"You don't know from tricky," Shirley said. "In salary plus commission sales, it's dog-eat-dog. If I had to cut in line to take a prosperous-looking customer, so be it. Sure, the other women complained, but I was driven to bring home the bucks so I could take care of you."

"Even if I didn't have a penny to my name, I would never butt in on another person's sale," Mitzy said.

"May you never find yourself in dire straits that force you to test your self-righteous attitude," her mother said wryly.

Mitzy jumped to her feet. "Just remembered I gotta go walk the dog."

"You don't own a dog."

"I'm heading over to the Anti-Cruelty Society right

now."

"Does your new condo association allow pets?"

"If not, I'll move."

"You'll do anything not to visit with your mother," Shirley complained.

Mitzy pounded her hand on the patio table. "Your sarcastic remarks make me nuts."

"What did I say?"

"That I'm a self-righteous bitch."

"I'd never say that to your face, honey," her mother joked.

Without another word, Mitzy headed for the door.

Shirley called after her, sounding miffed. "I apologize, oh sensitive one. While we're talking apologies, it's interesting that you're curious about a simple tea set, but don't give a hoot about what's going on with me."

A faint twinge of guilt reached down to Mitzy's toes. When was the last time she'd bothered to inquire into her mom's day, except to wheedle a dinner invite from her and Harry? "Of course I'm interested in what you're up to."

"I'm going to pretend you asked what I was working on today," Shirley said brightly.

"Quit blowing soap bubbles into a tidal wave, Mom," Mitzy said.

Shirley waved an oversized book in her daughter's face. "This book has the names of Jewish immigrants who came to this country through Ellis Island from 1900 to 1913."

"Why would you want that information?" Mitzy asked.

Shirley put her hands on her hips. "One guess."

"Um, you think our ancestors are a part of that group?"

"Exactly!" Shirley said.

"And this is important why?"

Shirley thumbed through the book. "Our little family needs to find its links."

"You could research our family tree on the Internet," Mitzy suggested.

"You gonna help me?"

"When I get a chance."

"Just like how you're going to make time to teach me how to access my email?"

"You could take a couple of classes at Wright Junior College."

"And feel more computer ignorant than I already do? I don't think so."

Mitzy eyed her mother's book. "How're you going to get information on peddlers who lived in the shtetls of Russia?"

Her mother smiled wistfully. "I want to connect with living relatives who would be the sons, daughters, and grandchildren of those immigrants who came through Ellis Island."

"Does Harry know you're researching this stuff?"

Shirley shook her head. "He'd say, 'Haven't you got better things to do?' "

"Why are you suddenly all over this ancestry stuff?"

"It's time for you to go buy that dog."

"Mother!"

"Wish me well, like you wanted me to do last August when you started your new teaching job."

That dagger hit its mark. Would she ever be able to respond to her mother as an adult instead of a rebellious adolescent? "Of course I care about you realizing your dreams in your old age…"

"Old age?" her mother said angrily.

Mitzy sighed. "Sorry, Mom. What can I do to help?"

Chapter 14

Mitzy maneuvered her soup and salad tray past the hordes of middle-school students scurrying into the cafeteria. After nudging open the door to the teacher's lounge, she slid into the last unoccupied chair.

A few welcoming smiles acknowledged her entrance. The other eighth-grade teachers were deep in conversation.

"Since Mr. Barge's death, the school nurse has gotten frantic calls from several parents about the air quality in the school," Edna Jurgenson said.

"Air quality is nothing to sneeze at, excuse the pun," Bill Haisley said. "Last week, up in Wauconda, dozens of middle school students and teachers were sent to the emergency room, complaining of dizziness and nausea."

"I remember reading about that in The Countryside Reminder." The comment came from Lynette LaFleur. "Exhaust fumes from a vending machine truck. Driver left the engine running while he restocked the machines."

"But no one else in the conference room became ill except Ellie's dad," Mitzy said, sprinkling bleu cheese on her romaine lettuce.

"That doesn't stop people from overreacting." Sour-faced

Ed Gimmel spoke as he chowed down on a roast beef sandwich.

The teacher's lounge door swung open. Principal Jerry Fillmore came in and took a seat at the lunch table. He looked tense, Mitzy noticed. "I just had a call from the police. The toxicology report indicates that Mr. Barge's death was drug-related."

Bill's eyes widened. "Legal or illegal drugs?"

Mitzy restrained herself from contributing to the conversation. It wasn't her place to share what Eric Whelan had told her.

"Prescription drugs mixed with alcohol."

"Do they think he committed suicide?" Ed asked.

"The police didn't say. This revelation affects us in two ways. First, we don't want to be the bearers of rumors. So we keep our mouths shut and refer all parent inquiries to the LFPD."

"What about when the papers get hold of it?" Edna asked.

"Even more so. We don't need any lawsuits over maligning the man's character."

"Although his character was easy to malign," Lynette said wryly.

Fillmore folded his arms on the table. "I realize that for some of you, Mr. Barge was your worst nightmare. But it's imperative we keep our personal opinions to ourselves when it comes to dealing with parents. That said, the police have notified me that a Detective Eric Whelan will be on school premises to interview teaching staff."

"Just the people who attended the IEP meeting?" Mitzy asked.

"That remains to be seen," Fillmore said. "You'll be notified whether or not you're going to be interviewed again. We'll have our attorney present during each interview, so you can safely share any information that might help the police in their investigation."

"So I can tell them how he banged on my classroom door, demanding to talk about his daughter's academic performance in health class?" Edna said. "My students had nightmares!"

"And how he explained away the pranks his daughter pulled?" Bill asked.

"The attorney will tell you what you can and can't say in that regard," Fillmore said. "You'll probably be advised not to go into particulars since Ellie is a minor. But general comments concerning her overall behavior can be shared."

"After all, the conference was addressing alternative high school placement for next year," Bill said.

Fillmore stood up. "I'll do my best to keep you informed."

~

As the other teachers somberly headed back towards their classrooms, Mitzy and Lynette stayed behind. "It's so nice having a planning period following lunch," Mitzy said.

"I'll say," Lynette agreed. "There's just so much of *The Outsiders* one can teach before you feel like strangling someone."

"In an upper-class suburb like Lake Forest, doing a class novel on a bunch of rebellious misfits is kind of odd."

"It was either that or *Maniac McGee*."

"How long have you been teaching?" Mitzy asked.

"This year makes ten."

"Have you been here all that time?"

Lynette shook her head. "I taught at the North Shore Cawley Day School for the first six years. We performed everything from *Romeo and Juliet* to original plays written by the students."

'Why didn't you stay?" Mitzy asked as she ran a pink marking pen over student worksheets.

"Higher salaries in the public schools, coupled with a change in administration."

"It must be a lot different here for you."

Lynette scowled. "With No Child Left Behind, there's too much emphasis on test-taking and not enough emphasis on poetry and literature. There's more to language arts than being able to write an acceptable expository, narrative, or persuasive essay."

"I read that Illinois standardized tests will now focus on math and science," Mitzy said.

"Which is strange, as college essays by incoming freshman have been abysmal. Actually, it's parents like Joseph Barge who make me consider permanently dropping out of teaching."

"His daughter's a hellion. But I admire her creativity."

Lynette nodded enthusiastically. "She's produced some topnotch essays. And her daily journals have been amazing."

Mitzy's ears perked up. "What does she write about?"

She noted Lynette's sudden shift in posture. "I can't share Ellie's journal entries with you. I promise the kids that whatever they write is private."

"Would you adhere to that promise if a dangerous event was looming?"

Lynette's eyes pierced her. "I'm offended you'd even ask such a question. If a student was in danger, I'd immediately seek out the school social worker."

"Sorry. I just wondered if Ellie had written anything about her relationship with her dad."

"Like I said, if she had indicated something nasty was going on, I would have taken action."

"So Ellie's behavior wasn't a problem for you," Mitzy said.

"Au contraire. Her behavior is what caused those 'F's."

"Can a student's grade be lowered solely due to behavior?"

"We're talking about a student who consistently fails to turn in her homework. A student who sits with her head down in class, randomly choosing which classroom assignments to complete. A student whose sarcastic comments constantly disrupt learning. A student who dunked a boy's head in the toilet bowl."

"A student on an individual education plan," Mitzy

reminded her.

"Who was being transferred to an alternative high school because her IEP didn't suffice," Lynette said.

"I'm confused. First you give the girl a glowing report, then you trash her?"

"I appreciate her writing talent, that's all."

"So her dad was constantly in your face."

"Twice during fall semester."

"Must have been scary as hell for you."

The English teacher shrugged.

"How did he get past the front office each time?"

"First time, the front office buzzed him in the school. He acted polite, yet reserved. But once he entered my classroom, he turned belligerent. Jerry escorted him out of the school.

"One month later, Ellie's father snuck in through the cafeteria door when the Mariott truck unloaded lunch. This time, he harassed both the health teacher and me. Jerry had him arrested and jailed overnight. He advised me to lock my door."

Mitzy looked up from grading papers. "How did that work out?"

"Sometimes I'd forget if I was running late to class. But I needn't have worried. His final verbal assault was directed at the physical ed teacher. This spring, Mr. C had the kids running laps outside in the back when Ellie's dad showed up."

"I bet you're relieved that chapter in your life is closed."

"I'll say! I'd wake up at three o'clock in the morning, panicking so much I could hardly breathe. The doctor finally put me on anti-anxiety drugs."

Mitzy scrutinized her. "Which ones?"

"I tried several, but they made me too dizzy. I need to stay sharp for my kids."

"Now that Ellie's father is dead, have the panic attacks stopped?"

Lynette gave a beatific smile. "I know I shouldn't be saying this," she confided, "but I've been sleeping like a baby who's nursed at the breast."

The bell rang. The door swung open. Another shift of teachers coming in for lunch.

Mitzy and Lynette hurried out the door.

~

It was 5:00 p.m. by the time Mitzy waved goodnight to the school custodian—did she imagine he'd hesitated a minute, like he wanted to tell her something?—and packed up the papers she'd been grading. Just as well he was leaving, and so was she. She felt too exhausted for a tête a tête. And a little depressed as well. No cute guy to rush home to. No dog to feed. With ten-hour workdays plus nightly lesson planning, any soul mate would die of neglect. Exactly two hundred and sixty-five days ago, Juron had vamoosed, too, but that wasn't really his fault. Investigative reporters had no set schedule. They couldn't pluck underworld characters from a midday stroll on the beach. Like worms emerging after a summer storm, the setting had to be just right for the corrupt to show their faces in public. Lucky for him, he'd moved up the food chain.

Though her teaching contract didn't require her to stay past 4:00 p.m., Mitzy enjoyed the late afternoon solitude as she leisurely marked her students' homework. Now, that task finished, her thoughts drifted towards the tall, blond, blue-eyed Detective Whelan. Would his lips taste of juicy caramel, the same as her chocolate-skinned ex-lover? Or would they feel dry and salty in the style of a guy who transferred all his passion into sleuthing? As in past months, she resolutely attempted to shed unbidden images of her and Juron lying on the beach, wrapped in each other's arms, as they shared tidbits of information about stories they were investigating. Those forbidden exchanges only deepened their mutual infatuation.

Quickly she reined in her memories, focusing instead on today's luncheon conversation with Ellie's English teacher. She never would have figured Lynette LaFleur for being on anti-anxiety meds because of Joseph Barge. Unwillingly,

Mitzy recalled those barely filled prescription drug bottles peeking from Beneath Ellie Barge's bed. Ellie had felt betrayed at her father's decision to pack her off to an alternative high school after he'd promised to do otherwise. For a girl with no immediate support system except a housekeeper and a comatose mother, her father's about-face must have felt unbearable.

If her aunt hadn't claimed her, Ellie would be in the clutches of the Department of Children and Family Services this very minute. Poor kid; her whole family decimated by tragedy.

Mitzy's thoughts went back to Joseph Barge. Did he purposely overdose? She bet Anya had some answers. On her first visit to the Barge home, Mitzy had been so preoccupied with Ellie's well-being, she hadn't thought to question the nanny about her own relationship with the girl's father.

She glanced at her watch, and then headed into the parking lot aglow in waning sunlight. Time for a return visit.

Chapter 15

Mitzy slurped cold purple broth from a white china bowl. "This borscht is marvelous!"

Ellie sat across the kitchen table, her bowl untouched.

"You have before?" Anya asked.

"On hot summer nights, my mother would serve borscht with sour cream for Shabbat. But she served it with shredded beets, no potatoes."

"What mean Shabbat?"

"Every Friday night at sundown starts the Jewish Sabbath. You have such a lovely accent. Where are you from?"

"Ukraine. I come here seven years ago. Ellie's family my first nanny job."

"You have family in Ukraine?" Mitzy asked, dabbing at her mouth with a paper napkin.

Anya nodded. "My daughter live there with my parents."

"That must be difficult for you to be apart," Mitzy said gently.

"It okay. My mom and dad both on pension. Love having granddaughter with them. In a few years, my daughter will go University of Moscow, study engineering."

"She must be a very smart girl."

Anya's eyes glowed at the compliment. "I am very proud of her."

"What did you do in Ukraine?"

Anya looked down. "I work at electrical factory, but plant close. No work. I think better to support family by come here."

"So you applied to be a nanny?"

"*Nyet*. When I first come to United States, my mother's cousin in Chicago take me in. I go to junior college, study computer. But not like data entry, so I search for something else. I help cousin take care of children during daytime. I like working with kids, but not enough money to send home to family. Cousin put nanny ad for me in Russian newspaper."

"How did that work out?" asked Mitzy.

"I nanny for two years Russian family in Skokie but the mother lose job and no longer can pay. So sad I must leave four-year-old girl."

"Did you try contacting a nanny agency?"

Anya shook her head. "Little girl's father and Ellie's father both work at bank in Lake Forest. When he find out they let me go, he interview me for nanny and housekeeper."

"Was Mr. Barge a difficult employer?"

Anya shrugged, though her tense expression belied the casual gesture. "At first, *nyet*. His wife just come into coma. He so sad. He stay with wife at nursing home, or in basement drinking. No time with daughter." She looked away nervously. "But then he start talk to me. Put arm around me. Kiss hair. Treat me like woman, not nanny."

Mitzy's eyes widened. "How did you feel about that?"

Anya shuddered. "Like frog teasing fly. I am fly."

Sympathy flooded through Mitzy. "Did you report him to the police?"

Anya shook her head. "I not want to lose job. Besides, police not always come to rescue."

Mitzy stared at her. "What do you mean?"

Anya pursed her lips. "In Ukraine, police take people to

jail if report someone."

"It's different here."

"Still, I am afraid."

"Did you tell anybody?"

"Not until soon."

Mitzy frowned, puzzled, then worked out what Anya must have meant. "You mean recently?" she asked.

Anya nodded. "Mr. Barge touch more and more, but I never say anything because I scared I be sent back to Ukraine. Also, I worry Ellie be with him alone. Shouting not good for child."

"So who did you finally tell?" Mitzy asked.

"Ellie's aunt come here last Christmas when Mr. Barge not home. I crying. She ask me what is wrong. I go past my fear and tell her Mr. Barge do bad things to me."

"How did she react?"

Anya swallowed. She looked ready to cry. "She look so mad, I think she kill somebody. She pick up phone, say she call police. I beg her not to call. Only make life harder for her niece. I am all Ellie has here."

"What happened then?"

"Ellie's aunt still hold phone in her hand. She ask—" Anya paused as if steeling herself, then went on. "She ask if Mr. Barge touch his daughter the way he touch me."

Mitzy felt faint. "And did he?"

Emphatically, Anya shook her head. "Mr. Barge love his daughter. When he drink, he use bad words. Yell and scream, but never hurt her that way."

Thank G-d, Mitzy thought. "What did Ellie's aunt say?"

"She put phone down and say from now on she email with Ellie. She be watching how Mr. Barge treat me and niece. If gets really bad, she do what she need to do."

"Did she say what she'd do?"

Anya shrugged, then got up and cleared away the borscht bowls. "You excuse me, I go now."

Mitzy stood as well. "I didn't mean to upset you, Anya. Again, thanks for your hospitality. Oh, Ellie, I forgot to give you something." She dug into her pocket, pulled out a blue "power" wristband and placed it on Ellie's lap. "Got this at the health club yesterday and thought you'd like it."

Ellie didn't respond. Not so much as a glance, or even the twitch of a muscle.

Unsettled, Mitzy followed Anya to the front door. "Is Ellie taking any medication for her condition?"

The nanny shook her head as she swung open the heavy wooden door. A melodic "Hello!" greeted them from the perfumed night air.

"Good evening, Ms. Fay," Anya replied. Mitzy noticed the nanny's behavior brighten as she stepped back, allowing the woman to enter.

Ms. Fay must be Fay Shimmer, Ellie's aunt. Trim and middle-aged, resplendent in a rainbow-colored poncho, she gave Mitzy an expectant glance.

Mitzy thrust out her hand. "My name is Mitzy Maven. I'm Ellie's special education teacher. I just stopped by to see how she's doing."

Smiling, Fay Shimmer shook Mitzy's hand. "And Anya plied you with her famous borscht?"

"Something like that," Mitzy said, smiling back.

Fay raised her poncho over her head and handed it to the nanny. Beneath it she wore an embroidered blouse and a flowing, three-tiered skirt. "Would you please hang this in my room, Anya?"

With a smile, the nanny disappeared down the hall.

Patting her short red hair into place, Fay gestured for Mitzy to join her in the living room. "Anya mentioned you first visited my niece last week. Have you noticed any change in her behavior?"

"Not really," Mitzy said.

Fay sank down on the sleek white couch. After a moment, Mitzy joined her. "Ellie's psychiatrist wants me to admit her to a residential treatment center, but I'm wary of institutions. My poor sister has been in a nursing home for the last five years. Little good it's done her."

The comment made Mitzy realize how Ellie's catatonia mimicked her mother's comatose state. Perhaps, in her own way, Ellie was trying to connect with her mother now that her father was gone.

"Last week," Fay confided, "her doctor started her on an intravenous drip of Benzodiazepine, but that's had little effect. He says the next step is electro-convulsive therapy."

Mitzy shivered. "That sounds frightening. Has her psychiatrist tried to talk to her? Determine the cause for her stupor?"

"Ellie has been seeing Dr. Ribaldi sporadically since her mother's accident. She's been on various antidepressant and anti-anxiety drugs since third grade. But the doctor feels her father's sudden death pushed Ellie over the edge, into a catatonic episode."

"Could she be schizophrenic?" Mitzy asked softly.

Fay shook her head. "He says once we find the appropriate treatment, the stupor and mutism will disappear."

"I've read that selective serotonin reuptake inhibitor antidepressant drugs can cause suicidal tendencies in adolescents," Mitzy said. "We ought to watch for that."

"My niece was off her SSRIs for three weeks, the necessary hiatus before starting her on a monoamine oxidase inhibitor for her destructive, acting out behavior."

"When did Ellie start taking an MOI?"

"She would have started taking it the week her father died, if my brother-in-law hadn't dumped her meds," Fay said. "He worried she'd get hooked."

"A non-medicated person suffering from moderate to severe depression is more likely to self-medicate: turn to alcohol, cigarettes, or illegal drugs."

"I fault myself for not being an active participant in Ellie's life," Fay lamented. "But Joe was such an obnoxious bastard when he was drinking; a daily routine since my sister's coma."

"Do you know whether he drank anything the morning of the day he died?"

Fay frowned. "Now that you mention it, Anya told me he had two shots of whiskey with breakfast. Six-thirty a.m. Disgraceful."

"Ellie said he'd received a new job offer?" Mitzy asked.

Fay nodded. "Two job changes in the five years since my sister's accident. Joe was nervous neither the bank nor the financial consulting firm would want him, once they got wind of his daughter's placement in an alternative high school. It's too bad because the structure and discipline at North Central Alternative High School would really help my niece."

"Sounds like you're familiar with the prospective high school program," Mitzy said.

"I checked into it after Ellie's last email."

"How did she and her dad get along in the weeks preceding his death?"

"Since Lani's coma, Joe has been an absentee parent." Fay paused. "You know, the detective who was here yesterday asked me those same questions."

"Sorry to pry," Mitzy said, rising from the couch. "I've overstayed my welcome."

"Not to be rude but after a long day at the art studio, I'm exhausted," Fay said, following her to the door. "It's difficult making the daily trek up here from Lincoln Park. But I'd do anything to help my sister's only child."

"May I keep in touch?" Mitzy asked.

"I'm sure Ellie would enjoy that. Dr. Ribaldi says she processes everything we say, even through her silence."

"She's lucky to have such a loving aunt." Mitzy stepped over the threshold and out into the night.

~

Fay briskly shut the oak door and strolled over to Ellie's huddled figure. She squatted down and looked for some sign of animation in the girl's eyes. A blank stare met her gaze. "Anya," she called down the hallway, her eyes never leaving her niece's face. "Make sure you flush Ellie's most recent prescription and throw the bottle in the trash."

"It done already," Anya called back.

Fay smiled. "You're a blessing."

Chapter 16

"Slow down!" Mitzy said as she pedaled down the bike path.

Maggie fell in beside her. "Man, are you out of shape! We've only biked from Emerson to Dempster and you're already panting."

"I dressed too warm." Mitzy grabbed the handlebar with one hand as she shrugged off her North Face jacket. "Thought it would be cooler by the lake."

"'North Carolina, come on and raise up,'" Maggie sang.

"Don't start! You know I hate that old rap song."

"My bad. So how's your student doing?"

"Ellie's still out of it," Mitzy said.

"And how has Ms. Snoop Dog been faring?"

"If this is going to be a Diane Sawyer special, can we at least take a break?" Mitzy pleaded.

Maggie laughed. "So much for getting rid of body fat."

They locked their twelve-speed bikes and headed for the boulders that framed the glistening lake by Northwestern University's Evanston campus.

"Check out the new graffiti," Maggie said, climbing across the boulders.

Mitzy peered down at a heart outlined in red and purple, its timeless message printed in gold paint. 'Will you marry me, Ashley? Love Dashmir.'"

"Sounds like love between the continents on that one," Maggie observed as she made her way across the adjoining rocks.

Mitzy paused at a boulder painted royal blue and sporting multi-colored lettering. "Each name's printed in a different neon color on this one: Megan. Seema. Patrick. Barry. Saul. Nikki."

"Here's a gigantic sunflower with each petal displaying a line of verse," Maggie said.

"I didn't know you were into poetry," Mitzy said, catching up with her friend.

"Just because I was a psych major doesn't mean I was ignorant in literature," Maggie said. Together they pored over the words, painted in elegant script:

To enter the path of righteousness,
Open the door to the waterfall,
Slide down to the base of consciousness
Then drink from the wisdom of the universe.
When you have been refreshed,
Seek to examine the wonders of the rainbow
Falling like glass from your fingertips.
Anonymous

"Beautiful," Mitzy gushed, sitting on the boulder alongside the sunflower.

"Know what it means?" Maggie plopped down beside her.

"The wonders of the universe are all around us if only we'd acknowledge them?" Mitzy said.

Maggie laughed. "You got it."

"Hey, I'm a pro at deciphering hidden meanings."

"Congratulations."

"Yet I can't decipher whether or not Ellie's dad committed suicide," Mitzy said. "The school staff thought he suffered a heart attack, but your detective friend said drugs and alcohol were a factor. We know Ellie and her dad had a big fight the previous night. Then there's Ellie's sporadic exposure to antidepressant drugs, plus her catatonic reaction to her father's death."

Maggie sat down beside her and stretched her legs. "Anything romantic between the nanny and the father?"

"Barge attempted some nasties. When Anya rebuffed him, he threatened to send her back to her homeland if she reported him to the police. FYI, the nanny had access to Ellie's drugs."

"But the nanny wasn't present when the event occurred," Maggie reminded her.

"Barge had two whiskies around 6:30 a.m., three hours before the parent conference was scheduled. A drug-alcohol interaction can occur two to four hours prior to a fatal reaction."

"Did you share your findings with Eric?"

Mitzy shook her head. "This is his gig, not mine. Anyway, Ellie's father habitually barged in on her math and English teachers, demanding to discuss Ellie's recent grades."

"The teacher with the French-sounding name, doesn't she teach English? You've mentioned her before."

Mitzy nodded. "Lynette LaFleur. A couple of days ago, Lynette and I chatted over lunch in the teachers' lounge."

"You discussed this case in a room full of teachers?" Maggie asked, incredulous.

Mitzy gave her friend a dirty look. "She and I were the only ones in the room. Turns out Lynette took anti-anxiety drugs during Barge's reign of terror. Once he was out of the picture, her panic attacks went poof."

"Maybe the English teacher is a suspect," Maggie said.

"My bet's on Fay Shimmer. She communicated with her niece by email on a regular basis, yet they only saw each other on Christmas because the father was so out of control. Maybe she convinced Ellie to put meds in her dad's coffee."

"With her brother-in-law out of the way, she'd become

Ellie's legal guardian," Maggie said. She frowned in thought. "Then again, Barge might have offed himself."

"If Barge howls at the moon every time his wife's sister comes near, he's not going to check out and leave her guardian of his little girl," Mitzy said.

"Five years of paying for an upscale nursing home must have walloped his wallet," said Maggie.

"I once did a story on nursing home fees. Medicaid only kicks in after you've totally exhausted your personal funds."

Maggie looked thoughtful as she worked her shoe back on. "A desperate father peering over a slippery slope and thinking it looks mighty tempting."

"If he jumps, Ellie receives a nice-sized inheritance guaranteed to keep her and her mother secure for a long time." Mitzy continued. "Auntie Fay still gets custody, but it's a price Barge is willing to pay."

Maggie whistled. "You could be barking up the right tree there, Sherlock."

Mitzy chuckled. "Sherlock sounds lots better than Ms. Snoop Dog. Can you run these other possibilities past your detective friend?"

"Okey-dokey. Anything for a friend. But it'll cost you three more miles."

Mitzy pulled the hoodie back over her head. "Why am I not surprised?"

~

Mitzy glanced at her watch. 6:00 p.m. Time to skedaddle. She shoved her lesson plan book and materials into her briefcase, flipped off the classroom lights and hurried out the door. She looked forward to visiting her former Tribune editor at the Glen Tree Nursing Home. Neil Grant recently had a hip replacement and had been moved to the nursing home for physical therapy.

Mitzy was surprised to see one of her students waiting for her in the hallway. "What are you doing here so late, Jordan?"

"Poms practice just ended. I know you stay late and I needed to talk to you."

"Isn't someone picking you up?"

"My mom will be here in fifteen minutes."

"All right then," Mitzy said, motioning for her student to follow her back into the classroom. She flipped on the lights. "What's up?"

"I visited Ellie at her house yesterday."

"How did it go?"

"Really weird. She just sat there. Didn't move the whole time. But when I said goodbye, Ellie made a weird noise and stared at this yellow-flowered journal on her computer table."

Mitzy's heart quickened. Ellie had attempted to communicate. "Then what happened?"

"I picked up the journal and put it in her lap. She used her elbow like a hockey stick and pushed it under her blue blanket. Her lips moved up at the corners a tiny bit, like she was trying to smile at me."

"Did anybody else see what was going on?"

Jordan shook her head. "Only Ellie and I were in her room. Do you think I should tell her aunt?"

"Is that what's bothering you?"

"Yeah."

Mitzy considered her student's options. "Well, since the journal can neither bite nor sting, that decision's really up to you."

Jordan laughed. "You're so funny. That's why you're my favorite teacher."

"Do you understand what I'm saying?"

"As long as the journal can't hurt Ellie, I don't have to tell."

"Although I'm sure Ellie's aunt would like to know."

"If Ellie wanted her aunt to know, she wouldn't have covered the journal with her blanket, right?" Jordan said.

"One would assume. But then you know what the first three letters of assume spell."

Jordan playfully kicked a student desk. "You always say

that! Well, I gotta go. Thanks for your help."

"Anytime," Mitzy said, once again grabbing her briefcase and hitting the light switch as they headed out the door.

As she slid into her silver Celica, she pondered what Jordan told her. What had compelled Ellie to reclaim her journal?

~

With its wide circular driveway and white pillars, Glen Tree Nursing Home looked more like a hotel than a rehabilitation center. "How can I help you?" asked a chirpy young woman in a pink cashmere sweater and a gray skirt.

"I'm here to see Neil Grant. He would have been admitted this week."

The receptionist typed some letters into the computer and scanned the screen for results. "That would be Room 302. Down the hall, to your left, take the elevator to the third floor."

Mitzy thanked her and turned to leave. A sudden impulse made her turn back. "Is this the only nursing home in Lake Forest?"

"The one and only."

"So if someone was in a coma for a long time, they'd be housed here?"

"Yep. On a floor with chronically ill patients or in our hospice wing, depending on the doctor's orders and the family's wishes. Is there someone you'd like me to check?"

"I think the mother of one of my students might be here. I'm not sure of her first name, but her last name is Barge."

The young woman scanned the computer screen once again. "Elana Barge. She's in room four-oh-four." She squinted at the screen. "She's been a resident here since July 1999. Oops! I'm new here. Pretend I didn't tell you that date, okay?"

"No problem," Mitzy said.

"Did you want to see Mrs. Barge?"

"Maybe later," Mitzy she said, then briskly headed down the hall.

A familiar baritone voice echoed down the hallway. "Hold that elevator!"

Mitzy turned to find a tall, lanky figure hurrying towards her. "Mr. Fillmore! Visiting a relative?"

"Yep," he said. He stepped in, and the elevator closed on them.

"What floor?"

"Can you press 2?"

"Sure."

"My grandfather's here," Fillmore confided.

"Alzheimer's?"

"You guessed it." He slumped against the elevator wall.

"How's he doing?"

Fillmore looked depressed. "He's on a new drug; makes him totally unresponsive."

"Have you talked to the doctor?"

"That's my next step." The elevator door opened, and Fillmore stepped out. "See you tomorrow."

You never know who you're going to run into at a nursing home, Mitzy thought, pushing the button for Floor 3.

~

Although the door was open, Mitzy rapped lightly. "Come in," said a subdued yet gruff voice. As Mitzy entered Room 302, she was momentarily blinded by the fiery sunset kicking through the window. "Hey," she said.

Her former editor lay atop a blue-gray comforter, his eyes intent on the news channel. Tearing his eyes from the 19-inch T.V. screen, he looked her way. "Well if it isn't the ghost of Mitzy Maven."

"Knock it off, Neil. It's been less than a year since I left the newspaper."

"A year can be a lifetime," her former boss said, wincing as he pushed himself into a sitting position.

"Word is you took a hammer to your hip," Mitzy joked.

"Would have done a better job if I'd known how it would pan out."

"How did it happen?"

"Slipped on ice."

"Rosemary said you guys just got back from Jamaica."

"On the sand, then."

"Right," Mitzy said, grinning. "How's the new guy doing?"

"Bradley's a fine reporter."

"How'd he do covering the Senate race?"

"He dug up info that made sure Keyes didn't get the keys."

"Sounds like he's doing his job."

"But he lacks your cutthroat instinct."

"Give him a chance, Neil. He only graduated Northwestern a couple of years ago."

"You were new once, too. But you had this intense desire to get down and dirty, infinite layers of questions in your eyes."

"As my mom would never say, you're making me blush."

"Hmph. Still can't take a compliment. So how's teaching?"

"I'm involved in REI. The Regular Education Initiative, mandating kids with special needs be taught in the least restrictive academic environment." She spent the next little while talking shop, fielding occasional questions from Neil about multiple intelligences, different learning styles and the challenges of team teaching. "Last week in geometry, a subject I almost failed in high school, the teacher presented a lesson on radius, pi, and diameter. I'm in there taking notes for one of my students. The students seemed confused.

"So next day, half the class works on circumference and diameter with me on one side of the room, the other half reviews the multiplication of decimals with Mr. Larson on the opposite end of the room. First I have my kids walk the circumference of a masking tape circle. Then I throw a string down the middle and we all walk the diameter, then the radius. We talk about pi. They put on flashcard necklaces and each kid role-plays a different part of the equation. Finally, these tall eighth graders stand in front of the rest of the class to perform their equation. What a blast!"

"Special ed and regular ed kids alike?"

"Yep."

"They learned the material better because they experienced it firsthand," Neil observed.

"Exactly."

"Bet you're a popular one at that school."

Mitzy shook her head. "Plenty of veteran teachers don't like sharing the podium with a special ed teacher. They think the principal planted me there to critique their lesson presentation and classroom management skills."

"If I know Mitzy Maven, a teacher not doing his or her job is going down."

"Not if the teacher listens to my insights and suggestions, given tactfully."

"You, tactful? How many times did the cops complain about your interfering with their interrogations?"

Mitzy sucked in her breath. Interfering. Was it possible she and Ellie's father shared a similar character trait?

A white-uniformed worker appeared with a dinner tray. Mitzy slipped on her tweed blazer. "That's my cue to wave adios. Hope you're up and running around soon."

"Thanks for stopping by. And kiddo?"

"Yeah?"

"When you first came to work at the Tribune, it took you awhile to establish relationships with the people who were going to save your ass out there in the big bad world. You gotta sow those politically savvy seeds now."

Mitzy leaned over to kiss him on the cheek. "Words of wisdom coming from the cliché slayer, himself!"

~

Her stomach rumbling, Mitzy headed out of Neil's room and down the hall. Hopefully she'd make it to Panera Bread before she passed out! First, a quick visit to the fourth floor. As she stepped off the elevator, the smell of urine, coupled with pitiful shouts, assailed her senses. This must be the floor where they kept the hopeless cases. The nursing station was vacant. Mitzy hurried past it, eager to pay her quick visit and leave.

The door to Room 404 was slightly ajar. Mitzy peered in. A woman not much older than herself lay in the hospital bed, her eyes closed, a feeding tube attached to her. Fay Shimmer was standing by the bedside, her multi-colored poncho wrapped around her like an angel's cloak.

"Please, Lani, you've got to wake up. If you're still inside that body, squeeze my hand. Flutter an eyelid. Anything. Dr. Klein says we should talk to you in a calm tone, but we're in a crisis, here."

Fay's voice shook as she continued. "Joe is dead and Ellie's not spoken since his death. Her psychiatrist is pushing for electro-convulsive therapy. You had a horrible time with that yourself when you were a teenager, remember? It's a lot safer now. But I still don't feel qualified to make this decision myself. You always took care of me when I was little. Please, Lani. If you're still in there, come back to us now."

Tears streaming down her cheeks, Mitzy retreated down the hallway.

Chapter 17

Mitzy attempted to hang the fourteen-inch fern planter onto one of the elongated hooks jutting out from the balcony ceiling. Making sure to stay far from the ledge, she turned up the volume on her iPod. In this way she could successfully ignore the dizzying sound of rush hour traffic ten floors below.

Fortunately, Mitzy's Evanston condo was situated on a second floor. Mitzy only had to contend with her fear of heights once a week, sometimes twice if her mom and Harry invited her for Shabbat dinner.

Although Shirley Maven had purchased her condo in a choice location overlooking Hollywood and Sheridan, the living room balcony provided the sole view of Lake Michigan. Four lanes of traffic needed to be crossed before you hit Lake Shore Drive. There you could walk by the boulders flanking the sparkling blue water, if you weren't killed by speeding cars.

Yet this condo was Shangri-la compared to the cramped one-bedroom apartment Mitzy and her mom had shared in West Rogers Park during her growing up years. Shirley could now afford to live here, thanks to Uncle Harry.

She glanced towards the sliding glass door and noticed her mother struggling to lift a twenty-pound potted geranium across the threshold. Last thing she needed to do given her herniated disc. "Need help hoisting that pot, Mom?" Mitzy asked, willing her voice into relaxed mode.

Shirley Maven shook her head and continued struggling with the potted plant. "I'm good. Just want to get this place looking good for Passover."

Although her mother immersed herself in a frenzied world of activities, Mitzy still had to contend with constant questions about her physical and mental health. Growing up as the only child of a young widow, her every owie had been subject to intense scrutiny. Yet when it came to her mother's health, the jury was on sabbatical, and there was no one to summon it back into the courtroom.

Up until her recent "accident," the sixty-nine year old Shirley had regularly hauled fifty-pound bags of mulch into the community garden she'd help design at Indian Boundary Park in their former neighborhood. *What a broad*, Harry would say with an admiring whistle. Yet now she was disintegrating into a senior citizen. What a tear jerker!

Shirley's tired voice brought Mitzy back to reality. "Actually, I think I'll take you up on your offer, sweetie."

"Huh?" Mitzy said. Once again, her mind had been hovering above another galaxy.

Shirley laughed. "And Harry says I'm the one who tunes out."

"Like mother, like daughter," Mitzy said, scooping up the oversized flower pot. "Where do you want this?"

Shirley straightened with obvious effort, her hands rubbing the small of her back. "The pot's too damn heavy for me to maneuver. Toss the monster over the balcony."

Sensing the angst behind her mother's ferocity, Mitzy set the flower pot on the ceramic patio table. Then she gently hugged the older woman. "It's weird seeing you like this, Mom."

Her mother dissolved into her arms. "Harry doesn't appreciate me introducing a herniated disc for a new bed partner either."

Mitzy blushed. "That's more than I need to know."

"Not to mention it's a real drag having to ask your daughter for help."

Mitzy swept a few stray silver strands of hair from her mother's forehead. "Cut it out, Mom. You know you can always count on me."

Shirley ducked beneath Mitzy's arms and wandered over to gaze across her living room balcony at the shimmering waters of Lake Michigan. "Someday in the not too distant future, you might regret those words, darling."

A shiver ran down Mitzy's spine. This conversation was derailing as fast as an Alfred Hitchcock movie remake. "Is there something you want to tell me, Mom?"

Her mother turned to go back inside, patting Mitzy on the shoulder as she passed. Moving cautiously, as if to avoid another pain flare-up, she slid open the patio door. "Clean up out here. I'm going inside to take a nap."

Mitzy yanked off her gardening gloves and tossed them on a flowered patio chair. "I'm not your slave. Clean the patio up yourself!" She shivered at the wave of hurt that crossed her mother's face. Where was this sudden hostility coming from? Her emotional control was eroding by the millisecond.

Her mother peered at her from the other side of the sliding screen door. "Here I am, attempting to bare my soul to my only child, and you've got the chutzpah to get in my face like some unruly toddler!"

The words stung like rubbing alcohol on a mosquito bite. Why was her mother showering her with this shit? They'd been so close when she was growing up. Her mother still bragged to her mahjong partners that Mitzy had never given her a moment's trouble. Sure, Mitzy had stifled her fighting words as a child. With one parent dead, it wasn't like she was going to risk driving the other parent away. A shiver ran through her body as she realized a similar connection between Ellie and her father.

"Earth to Mitzy," her mother said.

"Sorry. I was thinking about something else."

"If you're going to argue with me, you really need to focus," her mother said, a tinge of humor coloring her voice. Suddenly Mitzy felt tired of the game. "I don't want to fight, Mom. Like you used to say, give peace a chance." In Shirley's college years, she had marched on Washington on four separate occasions; the first time to protest the Viet Nam War.

Her mother stepped back outside. "Congratulations! I was testing you. You passed with flying colors."

"Huh?"

"I've been in a terrible muddle over whether or not to share a little problem I'm having."

Mitzy's fatigue vanished in a jolt of anxiety. She slapped the remaining plastic plant hangers on the glass table. "Out with it!"

"Shirl?" came a bass voice from inside the condo.

Shirley slid the patio door further ajar. "We're out on the balcony, darling."

Harry joined them outside, his white polo shirt slightly wrinkled. "How's my girls?" he asked, giving them each a peck on the cheek.

"Is that the best you can do?" Shirley asked. She looked up at him, her eyes filled with adoration.

"You don't like my kisses, babe, you can take your business to Walgreens."

Mitzy giggled in spite of herself, well familiar with the punch line.

Harry walked out onto the balcony, tennis racquet in hand. "Looks like an arboretum out here."

"Mitzy gets the credit," Shirley said. "My back's been giving me a run for the money. Of course, I never mastered the art of running, even when my back was in perfect condition."

Mitzy rolled her eyes at her mother's lame attempt to be funny.

"You still in pain, we better get you to the doc," Harry said.

Shirley waved off his concern. "So how was the game?"

Harry pulled a handkerchief from his khaki shorts pocket and ran it across his forehead. "What a scorcher! Barry slaughtered me out there on the courts."

"I can tell," Shirley said, eyeing his sweat-stained shirt.

"I'm heading for the shower, then you and I is heading down to Grant Park."

"I ain't heading anywhere if you can't talk right," Shirley joked.

Harry put his arm around Mitzy. "Must have been a barrel of laughs growing up with this woman. Speaking of laughs, listen to this one my buddy told me."

"You and your jokes," Shirley scoffed.

"Come on, Shirl. Don't be a killjoy. A guy walks into a convenience store armed with a shotgun and demands all the cash from the register. After the cashier puts the cash in a bag, the robber sees a bottle of Scotch on a shelf behind the counter. Waving the gun at the cashier, he orders her to put the whiskey in a bag. She refuses, saying she doesn't believe he's over 21."

"That happens to me all the time," Mitzy snickered.

"At this point, the robber hands the cashier his driver's license. She looks it over, agrees he's 21, and sends him off with his bottle of Scotch. The cashier then calls the police and gives them the name and address she picked off his license. The cops arrest the robber shortly afterwards."

"Anybody who walks into a store with a shotgun's got to be wacko," Shirley said. "Why in the world would the cashier play a game of Russian roulette with a dangerous killer?"

"Um, that's not Russian roulette, Mom," Mitzy said.

"Don't get stuck in linguistics," her mother said impatiently. "You catch my drift."

"Like I said, must have been a real gas having this woman for your mom," Harry said, chuckling.

Had it been fun growing up with a widowed mother who worked forty hours a week to support the two of them? Had her mother always been this crusty? Her thoughts centered on the summer of seventh grade when she and her best friend caught their first fish down at the pier. Her mom had allowed them to bring it back to the apartment. The big scaly fish had swum the length of their bathroom tub!

Every fall and spring, Mitzy had looked forward to going apartment hunting with her mother, daydreaming about renting a spacious, more cheerful living space for under $300.00 per month.

And then there were the summer Sundays they spent munching salami sandwiches and potato chips as they tanned together on the beach. Thanks to the CTA, she and Shirley frequented a different beach each weekend.

"We did have some good times," Mitzy conceded.

"Good, 'cause you only seem to remember the tough times," her mother said.

How could she forget the nights she'd meet her mom at the bus stop? If Shirley had sold a lot of women's suits that day, they'd stop at the broasted chicken food joint and chat on their walk home. But if her mother's day had been filled with frustration, the wrong word could set her off for the whole evening. Trouble was, Shirley's emotional barometer rose and fell like a tsunami. Those anxious moments ceased once Harry arrived on the scene, armed with emotional and economic support.

"Mitzy, I'm worried about you," Shirley said.

"What?"

"You fade off into the sunset more and more these days," her mother lamented.

Mitzy forced a smile. "Just got a lot on my mind, Mom." She looked at Harry. "We were kind of finishing up something when you came in."

"Mitzy," her mother said sharply.

Uncle Harry gave Shirley's shoulders a squeeze. "You lovely ladies enjoy. I gotta go shower."

Shirley glared at Mitzy. "When he comes back, you owe that man an apology."

"I'll phone him later, after you tell me your little secret."

Shirley looked perplexed.

"The one you said you'd been agitating over," Mitzy said, tapping her foot.

"I have no idea what you're talking about. I got a headache. I'm gonna rest until Harry gets home. Thanks for helping me out today, sweetie."

Mitzy's jaw dropped. "Harry's in the shower, Mom."

"Of course he is," her mother said cheerfully as she leaned forward to kiss her on the cheek. "Talk to you later."

Today, her mother had been the poster child for odd behavior, Mitzy thought as she headed through the living room and out the front door. Between figuring out who, if anyone, killed Joseph Barge and worrying about her mother's undisclosed health issues, something told Mitzy she'd be on the Internet all night.

Chapter 18

Detective Eric Whelan leaned forward in his chair. "First, I'd like to thank Dr. Ribaldi for sparing the time to talk to us this afternoon in an effort to shed some light on the family life of Joe and Ellie Barge."

Dr. Victor Ribaldi leaned back in his plush leather chair and smiled. They were in his office, a comfortable and expensively furnished room. His practice must be thriving, Eric thought.

"I'd also like to thank Mitzy Maven for tearing herself away from her students long enough to contribute her insights. Ms. Maven, you've already met Fay Shimmer, Ellie's aunt, as well as Anya, Ellie's nanny, right?"

Mitzy Maven gave him a thumbs-up. He felt an impulse to grin and quashed it. She was here as a professional, not as someone for him to get interested in. Not that he was looking, anyway.

"All right, let's get started." Eric pulled a yellow legal pad from his briefcase. "I called this meeting because at this point, we are in limbo concerning Joseph Barge's exact cause of death."

"Isn't the police department supposed to conduct the

investigation and then report back to the family?" Fay asked.

"Usually, yes. But I've found that occasionally the most efficient way of solving a case is to work as a team with family members and the professionals in their midst. My police chief supports this approach. Any more questions?" Eric glanced at the faces around the table, all staring at him in anticipation. "Then let's begin. Today's interview will be recorded for accuracy." He clicked on the cassette player in front of him. "Ms. Shimmer, are you the legal guardian of Ellie Barge?"

Fay nodded. "I am."

"Have you given Dr. Ribaldi written permission to share details with us today regarding Ellie's psychotherapy, as well as her pharmaceutical history?"

"I have."

"Have you given Ms. Maven written permission to share details about your niece's academic and behavioral history at school?"

"Yes, I have."

He turned toward the psychiatrist. "Dr. Ribaldi, when did you start seeing Ellie Barge as a patient?"

Ribaldi donned his reading glasses and scanned his patient's folder. "That would have been in May 1999. Ellie was eight years old."

"What precipitated that first therapy session?"

The psychiatrist continued to read. "Elana Barge became comatose following a head-on automobile collision. She was placed in a nursing home. Her daughter was distraught."

Both the aunt and the housekeeper grimaced.

"What was the cause of the collision?"

"The night of the accident, Ellie and her mother were caught in a downpour and the roads were slick. Ellie was strapped in the back seat, whining about stopping at McDonald's. Mom turned around to address the issue. At that moment, a truck ran through a red light and slammed into them."

Mitzy Maven stifled a gasp. Eric noted her reaction. Clearly, she cared about this girl. He admired her for that, but wondered if it would affect what she told him about Ellie Barge.

"Was Ellie injured?" he asked.

"Not physically."

"What were Ellie's symptoms afterward?"

Ribaldi glanced up from his papers. "Initially, she presented with post-traumatic stress syndrome, experiencing recurrent dreams of the accident. In play therapy, she repetitively placed her girl child doll in harm's way, then wrung her hands and trembled when her toy car pushed the mommy doll down, leaving the child doll untouched." He took a construction paper page from the folder and held it up. "As you can see, she depicted herself as a black butterfly with a human head, and her mother as an ant-sized stick figure."

Fay Shimmer covered her mouth.

"How about the father?" Eric continued.

"He's the black tree-like figure running towards them from the far right-hand corner of the page."

Eric saw Mitzy reach for the drawing and begin to study it quietly. Then he turned back to the psychiatrist. "Did you question Ellie about her drawing?"

Ribaldi nodded. "She said her father was too far away to save them."

"So much insight for a young girl," Ellie's aunt sniffled through tears.

"Did you counsel both father and daughter?"

"Yes. During the first few months following the accident, Mr. Barge attended a handful of sessions with Ellie. He also attended four sessions of individual therapy, then stopped."

Eric made a quick note on his pad. "What was the relationship between Ellie and her father?"

"Ellie mentioned that before the accident, she and her father played at the park, visited museums, and attended a few daddy-daughter Valentine's Day dances. But after the accident, he often worked late. When he was home, he'd leave Ellie to her own devices."

"How did she feel about that?"

"Her drawing indicates she believed herself blackened with guilt for causing the crash."

Poor kid, Eric thought. He turned towards Mitzy. "How was Ellie's behavior at school during that time period?"

The special ed teacher handed the drawing back to Dr. Ribaldi. Then she opened her student's school file and scanned several papers in it. "At the time of the accident, Ellie was in her last month of third grade. Her teachers indicate she changed from a cheerful, outgoing student into a solemn-faced little girl who no longer participated in class discussions or interacted with her peers."

He nodded and refocused his attention on the psychiatrist. "What type of treatment was Ellie receiving at this point?"

Dr. Ribaldi adjusted his glasses. "When no behavioral change occurred after six months, play therapy was discontinued. When Ellie was in fourth grade, we started her on anti-anxiety drugs, but those made her lethargic."

Mitzy interrupted. "Her files indicate she tested one-and-a-half years below grade level in math and science. Her father refused to sign off on special education services."

The detective politely nodded. "Thank you for that, Ms. Maven. Continue, Doctor."

"Ellie went through a selective mutism stage. Yet, she did speak to me during our weekly therapy sessions. She said she only felt alive while in school. Behavior modification proved unsuccessful. Her father was anti-medication. Ellie's selective mutism phase lasted six months, and then disappeared as suddenly as it had begun. Thereafter, Ellie refused to discuss that time frame with me during our counseling sessions."

The click of the tape recorder broke the silence. Eric deftly flipped the cassette and reinserted it in the machine. "Were there any changes in the family relationship or the school environment during the next three years?"

Mitzy flipped through the school file. "In sixth grade, Ellie received a one-week suspension for flushing another student's homework down the toilet. In class, she talked back to her teachers."

"She refuse to bathe," Anya said.

Mitzy nodded. "A note in her file mentions cleanliness was an issue."

"Ellie say she be bad so father come to school to get her," said Anya.

Dr. Ribaldi drummed his fingers on the desk. "Ellie fruitlessly attempted to engage her father through her acting-out behaviors. The more she acted out, the more withdrawn he became, with sudden rages."

Reading from the file, Mitzy said, "By seventh grade, the school stated that if Mr. Barge refused to allow his daughter to receive special education services, they would take him to court for child neglect."

"I recall during that time period, Joe came in for one counseling session," the doctor continued.

"What was his mental state?" Eric asked.

"He initially discussed his daughter's special education deficits, but conversation soon switched to his wife's medical condition. Elana was still in a coma. He was contemplating whether or not to take her off life support. He appeared depressed and withdrawn. Possibly suicidal."

That was interesting. Eric made another note. "Did you treat him for depression?"

"I advised him to first make an appointment with his primary care physician, whom he hadn't seen for three years, to rule out any type of medical condition."

"Did he follow up?"

The psychiatrist nodded. "Mr. Barge phoned me a week later and told me his doctor had given him a prescription to treat his hypertension. He confided that he had no intention of filling the scrip."

"Lani used to say Joe wouldn't even take Tylenol for a headache," Fay said.

"I urged Mr. Barge to set up additional therapy sessions, but he declined," Dr. Ribaldi said. "However, he did agree to have Ellie placed in her school's special education program."

"So Ellie's father was walking around with untreated

high blood pressure," Eric observed. "How did that affect his behavior with Ellie?"

"He often argue with daughter," Anya said. "Turn red in face. Complain of dizziness and bad stomach."

"In seventh grade, Ellie's records indicate twenty-three absences," Mitzy said. "She received negative check marks on the behavior/attitude section of her report cards, including 'stays on task' and 'completes homework on time'. Except for math and science, her grades were in the average range— atypical for a chronically absent student. In the comments area of the report card, her English teacher indicated Ellie participated with much insight during class discussion of literature and poetry."

Eric turned toward her. "How long have you known Ellie, Ms. Maven?"

"I've had her for resource room and math class since last fall."

"How would you characterize her behavior?"

The teacher stiffened. He thought of a cat, arching its back in warning. "Ellie has a behavior disorder identified as ODD, or oppositional defiant disorder."

"Can you explain what that behavior looks like?"

She gave him a challenging look. "Disobedient, hostile, defiant toward authority figures." He had the feeling she was daring him to think the girl a monster. Which was odd, if she cared about Ellie Barge as much as she'd seemed to. Maybe she was just the kind of person who laid all her cards on the table. She certainly had at the pizza place.

"Sounds like a perfect description of her father," Fay interrupted.

Mitzy shook her head slightly. "Ellie's defiance isn't the acting-out type, with hollering and screaming. Hers is more passive-aggressive: talking to teachers while burying her head in her arms on the desk, manipulating things to go her way, using threats like, 'My father will be pissed if you give me a bad grade.' "

Eric gave her a nod. "Thank you for sharing. Doctor Ribaldi, has Ellie been on any prescription medication?"

"Over the years, we treated her with various SSRIs, including Prozac, Paxil, Celexa and Zoloft."

"Why such a variety?"

"It takes a few weeks for a drug to start working, but Ellie almost immediately complained of feeling achy and drowsy, unable to concentrate in class. Each time her father noticed a drug's side effects, he'd discard the unused portion of pills."

"Don't antidepressants sometimes cause suicidal tendencies in children and teenagers?"

Dr. Ribaldi frowned. "SSRIs are prescribed to children and adolescents on a trial and error basis."

Eric nodded. "At the time of her father's death, was Ellie still taking these drugs?"

"She was scheduled to begin taking Nardil. Although using monoamine oxidase inhibitors with a non-hospitalized adolescent is highly unusual, a colleague of mine mentioned a depressed adolescent patient of his had experienced stellar results within ten days."

"So you switched to Nardil?"

The doctor shook his head. "There's a two-week waiting period between taking an SSRI and an MAO inhibitor. Ellie was in the second week of that waiting period when her father died. She arrived home from the hospital a few days before the event."

"What was she hospitalized for?"

"Attempted suicide."

Ellie's aunt sucked in her breath. "My niece and I emailed each other regularly during the last three months. But I had no idea she was so sick."

Eric noticed Mitzy perk up at the aunt's admission.

"When did you and Ellie start corresponding in that manner?" he asked.

"Halfway through eighth grade, Joe threatened to cut me off from visiting Ellie during the holidays unless I stopped seeing her regularly."

"Why was he against you communicating with his daughter?"

"He thought I was trashing him, but I'd never do that. I told Ellie she should contact me by cell phone in an emergency. She phoned me the morning she cut herself, but I was working at the studio and my cell was off, my land line down. When I saw her caller ID, I called her back, but Joe had confiscated her phone."

Eric clicked off the recorder. "Ellie is lucky to have such a dedicated group of individuals working together on her behalf. You've shared some valuable information that will aid our investigation." He stood, smoothing the crease in his pants leg. "Again, thank you."

Mitzy followed him out the door. "Detective, wait up. I never got a chance to tell you about my conversation with Ellie's eighth-grade English teacher. She had a lot to say about Ellie's father."

This woman was an enigma. One minute poised to break his neck, the next minute friendly as a purring cat. Not breaking his stride, he tossed out, "Got time for a Starbucks?"

"Sure. They hired a substitute teacher for the afternoon."

~

"So tell me about Lynette LaFleur," Eric said, when they were seated at a corner table with their coffees.

Mitzy licked the whipped cream from her caramel mocha. Now that she'd started this, she was having second thoughts, so she hedged. "Lynette personifies what teaching is all about."

"How so?" he asked, slurping his hazelnut chocolate latte. She'd expected him to drink his java plain black, but so far Eric Whelan didn't seem like a stereotypical cop.

"Her kids act out Shakespeare plays, write their own sonnets, play American Grammar Idol."

"Sounds like her methods are unorthodox."

"Not unorthodox, Eric. Creative. That's how kids learn best." Was it too soon, calling him Eric? He didn't seem to mind, though.

He was staring down at his latte, a hesitant look on his face. "Hey, you know how back at the doc's office you were talking about oppositional defiant disorder?"

"Uh huh."

"Well, my eleven-year-old nephew was diagnosed with attention deficit disorder and he shows some of those same behaviors."

"ODD is one of the conditions that seems to go along with ADD. Is your nephew always pushing the envelope with his parents and teachers? Does he rebel against following instructions or rules? Blame everybody else for his mistakes? Find it difficult to switch from one activity to another?"

"That's amazing. You've got him down pat. Yet he gets all A's and B's on his report card."

"Only thirty percent of ADD kids have learning disabilities. Famous inventors, scientists, artists, politicians, and entertainers were ADD or LD long before those acronyms came into existence."

"That is so weird."

Encouraged by Eric's show of interest in one of her favorite subjects, Mitzy leaned forward. "According to the neurologist who did the first MRI of the brain a few years ago, their brains are just wired differently. ADD people tend to think outside the box. Creative. Questioning. Processing information in unique ways. Yet as kids, they give their parents and teachers a rough time."

"So my nephew might turn out all right after all." Eric sounded relieved.

"More than all right, as long as he's given a structured environment and consequences for his actions," Mitzy said. "We're not talking physical punishment here; punishment for these kids is taking away their iPod. Was she talking too much? Telling Eric more than he wanted to know? Tough shit. She was on a roll. "These kids need adult supervision after school, right up through high school. Because ADD and LD are double-edged swords. Over fifty percent of jailed criminals have either undiagnosed learning deficits or attention deficit disorder."

"My sister-in-law's a former teacher," Eric said. "She and my brother are real structured with Darin. They use that '1,2,3 Magic' program that's on video."

"Good program," Mitzy said.

They sipped coffee, and then Eric switched subjects. "So... what did Ellie's English teacher have to say about Joseph Barge? When I talked to her, I got the sense they weren't on the best of terms."

Reluctantly, Mitzy nodded. "Confrontations with Mr. Barge took a real toll on Lynette. She was on anti-anxiety drugs, he frightened her so much."

"You telling me this because you think she might have been involved in Barge's death?"

It sounded so blunt, put that way. "Not sure. There's something else I forgot to mention, hottie." Abruptly, Mitzy covered her face. "Sorry. That just popped out."

"So you think I'm hot?" Eric said, grinning.

"Can we get back to business here?" Mitzy peeked out from beneath her hands.

"Your wish is my duty," Eric said.

"That's 'command'. When I first visited Ellie, I saw three half-empty bottles of antidepressant drugs sticking out from beneath her bed."

He looked at her, suddenly alert. "So she managed to hide some of her meds from her dad."

Damn. Now he was even more suspicious of Ellie. "Anyone at that house could have had access to them. The housekeeper, the aunt..." She paused, wondering how he'd take what she was about to say. "Or the father, for all we know."

He shook his head. "Ellie drugged her father."

Mitzy sat up straight. "Her mother's already lost to her. No way would she want to lose her father, too!"

"She could have killed him by accident. No way would a thirteen-year-old kid realize booze and meds combined with untreated hypertension can be fatal."

Mitzy jumped up so fast, the remains of her latte shot

onto the lacquered tabletop. "I'm not going to sit here and allow you to malign an innocent child."

He scowled at her. "Any defense attorney will tell you innocence is based on perception."

"I'm out of here!" Mitzy turned and stalked out of the coffee shop. She felt a passing moment of guilt—she'd meant to treat him, since he'd bought her pizza—but squelched it. Let the hotshot detective pay for his own damn coffee.

~

Eric pulled out a legal pad and laid it across his lap. "How would you describe Joseph Barge as an employee?"

Dexter James Stacey leaned back in his cherry leather chair and glanced out the window. His office was exactly what Eric would expect of a stuffy, old-school bank president: well-padded leather furniture, dark paneling on the walls, an oil portrait of some former bank bigwig on the wall behind Stacey's mahogany desk. "Joe was a real go-getter, especially after his wife's accident. He never balked at speaking engagements on behalf of the bank, or sitting through yet another Chamber of Commerce networking breakfast."

"Town Center Bank's golden boy," Eric said.

"You could say that."

"How did he get along with the rest of the staff?"

Stacey glanced at him. "Joe had a quick temper, but it dissipated just as quickly." He smiled faintly. "And he was a regular Tiger Woods on the golf course."

"You mentioned his temper. Any particular scenario come to mind?"

"Joe was in charge of our corporate clients. He'd complain we needed to update our computers to send out birthday and anniversary cards to company CEOs, and hold an annual vacation incentive raffle for executives who switched their personal, as well as professional, banking accounts our way."

"Sounds pretty innovative."

"The board of directors thought Joe's ideas were a bit far-fetched."

"What was his reaction?"

Stacey leaned forward, refocusing his gaze on Eric. "He was furious. Ranted and raved that he knew best how to increase this bank's revenue and the board of directors was making a big mistake, one they would regret."

"How did they react?"

"They took his words as a veiled threat."

"When did this conversation take place?"

"About a week prior to Joe's death."

"How about you, what did you think?"

Stacey sighed. "I chalked Joe's remarks off to his usual paranoia. He was one of those 'me against the world' guys. Not completely unfounded, I might add. Some bank employees felt he got away with murder when his temper flared up. Yet with customers, Joe was a prince. Charming and insightful.

"He was with us for four years. Loyal employee, knowledgeable about the future. We'd slotted him for VP of Marketing in our mutual funds division and he was scheduled to begin training in September. Then rumors started flying he'd been offered VP of Internet Marketing at a local financial consulting firm, for double his salary."

Eric whistled. "He must have been a valuable guy."

"Despite that fact, I doubt the board would have agreed to match that number."

"Anybody on the board have it in for him?"

"Nobody who would wish him ill, if that's what you're insinuating," Stacey said huffily.

"Why don't you let me be the judge of that?"

The older man held his gaze a moment, then looked thoughtful. "We initially considered offering the new position to Judd Jenson, V.P. of consumer services. He was miffed at being usurped."

"Judd got his dream job after all."

Stacey nodded.

Eric rose to shake his hand. "Thanks for your help," he said. "I'll be in touch."

"Glad we could assist."

Eric turned to leave, then stopped. "One last question. Would Barge's promotion have been in jeopardy had the bank found out his daughter was being placed in an alternative high school for students with severe emotional problems?"

The bank president's mouth fell open. "That's preposterous. Even though we are a family-owned institution, we pride ourselves on providing a variety of mental health-related options for our employees and their families."

"Okay. Thanks." Eric hurried out the door.

Chapter 19

As Mitzy gazed at her family and friends seated around the white linen-covered dining room table, a feeling of peace and calm engulfed her. She hadn't seen her aunt, cousins, and grandma since last Passover. They all lived in Scottsdale, Arizona, where the weather was hot and dry, unlike the volatile temperatures of Chicago.

Shirley had the video camera focused on Mitzy's nine-year-old cousin, Jessica, who was flawlessly chanting the Four Questions in Hebrew. Not bad after only one year of Hebrew school. Mitzy's eyes misted. After her father was killed, her mother had confined their observance of Judaism to holiday rituals, embarrassed to appeal to a temple's generosity for a Hebrew school scholarship. Fortunately, her cousins had been blessed with the economic means to follow a different path. They and their parents were totally immersed in temple life and learning.

Observing family tradition was like gluing the past and present together in one giant collage, even when the colors in those pictures clashed. For many kids at alternative schools, the holidays were days like any other, not worthy of being singled out for special celebration and festivities.

That first Passover following her father's death had been stark in its emptiness. Refusing to pretend their lives had been left unscarred, Shirley Maven had declined dinner invitations from extended family, who lived in nearby Skokie at the time.

Even at five years old, Mitzy had felt that isolation. The deep silence surrounding her and her mother as they read aloud to each other from the Haggadah. The wistful yearning of placing Elijah's oversized wine cup on the dining room table, then opening the front door for the biblical prophet to enter. Pretending Elijah, with his gray beard, was her daddy in disguise, like some masked figure at Purim. Elijah must have been busy elsewhere because her daddy only reentered their lives in her dreams.

Mitzy furtively glanced at Eric, whom she'd invited on the spur of the moment as a consolation prize for walking out on him at the coffee shop. Just because he'd questioned her about Ellie's meds didn't mean he was zeroing in on the girl as a suspect in her father's death. He was just doing his job, being thorough. He looked adorable in his black suit and gray striped tie, following along in the Haggadah as if his life depended on it.

Tonight's Seder was flowing effortlessly. The very meaning of the word Seder was "order". A verse from Ecclesiastes flowed through Mitzy's mind: "To every thing there is a season. And a time for every purpose under Heaven." If she could control her knee-jerk reaction to every single word Eric uttered, there just might be a season of "them." *Earth to Mitzy*, she yelled inside her head. *Concentrate on the book before you!*

Even back in biblical times, word choices had a power all their own. They could make or break the world. This was the season of Passover and the purpose was to remember how the Jews, through the Lord's constant prodding via Moses, had finally broken free from the yoke of four hundred years of bondage in the land of the pyramids. Moses and Aaron had been forced to go to Pharaoh ten times, proclaiming in G-d's name, "Let My people go!" When words failed to produce the necessary magic, Adonai visited ten plagues upon that ancient country. Even then, it took a tsunami at the Red Sea to free the captives from the Egyptians' advancing chariots.

The trick tonight, as at Passover celebrations throughout the generations, was to mold that remembrance into a meaningful experience for the children so that they would pass it along to their own children in the years to come. A trickle of anxiety went through Mitzy's chest as she contemplated whether she'd be the last in the line of Arnold and Shirley Maven.

Now Jessie's younger brother, Adam, hesitantly recited the first of the Four Questions in English. "'Why is this night dif-fer-ent from all other nights?'" Mitzy observed her Aunt Joanie's eyes shine with pride as her son made his way through the three-syllable word. "'On all other nights we eat bread or matzah. On this night, why do we only eat matzah?'"

Adam continued on to the second question: "'On all other nights we eat all kinds of vege'—What's that word?"

Jessie whispered in his ear.

"'Vegetables. Why on this night do we only eat maror?' Wait, what's that again?"

Jessie pointed to the Passover plate with all the special foods on it. "Horseradish, idiot."

The little boy hung his head.

Aunt Joanie gave her daughter a stern glance.

"Sor-ry!" Jessica said.

"I don't want to read anymore," Adam pouted.

Grandma Rose put her arm around him. "Let's all read the next question together."

Adam nodded, a smile on his lips. Together they began. "'On all other nights, we do not have to dip vegetables even once. On this night, why do we dip them twice?'"

"Darn it," Shirley screeched, fumbling with the video camera. "The battery died."

"Let it go, Shirl," Harry said.

"Can we eat soon?" Jessica begged.

"How about we all read the last question aloud?" Grandma suggested. In unison, they recited: "'On all other nights, we eat our meals sitting any way we like. On this night, why do we lean on pillows?'"

Mitzy glanced at Maggie, who sat next to her, and at Eric on the other side. She was pleased to see that, unlike earlier in the Seder, they were participating along with everybody else. Maybe it wasn't so boring for them after all.

"Jessie and Adam, you did a great job reading the Four Questions, with a little help from your friends," Harry said.

"I didn't need any help," Jessica protested.

Aunt Joanie gave her "the look."

"Now let's go around the table and read the answers," Harry said, turning to his friend. "Byron, did you want to go first?"

The former Camp Briarwood director picked up his Haggadah and read for the first time that night. "'This night is different from all other nights because once we were slaves to Pharaoh in Egypt, but Adonai took us out with a mighty hand and an outstretched arm. We had to leave so quickly, there was no time for the bread to rise.'"

Maggie read next. "'The bitter herbs remind us of our four hundred years of bondage in Egypt.'"

Harry nodded in Eric's direction. Eric read: "'Reclining as we eat our meal is a symbol of freedom.'" His low, confident voice made Mitzy tingle inside.

She glanced at her mother fiddling with the camera. *Don't say anything embarrassing about the investigation into dad's death*, she prayed. But who could say with Shirley? She was so unpredictable. Now Harry was signaling for Mitzy to read. "'Salt water is symbolic of the tears we cried as slaves.'"

Then came the retelling of the story of the exodus from Egypt. In minutes they had encapsulated in familiar words an event that occurred two thousand years ago. This year, Mitzy's mother had purchased one of the intricately illustrated versions of the Haggadah, with discussion questions framing each page.

Mitzy's ruminations stopped at Harry's next question. "How are we slaves today?"

"Oh no," Adam groaned, rubbing his tummy.

Her finger to her lips, Aunt Joanie handed her son a piece of matzah with butter.

Harry seemed not to notice the charade. With an almost imperceptible nod, he acknowledged Maggie's raised hand.

"Nowadays, we're slaves to money and power," Maggie said.

Mitzy smiled, recalling the intense political debate she and Maggie had enjoyed when she'd been on the news beat. That they were on polar ends of the election results bar had only made their discussions more passionate.

"People suffer from depression because although they slave away at their jobs to make ends meet, they still can't afford to feed their families," Eric offered.

Mitzy shot Eric a quick smile. So insightful.

Maggie leaned over and whispered in her ear. "Aren't you glad you invited hottie boy?"

Mitzy nodded. The concept of inviting a stranger to share the holiday came straight from the Haggadah. Remember that you were strangers in a strange land. The "asking for trouble" part concerned the seating arrangement. Sometimes an unexpected arrival had to sit on the piano bench at the far end of the table because every possible chair was occupied by somebody's tush.

The contrived set-up made her mom all crazy. That was no way to treat a guest. Ultimately one of the kids would be urged to exchange seats with the newcomer, resulting in more commotion because the kid's place setting would be inundated with matzo crumbs, a half-eaten hardboiled egg, and grape juice stains.

Mitzy surreptitiously glanced at Eric. Although he was slouching on the maple piano bench, he didn't seem uncomfortable. He was right in tune with tonight's theme, anyway: the whole idea of being able to slouch at the dining table because you were free. Of course everybody else was comfortably leaning back on pillows flanking their chairs, while he…

"Earth to Mitzy," Harry said, his eyes laughing.

"Sorry," Mitzy mumbled. "Are we still on the same discussion question?"

Her mother gave her a dirty look.

"Okay, okay." Mitzy did some quick thinking. "Some individuals seek relief by becoming slaves to prescription or illegal drugs."

"I've always been a slave to hugs," Grandma Rose piped in.

"She said 'drugs', not 'hugs', Mother," Shirley shouted. Everybody stared at her. "Sorry, she's not wearing her hearing aid."

"I'm hungry," Adam whined.

"Sh," Jessica said, passing him a hard-boiled egg.

"You're talking about the Type A personality," Aunt Joanie said.

"Wasn't it Henry David Thoreau who said 'People lead lives of quiet desperation'?" Eric asked.

Mitzy was dumb-struck. Hottie had just quoted one of her favorite philosophers of all time. The summer of her junior year in college, she and her best friend Cindy had driven all the way to Massachusetts just to see Walden Pond. Cindy's ability to attract cute guys overshadowed the fact she didn't have a driver's license. She and Cindy lost contact after college, but were Cindy here right now, she'd agree with Mitzy that Eric was a real "Yeah, yeah", and smart to boot.

Harry's eyes twinkled. "We could discuss this topic for hours. Instead, it's time to act out the Ten Plagues the Lord visited upon Pharaoh, urging him to let the Jewish slaves leave Egypt. We spill a drop of wine or grape juice from our cups as we say each plague—"

"—and then you put your plague thingie out on the table," Jessica said.

Mitzy stifled a laugh.

"Frogs," Adam said, tossing two plastic frogs across the table.

The list continued down the line.

"Cattle disease," Shirley said, placing a toy cow next to her wine glass.

Mitzy turned to her friends. "You guys having fun yet?"

"This Seder thing is sweet," Eric said.

"He seemed like such a superficial guy at the police academy," Maggie kidded.

"Target practice wasn't an appropriate setting for philosophical discussion," Eric countered.

Mitzy laughed. "Quit harassing the detective and eat your bitter herbs."

~

It was 10:00 p.m. Mitzy yawned as she stacked the last of the gold and white china dinner dishes in the dining room breakfront. "Mom, next year you should switch to paper plates."

"Who eats brisket on paper?" her mother said, running the sweeper beneath the dining room table.

"Lots of people," Mitzy said.

"Next thing I know, you're gonna ask me to serve matzah ball soup in plastic bowls."

"Sure beats running all these dishes through the dishwasher."

"Grandma Rose always served the Passover meal on china plates. So do I. And one day, so will you when you get married."

Mitzy paused, then shoved the last of the pots in the top cabinet above the stove. "Listen Mom, it's a school night. I gotta go. Thanks for a lovely Seder."

"How come I mention marriage and you skedaddle?" her mother asked, pulling up the white linen tablecloth.

"It's getting late."

"You're only twenty minutes away."

"Don't be pushy," Mitzy warned.

"What? I can't ask a simple question?"

"I start a new career and already you're nagging me

about getting married."

"You're the other side of thirty, sweetie. Those eggs don't stay fresh forever, you know."

Mitzy glared at her mother. "I'm out of here."

"So go. I had something important to tell you but, as usual, you're in a big hurry."

"Tell me quick. You located some of our living relatives?"

"Forget it. It's not important."

"Mother!"

"I guess it's better than you reading about it in the newspaper."

"Stop being such a drama queen, Mom," she said with a touch of anxiety. Had one of their long-lost relatives turned out to be a rapist or murderer?

There was a pregnant pause.

Shirley Maven's eyes sparkled. "Harry and I are getting married."

Now Mitzy felt energized. "Really? After all these years?"

"He's getting old. I want him to leave me something in his will!"

"Oh my gosh! I'm so thrilled for you guys!"

"Not so loud or you'll wake the old geezer up," her mother said with a laugh, pointing to Harry snoring in the living room La-Z-Boy chair.

"Did he tell his family yet?"

"His grown nieces and nephews are all he's got left. They'll probably be mad that they won't be able to get their hands on his millions when he kicks the bucket."

"Engineers don't make millions, Mom."

"I'm kidding."

"Well, I'm so excited for you, and for me. Uncle Harry was always there for me when I needed someone to confide in."

"So what am I? A piece of cake?"

"You were great, too, but you always judged me. Harry would listen to me chatter away until I eventually figured things out for myself."

Her mother put her hands on her hips. "I always judged you? What kind of baloney is that?"

Mitzy rolled her eyes. "Mom, I really gotta go. Talk to you tomorrow. Thanks for letting me invite Maggie and Eric tonight."

Her mother was all smiles at that. "My pleasure. Maggie's so insightful. And that young man she brought along is absolutely adorable."

Mitzy resisted the impulse to say she'd invited Eric separately, not as a pair with Maggie. That would only start her mother off on marriage again. Instead, she settled for, "Eric and Maggie are both detectives, remember?"

"So they're not boyfriend, girlfriend."

Damn. Mitzy's hackles went up. "Why do you ask?"

Shirley smiled a secret smile. "No reason. Listen, before you run off, I want you to sign up for a wedding dance class."

"I danced for a DJ company during high school, I think I know how to dance."

"I'm talking foxtrot, not rap."

Mitzy attempted to demur gracefully. "How 'bout I watch Dancing with the Stars?"

"Why can't you take a couple of dance lessons for your mother? You could even ask that nice young man to join you."

"Stop trying to control my every move!"

"Sh. Harry's sleeping. Listen, I already checked the Chicago Park District schedule. They're offering a ballroom dance class a block from here. Starts next Thursday."

Mitzy sighed. "If I decide to do it, and I emphasize 'if', I'd take a class in Evanston."

"There's no time for 'ifs'. Harry and I are tying the knot on July 25."

"So soon?" If that wasn't just like Shirley Maven, to drag her feet forever about something and then rush in once she'd decided to do it.

"We want to start our marriage out with a bang! I got a

great deal on a ten-day cruise to the eastern Caribbean."

"Hey, you never took me on a cruise," Mitzy kidded.

"I never was able to sock away enough money doing retail sales. And your thirty-three-year-old father never planned on dying, so there was no life insurance. You know, you really should buy yourself a life insurance policy. You're young and the premiums would be—"

"Mom!"

"Okay, okay. Listen, Harry would be happy to have you tag along on the cruise. He always says you're like the daughter he never had."

"Oh my gosh! That is so sweet of you, but I don't want to ruin your honeymoon."

"Honeymoon, shmunymoon. This heifer's already been milked."

Mitzy blushed. "Okay then, let me think about it. And thanks for the offer."

"And honey?"

"Yeah?" she said, her hand on the doorknob.

"With all of your word expertise, isn't 'oh my gosh' a bit childish?"

"Okay, I'm out of here."

"Drive safely," her mom called out sweetly, shutting the door behind her.

Sauntering down the hall, Mitzy giggled as she headed toward the elevator.

By the time she unlocked her apartment door, it was 11:00 p.m. The light on the answering machine blinked slowly. She yawned. If it was important, whoever it was would have called her cell phone. She stripped off her clothes, hit the night-light switch and fell into bed.

~

The furry pink alarm clock clanged six times. Mitzy awoke with a start. Visions of herself dancing with Joseph Barge at her mother's wedding filled her head. Trembling, she slipped into her silk robe and cheetah slippers and

headed for the shower. The blinking light on the answering
machine caught her eye. Her heart quickened.
      She pressed the replay button. "Hey Mitzy, it's Eric."
The detective's voice sounded tense. "I need to talk to you
regarding the Barge case. Meet you in your classroom at
8:00 a.m. If there's any problem, call me on my cell phone."
The second call was from her mother, telling her how much
she'd enjoyed their visit. The third and fourth calls were
repeats of Eric's first message.
      Mitzy shuddered. Thank God it wasn't The Call she'd
dreaded ever since her father was killed twenty-six years
ago. The Call saying her mother had also died. Her mom was
active, but with her health problems, life was unpredictable.
Nobody knew when the light switch would permanently flick
off.
      As Mitzy showered, she mused about Eric. This was the
first time he'd called her at home. She'd love to invite him
on a bike ride through Evanston or to a basketball game at
Northwestern, but she didn't want to appear too eager. His
actions today would determine whether or not she would
allow him to pursue her.
      As if. Mitzy laughed aloud, then coughed a mouthful of
water. Eric hadn't shown the least bit of interest in her, other
than attending last night's Seder. Even their professional
interaction was snarkly. Of course, she had it in her power to
change all that. She'd manipulated Juron, withholding sex
until he'd asked her to move into his downtown condo. Not
that sex was even on the table here. She giggled. Sex on the
table sounded electrifying! It had been a long dry spell since
her soul mate's body and hers had intertwined.
      Mitzy stepped out of the shower and wrapped herself in a
thick white terrycloth robe. Now, Detective Eric? He might
be a keeper, as her mother had so aptly put it. Comfortable in
his own skin, sensitive enough to quote Henry David
Thoreau. Pretty damned sure of himself, sometimes
annoying with it—though that was probably an asset for a
cop. A man who lived life on his own terms and refused to
capitulate to anybody. A guy definitely worth getting to

know. One thing Mitzy was sure of, though. If Eric remained convinced Ellie was responsible for her father's death, their relationship would be over before it began.

Mitzy finger-combed gel through her auburn hair, then slipped into black slacks and a salmon pink poncho. She grabbed her keys, along with a matzo and cheese sandwich and bottled water, and hurried out the door.

~

Mitzy shot Eric a quick smile as she dropped her purse and a stack of collated packets on her desk. "So what's with all the answering machine messages?"

Eric appeared in no hurry to respond. Instead he leaned back in the computer chair, his legs crossed. "Had a great time at the Seder last night. Thanks for the invite."

She rummaged in her top desk drawer for an ever-elusive permanent marker. "You made a positive impression on my mom. She said you're the kind of guy I should marry." She hadn't, exactly, but Mitzy couldn't resist teasing Eric a little as payback for the phone calls.

The detective's face turned scarlet.

Mitzy found the marker, turned to the white board, and jotted down instructions for this morning's lesson. "Don't worry. I told her I'm never getting married. So you had some breaking news on the Barge case?"

He nodded. "The custodian saw a kid pull the fire alarm."

Mitzy recalled that morning. Ellie had come in early, saying she needed a package of paper for Norman Stein. She looked ill and Mitzy had sat her down outside the nurse's office.

"You all right?" Eric asked, concerned.

"Was he able to identify the student?"

The detective stared back at her, his eyes expressionless. "Nope. Any ideas?"

"Not sure," she hedged. She sensed he knew more than he was saying. "Maybe one of the kids Ellie bullied."

"I know Ellie's your student, Mitzy, but don't let her blindside you."

She felt annoyance rising. "Ellie plays hooky from school. Pleads many an imaginary ailment. Pulling the fire alarm might have been her newest ploy. But she's a prankster, not a killer."

The school bell rang. Eric got up to go. "This is why I had reservations about bringing you in on the case. You're too emotionally attached, Mitzy. Ellie's not your own kid."

Anger shot through her, along with disappointment. So damned sure he was right and she was wrong. "Was the kid's name Sammy?" she called after him.

Eric threw his arms up in apparent disgust, and then vanished into the crowd of students and teachers.

Chapter 20

Mitzy swung open the car's passenger door. "Got all your stuff?" she asked cheerily.

"You're A-ok, kid, driving me home like this so my daughter didn't have to find a babysitter for the grandkids," Neil said, easing his body into the Celica.

Mitzy switched on the ignition and slipped in an Alicia Keyes CD. "No problem. We were off from school today anyway. Plus, I want to smooth the way in case I have to ask you for my old job back. How's that hip doing?"

"Much better. Only thing I'll miss about Glen Tree is the physical therapy."

"When do you go back to work?"

"In a couple of days. Now what's this about you wanting to reclaim the newspaper as your hearth and home?"

"I'm in a real quandary, Neil. It looks like that student I told you about might be involved in her father's death."

"Have you talked to the kid?"

"The girl's in a catatonic state."

"Think she offed him?"

Mitzy carefully pulled out of the parking lot. "Why would she remove her lifeline? Her mother's comatose. In

fact, she's at Glen Tree. Ellie's aunt is her only remaining
relative."

"Maybe she didn't mean to kill him."

"You sound like the detective on the case. I found some
partially empty prescription bottles of antidepressant drugs
beneath her bed."

"Any other evidence?"

"The nanny says Ellie and her father had a big fight the
night before her MDC meeting."

"MDC?"

"Every three years, school staff and parents of special ed
kids have a meeting to gauge a student's progress with
annual academic and behavioral goals and determine future
placement. At Ellie's MDC meeting, her father was poised
to sign off on alternative high school placement when the
fire alarm went off. Everyone fled the room. Minutes after
the meeting resumed, the father keeled over, dead."

"What did the coroner's report say?"

"Evidence of drugs and alcohol in the father's system,
along with liver damage. Untreated hypertension. Mix an
MAO inhibitor—"

"Huh?"

"A category of antidepressant drugs you take when all
other types of antidepressant drugs fail. Mix those drugs
with alcohol and untreated hypertension and you get a fatal
reaction."

"How would a kid suspect a fatal reaction would occur?"

"She wouldn't. But it gets murkier, Neil. The custodian
saw a kid lurking by the fire alarm the morning of the
conference. No ID was made. I suspect Sammy, a seventh-
grade student of mine. Ellie was suspended for dunking his
head in the toilet. Turns out his conference was scheduled
an hour after hers. He could very well have pulled that alarm
himself."

"Pulling a fire alarm doesn't make the boy a murderer."

Mitzy stopped at a red light and turned towards her
former newspaper editor. "At the very least, an accomplice.
Think about it, Neil. Ellie tells the kid she'll stop bullying

him if he helps her out. A harassed kid at his wit's end would have gone along with her plan."

"She could have badgered him into doing something worse than pulling a fire alarm," Neil mused. "Is there anyone else who had access to the father and the drugs prior to the meeting?"

"The nanny and the aunt had access to both. The school principal and the teachers attending the meeting had access to the father, but not the drugs as far as I know. But they've all been interviewed and cleared by Detective Whelan."

"My advice to you, kid, is to use your god-given and delve deeper."

"Neil, when I took this teaching job, all I wanted to do was help kids. If I knew I was going to continue to play investigator, I never would have left the newspaper. I should resign."

"As usual, you're selling yourself short."

"My mom thinks I can more effectively help students with special needs by writing about the challenges they face in society and the workplace."

"You're no quitter, kid. Give teaching a chance, why don't you?"

"I can't handle the possibility Ellie might have fatally drugged her father," Mitzy said, her voice breaking.

"You'll deal with it. As they say in Gamblers Anonymous, one day at a time."

Mitzy pulled over to the curb. "You finally started going to the meetings?" she said, hugging the newspaper editor. "I'm proud of you!"

"Ditto," he said gruffly, hugging her back.

~

Dr. Ribaldi leaned back in his chair and perched his horn-rimmed glasses higher on his nose. "My advice is to continue conversing with your niece and include her in your daily activities, despite the absence of verbal and kinesthetic response."

"But it's been three weeks," Fay said, wringing her hands. "How much longer will Ellie remain in this stupor?"

"It's difficult to say. She's quite depressed. Fortunately, catatonia responds well to treatment, no matter its cause or duration."

"She's pretty much stopped eating and drinking, and she's lost a lot of weight."

Dr. Ribaldi flipped through the medical records on his desk. "Ellie's in good cardiovascular health. When the nurse makes her home visit this afternoon, have her phone me. We'll up your niece's intravenous fluids and electrolytes and slightly increase the amount of lorazepam she's receiving. That should facilitate her food and fluid intake."

Ellie sat mutely beside her aunt, letting the adults' words wash over her. As if she ever wanted to eat or drink again. The house was deadly quiet now; no more of her father's bombastic yelling and her own tearful retreats. Only a few kids had come to visit since the funeral. Who could blame them? She'd used their souls as punching bags to get even with her father for emotionally abandoning her. Everyone had abandoned her. Everyone but Ms. Maven. She'd been to the house three times. And there was that cute detective with the piercing blue eyes and quick smile. He talked to her like she was still there, not just a shell of a girl lost in Neverland.

"Fay, I urge you to reconsider ECT. It is still the principal treatment for catatonic patients."

"You know how my brother-in-law felt about taking medicine. He'd go ballistic if he knew his daughter was being subjected to electric shock therapy."

"The correct name is electroconvulsive therapy, and Joe is no longer controlling Ellie's life. You alone have the power to take the steps necessary for your niece's full recovery."

Fay dabbed her eyes with a pink floral tissue. "I guess I have my own private reservations about ECT."

Silence pervaded the office. "Ellie can hear you, whatever you say," the doctor cautioned.

Ellie observed her aunt inhale deeply.

"I doubt even Joe knew of my sister's brief rendezvous with ECT when she was seventeen. Lani was a cheerleader in high school. Her senior year, she was dating a football quarterback. When her boyfriend found out she was pregnant, he took her to get an abortion. Afterwards, my sister went into a deep funk. She was out of school for weeks. Following the doctor's advice, my mother took Lani in for several treatments of electric shock therapy. She finally recovered, but according to her stories, the treatment was barbaric."

"ECT has come a long way in the last twenty years, Fay. The only caveat in treating adolescent depressed patients with ECT is that the rate of recovery may be slower than that of adults. But we should see some immediate improvement."

"Meaning?"

"Ellie may be verbal, attentive, and social for short periods of time. If we're lucky, the change could be permanent."

"Perhaps I should get a second opinion."

Dr. Ribaldi sat forward, elbows on his desk. "You're welcome to do so, Fay, but any psychiatrist will validate this method as the routine course of treatment for catatonia when lorazepam or another Benzodiazepine fails to work. Intravenous dosing of lorazepam relieves catatonia in 79 to 90 percent of patients. Let's try Ellie on the higher dosage for five days, in addition to facilitating her food and water intake. If we succeed, there'll be no need for ECT."

"I'll agree to that."

"I do, however, want to explain the procedure for ECT so we can move directly into that mode of treatment should the other fail."

"All right."

Dr. Ribaldi reached into his bottom desk drawer and pulled out a picture of the skull. "Seizures are induced daily until symptoms substantially abate." He pointed to the side of the head. "We use bi-temporal electrode placement with brief-pulse currents. Due to Ellie's youth, she'd receive 6.5 percent of the ECT device's maximum energy output. Her seizure threshold might be heightened following the lorazepam treatment, and the first seizures may not fully take effect. We would then introduce the Bendiazepine antagonist, Flumazenil, into the ECT induction process."

Ellie watched from beneath partially closed lids. She anticipated with welcome relief the pain of electricity infiltrating every organ and tissue of her body. A fitting punishment.

Aunt Fay stifled a yawn. "I don't understand all this jargon, doctor. I just want to make sure the treatment is safe and won't leave my niece brain-damaged."

"ECT is so safe, it's used on patients who are pregnant. It is an effective alternative to reducing severe depression and catatonia, and actually relieves the underlying psychopathology in patients with manic-depressive disorder."

"So you'd automatically start my niece on this treatment?"

"If all else fails, yes. First Ellie would undergo a pre-ECT general medical examination. Then she'd be referred to a neurologist for further assessment, including an EEG, MRI, and a CSF. If all goes well, ECT treatment would ensue."

Rising from her chair, Aunt Fay thrust her hand forward. "I'm placing my niece's life in your hands."

Dr. Ribaldi stood up, warmly clasping her hand with both of his. "If Ellie was my own child, my choice of treatment would remain the same."

Fay smiled faintly, then helped Ellie up and turned them both towards the door. Then, hesitating, she turned back to face the doctor. "There is one more thing."

The doctor looked up from his files. "Yes?"

"I suspect Ellie drugged her father."

~

A ringed index finger zig-zagged down the front page of the Lake Forest Review, stopping midstream:

> *Three weeks ago, Town Center bank executive Joseph Barge suffered a fatal heart attack while attending his daughter's IEP meeting. At that time, it was thought Barge died of natural causes. However, an undisclosed source from the Lake County coroner's office now confirms cause of death was a fatal reaction resulting from alcohol, prescription drugs, and untreated hypertension.*
>
> *According to Paul London, medical examiner for the Lake County coroner's office, it would take a cocktail of alcohol and pills of the SSRI category of anti-depressant/anti-anxiety drugs to cause a fatal reaction. London says an MAO inhibitor, also used as an antipsychotic drug, works on a different part of the brain and would take a smaller number of pills to bring about death.*
>
> *Sources say Barge would have ingested the alcohol and drugs one half-hour to four hours prior to the school meeting, which was held at 8:30 a.m. If anyone has any knowledge concerning this case, please contact the Lake Forest police department at 565-0375.*

Manicured fingers crumpled the newspaper and threw it against the office wall, landing a hole-in-one in the oversized trash can. *That's what happens when you mess around with people's lives.*

Chapter 21

Mitzy paced the far recesses of the dance floor, waiting for the teacher to begin. A dozen or more couples huddled throughout the brightly lit room. "Come on already," she mumbled.

"Welcome, everybody," Ms. Valerie finally began, in a cheery voice that went with her ruddy cheeks. "In this eight-week class you will learn to dance the foxtrot, waltz, and swing. Any upcoming weddings?"

Mitzy raised her hand. Everybody applauded.

She blushed. "My mother's." The applause quickly dissipated.

"You'll be the belle of the ball," the instructor said, smoothly rescuing her from the awkward silence.

Mitzy nodded.

Miss Valerie continued. "Gentlemen, you'll need to wear thin-soled shoes so you can slide across the floor easily. Ladies, heels or dance shoes will be fine. Regardless of what happens outside this class, the men lead and the ladies follow." Smothered giggles.

"The girls want you to lead, guys," the teacher encouraged. "Place your right arms around their backs just below their shoulder blades. That way, you can guide them in any direction you choose." Snickers.

Another great couple sport, Mitzy thought ruefully.

"Okay. Let's start with the foxtrot. We're going to be drawing two right angles, or a square, with our feet. Gentlemen first. Step together, step forward. Step together, step backward."

Mitzy watched the other young women exchange humorous glances as their guys clumsily attempted to move their feet in rhythm. When it was her turn, Mitzy hung back. She'd hoped to just observe from the sidelines, but Miss Valerie grabbed her hand. "Watch how it's done, ladies," she said, guiding Mitzy through the foxtrot. "Quick quick slow, quick quick slow. Ladies step back as your guy steps forward."

Her cheeks felt hot as the teacher relinquished her hand, then spun around towards the middle of the dance floor. "Your turn, ladies! Keep those arms out as if you're encircling your partner." Her arms extended in a mannequin pose, Mitzy moved in an imaginary square, progressively inching closer to the door. *Wedding or no wedding, I'm out of here!*

As Miss Valerie assisted a klutzy couple at the far end of the room, Mitzy seized her black North Face jacket from a folding chair, then danced backwards through the open doorway. She collided with someone and turned to apologize. She found herself looking up into the stunned face of Eric Whelan.

"What are you doing here?" she sputtered, pushing him out into the hallway.

Eric looked half irritated, half amused. "You don't have to get physical about it."

"Wait! You've been invited to the wedding?" Mitzy asked.

He grinned. "No big surprise there."

"Boy, she works fast."

"Who?"

"Next thing you'll be telling me you're best man."

Eric gave a little grin and shrugged.

"I'm going to kill that woman!" Mitzy said angrily. "She just met you!"

Eric laughed. "Thirty-two years ago."

"Excuse me?" Mitzy felt bewildered. Did her mother have a child from a previous marriage? As a reporter, she'd once done a story on a married guy who had a second household.

"My sister was five years old when I was born. We've always been close. Naturally she'd ask me to be her best man."

Mitzy shot him a beatific smile, started laughing and quickly stepped away from the music coming from the other side of the doorway.

Eric followed her past the gap. "Wait a minute. You thought I was invited to someone else's wedding?"

Mitzy nodded, giggling.

"Okay, I'll bite. You're getting married and you thought your fiancé invited me without mentioning it to you first."

She shook her head. "Actually, it's my mom who's getting married for the second time. Harry, the older gentleman who led the Passover Seder, he's the lucky groom."

"Oh yeah, that whole discussion on freedom was really thought-provoking. Harry's a great guy. But why'd you think your mother'd invite me to their wedding?"

"She's impulsive."

"Or very friendly."

"By the way, I'm not attached," Mitzy said, "which you probably figured out by my lack of a partner at the Seder."

"Which is why you were backing your way out of a couples' dance class," Eric said.

"Exactly." She paused briefly, then thought, *What the heck*? "Look, since we're both in a similar situation, how about going back in there as a couple? That way, we'll both learn the dance steps for our respective big days."

Eric gawked at her.

Mitzy's eyes burned with humiliation. "Forget it."

Clumsily, Eric reached to touch her shoulder. "It's a fine idea. I'm just a little taken aback, that's all."

Mitzy pulled away. "Why?"

"I mean, one minute you hate me because I won't give Ellie Barge the benefit of the doubt, the next minute you invite me to be your dance partner."

"What's a guy to think?" Mitzy said, her words edged with sarcasm.

Eric laughed wryly. "Those are the exact words my ex-girlfriend used on me, except for the gender thing."

Mitzy observed him from beneath hooded eyelids. He looked so miserable standing there, his frown as deep as the Napa Valley. Her heart softened. "Sounds like you've got some major trust issues."

"Let's just say I don't need a woman to make me whole."

Mitzy did her best to stifle the laughter welling up inside her. He was spouting her mantra, almost verbatim. "No new girlfriend on the horizon?"

"I've taken a vow of chastity," Eric said, the muscles around his lips twitching.

Now she was laughing so hard, boogers dangled from her nose. Eric chuckled as he handed her a tissue and a mini hand sanitizer.

A guy after her own heart! Mitzy blew her nose and tossed the used tissue in the trash. Then she massaged antibacterial lotion into her palms. "I can't believe you actually carry sanitizer around with you."

"Blame my sister. She's germ-phobic."

Hard boiled, yet funny as hell. Mitzy swung open the door and pushed the handsome detective into the dance room. "Miss Valerie's got to be teaching the next dance step by now."

Chapter 22

Mitzy checked her watch. Only ten minutes until the first bell. She hurried down the hallway to her classroom. She felt a sudden tap on her shoulder and turned.

"Where have you been?"

"Hey, Lynette," Mitzy said warmly. "How's it going?"

"Good," the English teacher said, falling in step with her.

"Looks like we're both running late this morning. What's your excuse?"

"I stayed up late last night to watch *Shakespeare in Love* on HBO."

"I watched *Dangerous Minds*," Mitzy said.

"That's the one about the inner city kids who had lots of behavior problems?"

"Yep."

"Speaking of problem kids, what's the story on Ellie? I was filling out progress reports yesterday and noticed she's been out for five weeks."

"She's still catatonic," Mitzy said. "Her aunt's supposed to take her to the hospital this week for some special kind of treatment."

"I read they still use shock therapy with severely

depressed patients. But they don't do it on adolescent kids, do they?"

"Even if they did, I doubt Ellie's aunt would allow such a controversial procedure."

"You never know. Listen, I'm concerned about Sammy Cooper. I figured he'd do better during Ellie's extended absence, but he's off on Pluto."

"Pluto's not a planet anymore," Mitzy joked.

"Exactly."

"He seems a bit quieter in resource room, too," Mitzy said. "Want me to talk to him?"

"I'd appreciate it." They reached Lynette's classroom. Mitzy's was a short way beyond it. Lynette set her briefcase on the floor and unlocked her door. The light blue gem of her ring reflected on the wall.

"Nice class ring," Mitzy said. "Where'd you go to school?"

"University of Illinois at Champaign. You?"

"Northwestern. But I had friends who went to U. of I. They found it too impersonal and transferred to Illinois State."

"I played women's basketball, so I had a ready niche of friends to hang with," Lynette said.

"How many of your basketball buddies grew up to become English teachers?" Mitzy teased.

Lynette smiled. "I guess I illustrate the old cliché, 'Never judge a book by its cover.'"

~

Ellie dreamed she was lying on the beach, the hot sun searing her every pore. The sand molded itself around her body in a loving caress. Suddenly, twenty-foot waves surged through her, rocking her high above the waters, then to the depths of the sea, high, then low. Again and again, the roller coaster of waves jolted her to its rhythm. Fantastic! Exhilarating! Then a wave crashed upon her, a thousand times stronger than the others. A tsunami dragged her down into its underwater cavern of darkness from which no breath could arise. Ellie thrashed around. Her eyes flew open. The tsunami disappeared. Feeling an unfamiliar pull on her arms and legs, she looked down to find herself strapped onto a hospital gurney under bright operating room lights. Too bright. She attempted to scream, but fear choked off the sound.

A hand smoothed her brow. "Mama?" she called out.

"Sh, you're all right now."

Ellie's eyes followed the deep voice. She saw nothing.

"You did just fine," Dr. Ribaldi said. "As soon as you calm down, we'll get these uncomfortable straps off you."

"What happened?" she croaked, each word pushing through her parched lips as slowly as a hippopotamus wading through a mud pool.

"It's been a long time since you've spoken."

"Where am I?"

"You're at Lake Forest Hospital," the doctor said.

"Where's Mama?"

"Breathe in, breathe out, breathe in, breathe out," the nurse instructed.

Something jarred her gurney. A woman's caressing voice floated over her. "Hello, darling!"

Ellie felt someone try to hug her. She pulled away. "Who are you?" she screeched, tossing her head from side to side.

"Oh my lord," a voice cried.

"Not to worry. Your niece is doing just fine."

"But she doesn't know me!"

"Short-term memory loss. Temporary blindness."

Ellie felt a jolt of exuberance. "Mama? Is that you?" She struggled to sit up as she shot a beaming smile into the darkness, but the arm restraints held her down. "I've missed you."

"It's Aunt Fay, darling." The answering voice sounded shaky.

"I'm dreaming, right, Mama?" Ellie said excitedly.

"How long will she be like this?"

"She should be back with us in an hour or so."

The woman's voice shuddered with tears. "I never should have given permission for Ellie to undergo ECT."

"Mama? Where are you?"

"I can't bear this!"

"Did you notice that your niece is speaking?" Dr. Ribaldi said.

"Oh, my god." The woman's voice shook. "I was so focused on Ellie's reactions, I didn't even realize that miracle."

"Where's Daddy?" Ellie asked.

"Courage, Ms. Shimmer, courage," the doctor said.

~

Mitzy stepped inside the Barges' Lake Forest mansion. "Just wanted to see how Ellie's doing."

"Miss Fay bringing niece home from hospital this afternoon. You wait?"

"Sure. May I use the bathroom?"

"Downstairs toilet plugged up. Plumber come today. You use Ellie's bathroom?"

"No problem."

The doorbell chimed. "Please excuse," Anya said, rushing to answer the door.

"XYZ Plumbing," said a deep rumbling voice.

Anya briefly reappeared. "I need show plumber inside. You okay find bathroom?"

"Go ahead. I know my way around."

~

It was eerie walking down the long hallway leading to the back wing of the house, Mitzy thought. The solitude must have been deafening for an adolescent starved of parental affection. Thank goodness for Anya. The nanny's adoring tone when speaking of her young charge demonstrated the bond of love between them.

A non-judgmental harbor was what children needed in order to bloom, especially a girl whose behavior stirred up a hornet's nest of negativity in those who dealt with her on a regular basis. Then again, what percentage of parents with healthy, normal children offered their offspring that utopian womb of acceptance? Mitzy's own mom had been lots of fun when she was growing up, with infinite board and card game tournaments of Chinese checkers, Scrabble, Monopoly, and gin rummy.

But Mitzy had sensed that when it came to games of all sorts, her mother's love was conditional. Visions of her thirteen-year-old self lying motionless on the couch as mononucleosis sucked away her energy. Mom, forced to forfeit her daily wages, urging her to come to the table and play Parcheesi. With excruciating effort, a pale, quiet Mitzy had moved each marble into place. Shirley had seemed oblivious to her exhaustion. If she had to while away the hours with an invalid, she required entertainment. Her mother was needy in those days.

Not that she wasn't needy now!

Mitzy headed down another hallway. The plumber's booming voice reverberated throughout the Barge mansion like an aural compass. So dark in this wing of the house. She entered a short hallway leading to Ellie's bedroom. A whoosh of fresh air beckoned her into the lavender-drenched room. Lavender curtains billowed in the wind. A navy blue Bears football blanket lay neatly folded at the foot of a lavender-and-blue flowered bedspread. On the lavender sham lay a clown bear, its eyes poked out. Obviously this Shangri-La had failed to extinguish Ellie's anger and fears.

Being an only child was no great shakes, Mitzy could attest to that. Mining for playmates who'd even remotely shared her interests. Frantically attempting to set up play dates, so as not to be alone while Mom worked.

In one respect, Ellie was lucky. She had taken martial arts, played basketball, and interacted with action figure dolls without having to worry about appropriate gender roles. Mitzy had done the girl thing, performing in dance recitals to her mother's proud applause echoing throughout the park district gymnasium. Given Ellie's disjointed family life, applause at her accomplishments was unlikely.

Her kidneys about to burst, Mitzy rushed into the bathroom adjoining Ellie's bedroom. As she turned to flush the toilet, her gaze fell on a lone yellow and blue capsule lying at the base of the toilet bowl. She picked up the squished capsule and read the inscription. Nardil.

What was that doing here, she wondered, washing her hands at the tiled sink. Ellie's dad flushed meds down the toilet, but he'd been out of the picture for almost four weeks now. Gently fingering the capsule, Mitzy headed back into the bedroom and glanced beneath Ellie's bed. The prescription bottles were gone. Mitzy bent down and peered into the dark, hidden corners. Nothing there.

Straightening up, she wrapped the squished capsule in a tissue she found on the girl's computer desk. Then she remembered the yellow-flowered diary. Where was it? Mitzy peeked into the hallway to make sure she was still alone. Good. She checked the computer desk, then inside the dresser drawers. Nada. The girl's stuffed animals appeared well-dusted, with nothing underneath them.

Mitzy unfolded the Bears blanket lying atop the bedspread. Nothing. She carefully refolded the blanket. "Mees Maven?" came Anya's voice down the hall. She quickly checked beneath Ellie's pillow, and between the mattresses. Where could Ellie have hidden the diary?

"Mees Maven," Anya said, stepping into the bedroom. "You get lost?" Mitzy saw the nanny glance at the crumpled tissue in her hand.

"Bad cold," she said.

"I get you tea?" Anya asked.

"Thanks anyway. I have to be going. Please tell Ellie and her aunt I stopped by."

Outside, as she unlocked her Celica, Mitzy prayed Anya and Fay Shimmer had nothing to do with the death of Joseph Barge.

Chapter 23

Anya knelt and peered beneath Ellie's canopy bed. No loose pills or capsules. At least it appeared so. Her mind ran back to the startled expression on the teacher's face as she'd squeezed past, crumpled tissue in hand. The look of a guilty person.

Anya sighed. She'd done what she could. There should be nothing left for Ms. Maven, or anyone else, to find.

She felt between the back panel of the bed and the wall. Only a smattering of dust bunnies filled her palm. In the early years, she'd found printed notes in a childish hand hidden behind the same bed in which her girl had taken refuge since her mama's accident, the accident for which she blamed herself. Each note was folded into a dozen squares, each tiny square containing a letter of the alphabet. Some sort of code, it was, for when Anya tried to string the letters together, the result was gibberish. Such a dichotomy. While the girl clearly wished to communicate with the outside world, she only used consonants, as if vowels could not be trusted. Keeping her own counsel, even at an early age, fearing some horror would occur if those consonants and vowels combined. Ellie had finally exposed that horror in the pages of her yellow-flowered diary in the days leading to her father's death. It was those words that gave Anya the impetus to do what she had to do.

With a mighty effort, Anya shook her unruly thoughts back into submission. She reached for a dust mop and dragged it back and forth beneath the bed, then along the hardwood floors of the spacious bedroom suite. Such a stark contrast to her family's one-bedroom apartment in Ukraine. She thought of recent pictures her parents had sent of Tatiana, her daughter whom she hadn't seen in seven years, only three years older than her young charge. Anger rose within her. Not against Ellie. Never against the dear girl whose every whim she attempted to fulfill. How little did wealthy people like the girl's father appreciate what they had. She debated which of the two children had a better life, Ellie or her own flesh and blood, and smiled sadly.

Anxiety choked this house to its very foundation. A father who barricaded his soul from his only child. A violent silence that erupted from a sea of despair. How could it be otherwise with the poor girl's mother lying comatose, her body available to touch, yet her mind existing in a place where nothing else did.

Was it not ironic that Anya's own daughter could see her but not touch her? Tatiana, whose mind also dwelled elsewhere. Though at least Tatiana was living her life back in Ukraine. It was no easy feat for Anya to be parted from her child. She had told Ellie's teacher that monetary concerns caused her to leave her homeland. Certainly she had no intention of sharing the true motive for her exit. She had been an activist, calling for the separation of Ukraine and Russia. The government had begun covertly tracking her family's every move. And so she had left home, moved to America to keep her family untarnished by intrigue. The money she sent home enabled Tatiana to attend a fine boarding school. And her daughter was nurtured by two adoring grandparents who lived for her every smile.

Nothing could threaten that. Nothing and no one. Including the Joseph Barges of the world, who believed they could take what they wanted with no regard for what others thought or felt.

Anya shivered, remembering how the man had come up behind her while she was dusting art pieces in the hallway and lifted her skirt. She'd turned in shock to find him half-dressed, his face red and his breath smelling of alcohol. Her face blazing, she'd run from the room. His thunderous laughter at her embarrassment had seemed to follow her, ricocheting through the house. Yes, Joseph Barge had deserved his fatal punishment. Of this she was certain.

~

Mitzy leaned back in the gold velvet fireside chair and propped her shoes on a matching ottoman.

"Aren't you forgetting something?" her mom asked, glaring at her from the couch, a towel-covered ice pack pressed against her right calf.

"Fine!" Mitzy said as she slipped off her pink rhinestone high-heeled sandals. "So how's your ancestry research coming along?"

"We've got a good shot at digging up your grandfather's family tree since Lishbitz is an unusual last name," Shirley said.

"There is no 'we.' This ancestry thing is your deal, not mine," Mitzy cautioned.

Shirley winced. "Strictly a slip of the synapses, darling. I know you're not interested in helping little old me."

Mitzy felt a twinge of guilt. "I guess I could spare a couple of minutes researching that surname."

"How generous of you," her mother said wryly.

"Again with the sarcasm!"

"Sorry, darling. It comes naturally. Your grandfather passed it down the pike."

"That's no excuse, Mom. Words do more damage than fists because they poison the brain."

"So how's it going with Ellie?" Shirley asked, massaging her thigh muscle.

"Her aunt took her to the hospital this week for some kind of treatment."

"The girl still not talking?"

Mitzy shrugged. "You know, I always took it for granted you'd be around when I grew up. I really feel sorry for this kid, her mother good as dead, her father gone."

"Did you hear about that woman who was in a vegetative state for twenty years?" Shirley asked, wincing as she adjusted her leg position. "One day she woke up and just started chattering away."

"Bizarre," Mitzy said.

"If that ever happens to me, unhook my feeding tube. I'll look forward to joining your dad up in heaven."

"You gotta stay alive for Uncle Harry!"

Shirley silently debated the issue. "Better keep me going an extra six months."

"Thanks for sharing your last will and testament," Mitzy said wryly.

"Darling, can you bring me a new ice pack? This one's warm."

"Mom, the chiropractor said twenty minutes on, twenty minutes off."

"I know, but this sciatica's driving me crazy!"

"First a herniated disc. Now this. You're really falling apart, lady!"

Shirley groaned. "Thanks for the reminder."

"Let's try this first." Mitzy placed her mother's leg on her lap and began to massage it gently

"Mmm. Feels good." Shirley leaned forward, her eyes sparkling. "Gotta tell you Harry's latest joke. A motorist unknowingly gets caught in an automated speed trap on the Tollway. He receives a ticket for forty bucks, along with a photo of his car. Instead of paying the ticket, the motorist sends the police a photo of forty bucks. Several days later, he receives a letter from the police containing a picture of handcuffs. He mails in his forty dollars."

Mitzy giggled. "You pooh-pooh his jokes."

"I don't want him to think I'm so easy to entertain," her

mom said, then winced in pain. "Why'd you stop massaging?"

"Sorry," Mitzy said. She picked up a small tube of homeopathic ointment and squeezed some into her palm, then gently rubbed it onto her mother's leg. "Anyway, Ellie's in this catatonic state for now. It gets worse once the protective cocoon bursts."

"What do you mean?"

Mitzy sighed. She didn't like thinking about it, let alone saying it. "The police will question her as a suspect in her father's death."

"How awful! But if this child did kill her father, you shouldn't visit her anymore."

"This is why I don't tell you anything," Mitzy complained. "You always overreact!"

Shirley teared up. "Your father's death almost snuffed out my will to exist. Many a time I looked longingly at the gas oven. But I kept that pilot lit because I had a little girl to raise. My heart couldn't take it if something happened to you."

Seeing her mother in such anguish, Mitzy's anger quickly dissipated. She handed her mother a tissue. "Nothing's going to happen to me."

"You got ESP?" Shirley said, her voice quavering.

"Gut feeling. Do you think about him much?"

Shirley dabbed at her eyes with the tissue. "Who?"

"Joe Blow."

"Now you're the one who's being sarcastic."

Why do I even bother? Mitzy asked herself. Still, she wanted to know. "Do you reminisce about the good times you and Dad shared?"

"Oh yeah," Shirley said, fresh tears glittering on her cheeks. "In high school, your father and I rallied together in Washington, D.C. for passage of the Equal Rights Amendment. Then again to stop the war in Viet Nam. No surprise that he became a pharmacist. His way of atoning for all those illegal drugs he downed during our hippie days."

"Too much information!"

"By the way, there's a new Vietnamese-owned nail salon on Sheridan just north of Devon. Get your nails done there for my wedding."

"Is that an order?" Mitzy asked, bristling.

"Just a request."

"I'll think about it."

"By the way, your nice young detective sent me a thank-you note."

"You're kidding!" What a suck-up, Mitzy thought.

"Evidently he was raised in the Unitarian Church. His family encouraged him and his sister to explore various religious traditions."

Hell of a lot of information to include in a thank-you note. "Eric's in my dance class at the park district."

"Small world. Are you inviting him to the wedding?"

Mitzy evaded the question. She hadn't decided yet, and had no intention of discussing it with her mother. "So where's your reception going to be held?"

Shirley pointed to a lamp table drawer. "Garden Banquets. The particulars are in there."

Mitzy dug out the brochure and skimmed through it. The first few pages held photos of tables dressed in white linen and ornate trees surrounding a spacious dance floor. Vases of fresh flowers adorned each table. "Fancy."

"Well, we only invited forty-five guests so that should keep the costs down. Plus the menu's to die for," her mother said, the excitement in her voice overriding her pain.

Mitzy flipped a gilt-edged page. "You can start off with cream of chicken, chicken noodle, or cream of mushroom soup."

"Invite Eric. Do it for your mother."

"We're talking menu here, Mom." Mitzy scanned the list. "Sliced tomato and cucumber in vinaigrette or the Hawaiian fruit salad?"

"Something tells me this guy's a keeper," her mother said.

"Aren't you the one who's always telling me to only date Jewish men?"

"Converts make the most observant Jews," her mother countered without missing a beat.

Mitzy rolled her eyes.

"What, you don't like this boy?"

"Liking has nothing to do with it, Mom. You want to order family style or individual main courses?"

"We'll order from the individual menu, just like they do for bar and bat mitzvahs."

"A celebration I never got to enjoy," Mitzy reminded her mother.

"Who had money for extras like religious education when you were growing up? Besides, you can still get bat mitzvahed as an adult. This ninety-year-old woman at Temple Emanuel just got bat mitzvahed."

"Thanks, but no thanks. You can choose from the roast leg of island duck à l'orange, breast of chicken Kiev, or boneless breast of chicken baked in butter, garlic and oregano. Gosh, they all sound so good."

"Darling, I'm feeling tired. Let's talk menu next week."

"Just a couple more minutes, Mom."

"I thought you had to get to dance class."

"I'm doing this for you!" Engrossed in the menu, she perused the list of veggies. "They've got whole green beans almondine, or you can go with peas and mushrooms. Then you get to choose baked potatoes or rice *arroz*."

"I wonder if they throw rice at second weddings," her mother mused.

"No clue. For dessert, you can order lime, orange or rainbow sherbet, or their famous kolackis."

"That's a sticky choice," Shirley said with a straight face.

"You're as bad as Harry, Mom." She held up the brochure so her mother could see it. "Check out this fruit salad volcano with smoke coming out of it."

"Darling, my pain medicine's kicking in and I'm finding it really hard to concentrate. Let's talk about it again next week."

Mitzy set the booklet down. "Sorry. I was so into the menu, I wasn't thinking about your needs."

"So what else is new?" her mom said mildly.

Mitzy gaped. "Oh, my gosh. That is so mean to say."

"Again with the 'oh, my gosh'."

Mitzy glanced at her watch, then rushed into the kitchen and plucked a fresh ice pack from the freezer. "Listen," she called, "I've only got twenty minutes to make it up north for dance class." She hurried back into the living room and handed the ice pack to her mom. Then she headed for the door. "Give Harry my love."

"Darling?"

"Yeah?" Mitzy called back, impatiently.

"Thanks for keeping me company today."

Mitzy gave her a genuine smile. "Not a problem." She closed the front door softly behind her and headed into the hallway. No matter their ups and downs, there remained an elastic bond between her and her mom; one that would not be broken.

~

Long fingers retrieved a newspaper from the trash can the custodian had not yet emptied, then smoothed the crumpled front page: *Yesterday, thirteen-year-old Ellie Barge emerged from a cocoon-like state following the death of her father one month ago. According to Victor Ribaldi, the girl's psychiatrist, the eighth-grade student fell into the stupor upon learning her father had suffered a fatal heart attack during a special education conference held on her behalf.*

A spontaneous act intended to end the terrorizing of students and teachers had produced a web of unintended consequences.

Chapter 24

Miss Valerie's voice rang out across the gymnasium as she confidently directed her adult students across the dance floor. "Side, side, back, side, side back."

"Look out, we're going to bump into another couple," Eric cautioned.

"Um, it's kind of difficult to see when I'm moving backwards. You're supposed to be doing the leading," Mitzy said, her eyes laughing. *If you only knew what a hunk you are, no matter how you move!* Not that she would tell him. It would only puff his ego.

"Okay, sorry."

"Guys," the teacher called out, "I'm hearing the crunch, crunch of heels. Try to stay on the balls of your feet as you maneuver across the dance floor."

"Man, there's so much to remember," Eric said, tensely guiding Mitzy into an open spot.

"Chill! It's only the third week of class," Mitzy reassured him. How sweet to see this strong, silent guy admit his weaknesses.

"Let's practice the ladies' turn while we're still promenading. Guys, as you move back on your right leg and your lady moves forward on her left, direct her underneath your raised left arm like a bridge. Girls, move into the turn during the side, side counts, then backwards on your right leg to complete the waltz step."

Mitzy stepped forward and banged her head into Eric's partially raised left arm. "Ow!"

"Sorry. Guess you're taller than I thought," he said.

"Okay, now we'll try it to music." Miss Valerie popped a CD into the boom box. "This one's a first-dance favorite at weddings."

The song poured into the room. "'Can I have this dance, for the rest of my life—'"

Eric held her closer than before, his eyes partially closed as he moved to the beat. In his arms, Mitzy flushed with pleasure. "Hey, I think you're finally getting the hang of this," she whispered, reaching up to give him a peck on the cheek.

His eyes flew open. He looked startled.

Mitzy blushed. "Sorry, it's a romantic song. The moment just seemed right."

A grin crept across his face. "Don't be sorry. I just thought—"

"That's your trouble. You think too much."

He looked down at her, his eyes twinkling. "Thank you, doctor."

"No charge. I should be angry at you, anyway."

"Me? Why?" Eric asked.

"Fifteen-minute potty break," Miss Valerie called. "Can you tell I used to teach pre-school?"

Several class members chuckled as they exited the room. Others hung in the back to chat. Mitzy headed toward a row of black folding chairs, sat down and patted the empty chair to her right. "Take a load off." She pulled two water bottles out of her dance bag and handed Eric one.

"So why should you be mad at me?" he said as he took it.

"I had to read in the newspaper that Ellie awoke from her comatose state."

Eric fiddled with the bottle cap. "It slipped my mind."

She raised an eyebrow. "Really?"

"My sister's wedding is coming up soon. She's been nagging me about renting a tuxedo."

"Now I see why they say men have difficulty multi-tasking," Mitzy said, laughing.

Eric frowned. "Have I ever in the short time you've known me made a sexist comment about women?"

He had a point, she realized. "I apologize. Can we get back to Ellie?"

He paused long enough to gulp down half the bottle. "It's difficult to believe this quiet, disheveled kid was ever a terror to anybody."

"Sammy Cooper would vehemently disagree."

Eric fished a memo pad and pen from his pocket. "The kid Ellie bullied?"

"One of many."

"Ten more minutes," Miss Valerie called out.

"Sammy's a student of mine. He's got learning disabilities, not behavior disorders, and he's a lot easier to teach than a kid like Ellie. His IEP meeting was scheduled right after Ellie's."

"What's an IEP?" Eric asked.

Mitzy sighed. "Parent-teacher conference. Anyway, Ellie was jealous because he's scheduled to be totally mainstreamed this fall."

"Mainstreamed meaning?"

"He'll be in all regular classes."

"As opposed to what?"

Mitzy felt her patience wearing thin. "As opposed to being in special ed classes."

Eric threw his hands up, obviously confused. "Whatever."

She felt a pang of remorse. Would she be able to understand the jargon cops used without being briefed first? "Sammy's only in seventh grade, but he was put in Ellie's eighth-grade class because he's advanced in math. Sammy works tediously slow on his pre-algebra equations, but he still gets the answers right. Ellie, on the other hand, zooms through each page like a supersonic jet. Yet her answers are often wrong."

"Which is why she constantly bugs the shit out of him," Eric said.

"Yep, snide remarks and bullying, culminating in the toilet bowl escapade."

Eric appeared deep in thought. *This guy is so hot*, Mitzy thought, struggling to maintain a neutral expression.

"Could Sammy despise Ellie enough to kill her father?" Eric asked.

"Five minutes," the dance teacher called.

Mitzy checked the room for a recycling bin. When she saw none, she tossed her empty water bottle in the trash. "Sammy is what they call a wuss at school."

"You can't judge a book by its cover."

"Lynette made that same comment to me just a couple of days ago."

"Lynette… the English teacher with the French last name, right?" he joked.

"Right." She took a deep breath. "Look, there's something you need to know."

"You're married."

Mitzy rolled her eyes, then sobered. "During my last visit to Ellie's house, I found a Nardil capsule on the floor behind the toilet bowl."

"Probably fell out of a prescription bottle," Eric said.

"Remember the three half-empty prescription bottles underneath Ellie's bed?"

"Okay, people," Miss Valerie said. "Everybody back on the dance floor."

Mitzy followed Eric into the middle of the room. "The bottles were gone."

Eric looked alert. "You think somebody disposed of them?"

"If Ellie was at the hospital with her aunt, it had to be the nanny."

"Perhaps Ellie's aunt flushed whatever was in the bottles before leaving for the hospital," Eric said.

Mitzy glared at him. "Those prescription bottles went missing prior to Ellie and her aunt's hospital visit. The kid was still comatose! Besides, Anya's employer came on to her on several occasions."

Eric raised his eyebrows. "She report him to the police?"

Mitzy shook her head. "Afraid she'd lose her job. Plus, she views herself as Ellie's protector, which could prompt her to take a risk if she thought it would help Ellie."

"You're sure Ellie didn't get rid of those bottles herself?"

"Stop blaming the victim!"

"Okay, class," Miss Valerie called out. "Let's move on to the Swing."

~

"Hey, Sammy."

"Hey, Ms. Maven." The seventh-grader pulled a study guide from his social studies folder. "Could you help me finish some homework for next period instead of doing phonics? We're supposed to read Chapter Seven, then complete these worksheets."

"That's fine. Let's take a peek." Mitzy ruffled through the textbook pages. "The Industrial Revolution. It's only the beginning of May and you guys are already starting the eighth-grade curriculum. Impressive!"

Sammy nodded, pulling a black gel pen from his pencil bag.

"Would you prefer for me to read aloud and you take notes, or do you want to read aloud and tell me what to write?" Mitzy asked.

"You read," Sammy said, smiling in obvious relief.

"Just a quick question. How's it been going since your IEP meeting? Are you excited to be going into all regular classes in the fall?"

"Sort of."

Mitzy noticed the smile leave the boy's lean face. "You think your teachers are going to place unreasonable expectations on you?"

Sammy shrugged.

"How about your mom?"

"I can deal with her."

"Then where will this pressure be coming from?"

"Me."

"Oh," Mitzy said thoughtfully.

Sammy fidgeted with his pen. "I'm scared of failing."

"In eighth grade, you're going to be in a supervised study hall instead of Spanish, so you'll have time to catch up on anything you don't finish in your regular classes," she said reassuringly.

Sammy hesitated. "There's something else."

"What?"

"The regular ed kids don't hang out with me."

"Well, Jordan and Tremayne will be in supervised study hall, too."

"It's not the same. I have these dreams of being swallowed up by a whale."

"Sometimes that can be a good thing," Mitzy joked. "Think of Pinocchio and Gepetto."

"Huh?"

She was incredulous. "You never read *Pinocchio?*"

The boy shook his head.

"So you feel like you'll be alone in an ocean of faces."

Sammy nodded.

"Supervised study hall will be your anchor. You'll have an LD teacher in there to help you with your homework. And Ms. Walker's always available, too."

"Aren't you going to be here next year?"

Mitzy briefly averted her eyes. "I'm not sure yet. Anyway, it's natural to be scared of change, even good change. Your other teachers and I have confidence in you. No one's expecting you to be perfect. Just do the best you can. And no more bullying! Ellie will be at a different school."

Sammy bit his lower lip.

"Something bothering you about Ellie?"

"Maybe."

"Out with it."

"I need to do my social studies."

"Sammy, you can trust me."

"But you like her."

"I like you, too. What's going on?"

"She asked me to do something that day," he said, his words rushing out in a blur.

She didn't need to ask what "that day" meant. "What did she ask you to do?"

"Pull the fire alarm," he said loudly, one word tumbling over the next.

Together, she and Sammy sat in silence, recalling the consequences of that command. "You pulled the fire alarm?" Mitzy murmured after a while.

Sammy nodded. Tears welled up, and one spilled over onto his red-splotched cheek.

"Why?"

Roughly, he wiped the tear away. "After she dunked my head in the toilet, I knew I had to do something to protect myself."

"Did you tell the social worker?"

Sammy shook his head. "Ellie was temporarily suspended, so I figured I was safe."

"How did it go when she returned to school?"

"All the bullying stopped. Her first day back, she even apologized for having been so mean. She promised to buy me a Blizzard from Dairy Queen after school."

"Did you go?"

"At first I said no, but she looked sad so I said okay."

"How did it go at the ice cream parlor?"

"The M & M Blizzard was great."

"I meant with Ellie."

"She was really nice. I was thinking that all this time maybe she just needed a friend."

"What did you guys talk about?"

"She said her dad blamed her for putting her mom in a coma because she was pestering her about going to McDonald's when their car crashed."

"Anything else?"

"How her dad was hardly ever home. How he screamed at her when he was home. How she'd been doing lousy in school and was scared he'd send her to a high school for kids who committed crimes and did drugs. She asked if, now that we were friends, I would help her out."

"What did you say?"

"I knew if I gave Ellie the answer she wanted, she'd permanently stop bullying me. So I said sure."

"Is that when she asked you to pull the fire alarm?"

Sammy shook his head. "She said she'd email me if her dad decided to send her to the alternative school."

"Then what happened?"

"The night before her parent-teacher conference, she emailed me. It was like 10:00 p.m. and I was just about to sign off. She was upset because she and her dad had a big fight. He told her he was going to sign the papers sending her away. She asked me to meet her at 8:20 a.m., right before school started. She'd tell me what to do."

"Did you meet her?"

"Actually, I overslept; my mom had to wake me up."

"So what happened?"

"I got to school at 8:25. Ellie was really pissed off, talking about how she could never trust anyone. Then she said, 'Let's synchronize our watches. Prove to me you're really my friend. At eight-forty, ask your teacher for a bathroom pass, then go the teachers' bathroom behind the conference room. At eight-fifty, pull the fire alarm, then run outside. I'll take care of the rest.'"

"Why did Ellie want you to pull the fire alarm?"

"She said she was going to make her dad too sleepy to sign the papers."

"Did she say how?"

Sammy shook his head.

"What happened next?"

"I was creeped out, but I didn't want to let Ellie down because I was scared she'd turn back into a bully and do even worse things to me than before. So I pulled the alarm and the whole school cleared out. That part was cool!"

"You felt powerful, huh?" Mitzy said.

"Oh, yeah!"

"Afterwards, did you tell anyone?"

"I was going to tell my mom, but then Ellie's dad died and she freaked out. I figured the best way I could help her was to forget the whole thing ever happened."

"So you've been carrying this load of concrete on your thin shoulders for the last six weeks."

Sammy felt his shoulders, then looked at Mitzy, obviously perplexed. "There's no concrete on my shoulders, Ms. Maven."

"I meant 'big secret.' That's why your grades started slipping. We'll get you to Ms. Walker after social studies. She'll contact your mom."

An insistent *bing* echoed overhead. "Oh, no! We never got to work on my work sheets. I'm dead!"

Not as dead as some, Mitzy thought.

~

The morning breakfast traffic was just kicking in at the fast food restaurant. Eric sprinkled Tabasco sauce on his Egg McMuffin. "I'm not rummaging through the Barge family's garbage for the missing prescription bottles. We don't even have a set time frame."

"Wait 'til I finish my food before you second-guess my suggestion," Mitzy said, her voice garbled.

Eric's eyes twinkled. "Didn't your mother teach you never to talk with your mouth full?"

"Gotta be at school in ten minutes," she said, slurping down her orange juice.

Wolfing down his breakfast sandwich, Eric said, "So why'd you ask me to meet you?"

Mitzy set aside her used plate and crumbled the napkin into a ball. "Sammy Cooper, that seventh grader I told you about? Turns out he pulled the fire alarm the morning of the teacher conference, clearing out the school."

The detective whipped out a mini-notepad from his pocket and commenced writing. "Thanks for the ID. Your school principal will determine the punishment on that one."

"He's looking at school suspension." Mitzy leaned forward. "That's only the tip of the icicle."

"Even I know that's 'iceberg'," Eric joked.

She looked at him solemnly. "Sammy pulled that alarm at Ellie's emailed request. She told him she was going to give her dad something to make him too tired to sign off on the alternative school papers."

Eric punched his fist into an open palm. "So Ellie did drug her father."

"If she did, it was by accident," Mitzy said softly.

"Justice is blind, Mitzy. If Mother Teresa had killed someone, she'd be handcuffed the same as me or you."

The thought of Ellie in handcuffs made her shudder. "We only have the word of a kid she bullied."

"I'll bring Ellie and this boy in for questioning," Eric said.

"Not yet. Listen. Whatever really happened, it's in her flowered diary. The one I gave her last Christmas. She was a prolific writer. She shared a lot of her entries with me at school."

"I'm on it," he said, rising from his swivel chair.

Mitzy touched his arm to restrain him. "The diary's gone."

"She probably hid it somewhere in her room."

Mitzy glanced down. "I searched her room. Thoroughly. Nada."

Eric gave her a disgusted look. "You're a regular Nancy Drew, aren't you? She must have taken it with her to the hospital."

"How would someone in a catatonic stupor do that?"

"I have no idea. Mental illness is not my area of expertise."

"Let me clue you in," Mitzy said. "A person in a stupor is pretty much immobile."

"So we're back to the aunt or nanny, this time as an

accomplice."

"The diary pages for the two days leading up to her father's death were blank," Mitzy whispered.

Eric stared at her. "And how would you know that?"

Mitzy ran her fingers through her hair. "Because I saw it. The first time I visited Ellie after her father died."

"I get it. In between seeking out prescription bottles, you took the liberty of thumbing through the girl's personal life."

His tone made her defensive. "Something like that."

"You're a real piece of work, you know that?" Eric shook his head. "I ought to take you in for tampering with evidence."

"It's not like I broke into the house."

"You went way beyond 'snoop' on this one. I'm sure Ellie's aunt wouldn't be too thrilled to hear about your little escapades."

"Prosecute me later, detective. First, find out who killed Ellie's father."

"The answer could be in the diary."

"I just told you the diary pages leading up to the poisoning were blank."

Eric smirked. "When she was planning her father's demise, she was smart enough to not tip her hand."

"Now that she's out of her mental cocoon, she could be filling in entries as we speak," Mitzy said. "Writing down what really happened."

"You just said the diary's missing."

"Maybe it's only missing from our sight."

"So you think Ellie hid it."

Mitzy shrugged. "Have you checked the emails between Ellie and her aunt?"

"You still believe Fay and Anya enabled Ellie to do the deed?"

"They're the only three people who knew Joseph Barge bought a Starbucks every morning on his way to work."

"You can't accept that your little darling pulled this one off all by herself, can you?"

"Think what you want. Just check it out, will you?"

"Fine," Eric said. "Tomorrow I go back to the house and search their computer."

"And if the history's been erased?"

"I'll check Fay Shimmer's computer at her art studio."

"Can you secure a warrant that fast?"

"That's affirmative." Eric's blue eyes turned somber. "Until then, no more sleuthing on your own. Hear?"

Mitzy tossed her breakfast bag into the garbage. "Scouts' honor."

Eric smiled. "All right then."

Not that she was ever a Scout.

Chapter 25

Ellie watched the tulips coming up outside her bedroom window. Purple, red, pink, and yellow. All bravely forcing their way through the ground and upwards, in search of yet another new beginning. Pinpricks of joy skittered across her chest as she imagined rolling down grassy hills and tramping through the forest. Could she shed her sorrow like a turtle crawling out of its shell, and resume her life as a kid?

Since her second visit to the hospital, joyous feelings had watered her parched soul, enabling it to bloom once more. Ellie's father had hovered in the ceiling of her hospital room as waves of electricity coursed through her like a high-speed train. He apologized for the deep sorrow his neglect had caused her. Best of all, he absolved of guilt over her mother's tragic accident. His forgiveness permitted her to free herself of the need to cut herself.

Tomorrow, she'd ask Aunt Fay to take her to the nursing home to visit her mom.

Footsteps clonked down the hardwood hallway towards her room, Ellie turned to face the one person she didn't want to confront. Fleetingly, she entertained the thought of retreating to that silent place within.

"Hi, Ellie."

"Hey, Sammy," she croaked. Dr. Ribaldi said it would take a while for her parched throat to heal.

"You've been gone so long. Everyone at school's been asking about you, so I made my mom bring me by to see how you're doing."

"Thanks for coming," Ellie said. She eyed the thin package he was holding. "Is that for me?"

"Oh, sorry," Sammy said, thrusting the gift into her hands.

Ellie carefully tore off the decorative paper. She smiled hesitantly. "How did you know I like Panic?"

"Ms. Maven said you saw them in concert, so I figured you'd like their CD. You don't have it, do you? I mean, their CD?"

Ellie shook her head. "That was really nice of you, especially after the bitch I've been."

Sammy's face reddened. "Uh, I'm really sorry about your dad."

"Thanks. Did you come to his funeral?"

He looked surprised. "Our whole resource room class came. Didn't you see us?"

She looked down. "Guess I was in another universe."

"Which one?" Sammy asked, excitement in his voice.

Ellie giggled. "It's just something people say. I really didn't visit another universe, Sammy."

"Oh."

"I'm really sorry I made you pull that fire alarm at school."

Sammy looked away. "I was scared that if I didn't do it, you'd be mean to me again."

"You were brave to come here today and tell me that."

Suddenly, Sammy's words rushed out. "I just want to do good in school. I want to know when someone's kidding when they say 'being in another universe.' I want to have friends, and I don't want to have to be scared anymore."

Ellie was taken aback at his outburst. He was usually so timid. "I know how that feels," she confided. "I've been scared forever."

"You're a bully. Bullies don't get scared. Oops! Are you going to beat me up again?"

She laughed. "You're my bud now. I'm done doing all that weird stuff."

Sammy sighed. "I think I just figured out what you were scared about."

"Let's play the Panic CD," Ellie said, attempting to distract him.

"When we were at the ice cream shop, you said you felt like you were a bad person because you were pestering your mom for a Happy Meal when she lost control of her car."

"For an LD kid, you're pretty smart," Ellie said warily.

"Lots of kids pester their moms to take them to fast food restaurants and nothing bad happens to them," Sammy persisted. "It was just an accident."

"Lots of things are accidents, Sammy," Ellie whispered.

Sammy's face blanched and he started to back away from her. "I kind of told Ms. Maven you asked me to pull the fire alarm."

Ellie's eyes blazed for a brief second, then she breathed in deeply. "It's okay, Sammy.   Could you ask Ms. Maven to bring that school detective here?"

"Why? Did you do something bad?" Sammy asked, his lower lip trembling.

"I'm not sure. That's why I need to talk to them."

Sammy's eyes grew wide. "Are you going to jail?"

Ellie's eyes turned dark. "Quit asking so many questions!"

Sammy backed away from her. "You promised you'd be nice to me from now on."

Ellie at once was penitent. "Sorry. Listen, you were brave enough to tell me how you felt when I was mean to you. You can do this. Besides, you taught me a lesson."

Sammy looked down the front of his shirt. "Me?"

"Uh huh. Friendship is like dental floss, you have to get between each tooth to find out what's really in there."

He frowned. "But what does friendship have to do with

dental floss?"

Ellie reached over to hug Sammy, smiling when he returned the hug. "It means you can't scare people into being your friend."

"'Cause friendship isn't thin like floss." He looked proud of himself.

"But like floss, friendship is invisible to the naked eye," she finished.

Sammy giggled. "How can an eye be naked?"

Ellie's laughter bubbled forth.

"I promise I'll talk to Ms. Maven tomorrow," Sammy said. "Hey, Ellie?"

"Yeah?"

"You've taught me something, too."

"What?"

"Bullies act mean to other kids 'cause they feel lousy about themselves."

"You got it!"

"Bullies need friends, too!"

Ellie laughed. "Just don't spread it around."

"Can we listen to that CD now?"

Ellie reached for her CD player. "Let's do it."

~

"Well hello," Fay Shimmer said. Mitzy could tell by her raised eyebrows their visit was unexpected.

"I take it your niece didn't mention she'd invited us," Eric said. Mitzy wondered why Ellie hadn't confided in her aunt, and suppressed a sense of unease. They would know from Ellie herself soon enough.

"No problem. I'm thankful Ellie can communicate again. Please come in."

As Ellie's aunt ushered her and Eric through the spacious hall and into the living room, Mitzy stopped to admire a colorful Indian sculpture. Any distraction, no matter how minor, was welcome. "Is this totem pole one of your creations?"

Fay nodded. "I modeled it after the one on Montrose and Lake Shore Drive."

"I knew the design looked familiar," Mitzy said. "When I was a kid, my mom and I would take the bus to the beach and picnic by the totem pole. Is it my imagination or has the real totem pole shrunk?"

"The wood has rotted over the years," Fay said. "The whole structure will eventually be restored to its original height." She led them into the living room and gestured for Mitzy and Eric to settle on the soft white cushions of the sprawling couch. "Anya's off today. Iced tea or cranberry juice?"

"Iced tea would be great," Eric said.

"Cranberry juice for me," Mitzy said.

"That's Ellie's favorite. She's in her room. I'll get her."

They heard Fay's stiletto heels click down the hall.

"There's only one reason Ellie would have asked us to come," Eric mumbled under his breath.

"She's starved for visitors."

"My cousin has a thirteen-year-old daughter. The last thing she wants is to hang around adults."

"Ellie's been encased in an adult world her whole childhood."

Eric leaned back against the cushion, stretching his arm along the top of the couch. "Odd that the invite came on the day I'm preparing to take apart the computer."

"What's even more amazing is that this quiet kid with learning disabilities actually had the chutzpah to contact you."

"Maybe she bribed him."

"Hey, up until four days ago, the girl was in a catatonic state. Remember?" Mitzy said.

"Stranger things have occurred."

They waited in silence. Whatever Ellie's reason for asking them here, she would need someone to be strong for her. Mitzy intended to be that someone, no matter what happened.

Chapter 26

Mitzy tried not to stare at the subdued Ellie inching towards them, her aunt's arm protectively encircling her shoulders. "You've lost some weight, sweetie. Think you can use these?" She took a package of cherry Twizzlers from her pocket and held it out.

Ellie reached for it. "Thanks!" she said, yanking off the wrapper with an unexpected spurt of energy.

"I guess those won't keep her from fitting into her new graduation dress," Fay Shimmer replied cheerfully.

Ellie eyed the couch. "Can you guys move over?"

"Not a problem." Eric got up and reseated himself in a hard-backed chair.

Mitzy patted the cushion he'd vacated and Ellie sat down. "Thanks for inviting Detective Eric and I to visit you today."

"Ellie was so energized yesterday when her school chum came to visit," her aunt said, peering down at Ellie. "I think she's coming down now."

Mitzy and Eric shared a quick look. "Was Sammy the friend who stopped by?" Mitzy asked.

Ellie nodded. "He brought me the Panic CD you told him

to buy."

Eric gave Mitzy a quizzical look. She shrugged.

"There's something I want to tell you guys. It's really been infiltrating my mind since I got sick," Ellie said, tearing off two Twizzlers. She gave one to Mitzy, the other to Eric.

Mitzy smiled at Ellie. "That was one of our vocabulary words. Do you remember how I taught the class 'infiltrate'?"

"You had us repeat this phrase printed in red magic marker on a long strip of paper. It said, 'Ants infiltrated our room!'"

"How creative!" Fay said.

"Then what?" Mitzy coaxed.

"You gave each of us a handful of black plastic ants. Then you turned off the lights. On the count of three, we tossed the ants into the middle of the room. You shined a flashlight on the ants and we all yelled, 'Ants infiltrated our room!'" Ellie's voice was soft as she told the story. Gentle, not like a bully or a rebellious teenager.

Eric applauded. "You're a terrific storyteller."

Ellie blushed.

Mitzy noted with pleasure the effect his approval had on Ellie. Maybe he didn't think she was a killer after all. Maybe he understood she was just a kid. "Great memory," she said, ruffling Ellie's hair. It still looked straggly, the purple streaks faded to lavender. "So what's been infiltrating your mind?"

Ellie looked up at her aunt, as if to send her from the room.

"You talk to Detective Eric and your teacher in private, honey," Fay said. "I'll fetch the cranberry juice and iced tea."

Ellie shot her aunt a wan smile as she squished the remaining Twizzlers into one gigantic, sticky red ball.

As soon as Fay left, Mitzy tilted Ellie's chin up and looked into her eyes. "What's wrong, honey?"

The fidgeting stopped. Ellie took a deep breath. "I killed my father."

Shock whipped through Mitzy like an arrow through her heart. She glanced at Eric. His face was impassive. "I'll get your aunt, Ellie."

The girl squirmed away from her. "No!"

"Should she have an attorney here, too?" Mitzy asked frantically.

"Her aunt will suffice for now," Eric said, his voice calm.

"If you call her in, I'll say you made it up!" Ellie sounded agitated.

Mitzy forced herself to relax. "Your aunt is your legal guardian, sweetie. She needs to be in on whatever you have to say."

"Aunt Fay's the only one who loves me," Ellie shouted. "She'll send me away!"

"Is something wrong?" Fay called from down the hall.

"No one's sending you anywhere, Ellie," Eric said. "We just want to protect your legal rights."

"Illinois doesn't have the death penalty anymore. We discussed that in social studies."

Mitzy felt faint at the thought that Ellie could actually go to prison.

"Let's all calm down," Eric said in a soothing tone.

Fay entered with a tray of beverages, and Ellie broke into tears at the sight of her. Fay put the tray down on the cocktail table and went to her niece's side. "What happened?"

"Ellie confided some pertinent information regarding her father's death," Eric said. "As her legal guardian, you need to be here."

Fay pulled Ellie upright, an arm around her shoulders as Ellie hid her face. "She's upset. She needs her rest."

"She needs to continue, either here or at police headquarters."

"What do you mean?"

"Your niece just admitted to killing her father."

Fay wrapped both arms around Ellie. "You believe the admission of an emotionally disturbed teenager?"

Alarm bells went off in Mitzy's head. Ellie's aunt hadn't missed a beat. She should be demanding an attorney before allowing her niece to speak to the police.

"I can't live knowing I killed Daddy!" Ellie screamed, pulling away from her.

"Sweetheart, you weren't even at your parent-teacher conference," Mitzy said. Unbidden memories rose of Ellie in the school office, looking shaky and sick, not long before the MDC meeting.

Ellie looked at her and swallowed hard. "Remember when the fire alarm went off, Ms. Maven?"

Mitzy nodded. Her heart sank as Ellie echoed what Sammy had told her. "I made a deal with Sammy that if he'd pull the fire alarm, I'd stop bullying him and be his friend. He almost missed getting to school on time and I was afraid I'd have to do it myself, but he came through in the end."

"Don't say anything else until we get you an attorney, honey," her aunt said.

Ellie stuck her chin out. "I've been watching a lot of Court T.V., Aunt Fay. Lawyers tell you not to talk. I want to talk. I've been waiting for this moment for so long. If you stop loving me, I'll cry for the rest of my life. But I have to tell right now."

Fay choked up. "Oh, darling. I'll always love you."

Detective Whelan pulled a mini-cassette recorder from his pocket. "Go."

"I snuck into the conference room four minutes after everyone cleared out," Ellie whispered.

Mitzy fought to keep her voice calm. "How are you so certain of the time?"

"I had a new second-hand watch I bought for track practice. I started running track a couple of weeks before Dad died."

"Go on," Eric said.

"After I got into the conference room, I noticed the Starbucks coffee on the table where dad was sitting."

"How did you know it was his cup?" Eric asked.

"His leather coat was over the chair."

"Then what happened?"

"I emptied two capsules of Nardil into his coffee." Ellie hugged her body. "The coffee was steaming hot and the granules disintegrated. I swirled the coffee around, then ran out of the room."

"Who did the capsules belong to?" Mitzy asked.

"Me."

Eric nodded. "How were you and your father getting along at the time?"

"We had a big fight the night before."

"Did your father hit you?" Mitzy asked. Though she hated the idea, part of her almost hoped the answer would be yes. What did they call it in court proceedings, extenuating circumstances?

Ellie looked at her aunt, then down at the floor. "He pushed me down. Then he started swearing and calling me scary names. He said if I ever try to kill myself again, I should finish the job. That hurt me worse than if he would have beat me up."

"Before the night of your fight, did your dad talk about sending you away to school?" Eric again, still in full detective mode. Mitzy's stomach churned as she watched him.

Ellie scratched her arm. "He said he'd decided the best place for me was an alternative high school. He didn't know how to handle me anymore. I promised I'd do better in school, but he stomped out of the room. I had to do something."

"Did you plan to kill your dad, Ellie?" Mitzy asked softly.

"No! Two Nardil capsules make me sleepy. I figured my dad would have the same reaction. He'd be too tired to sign off on my alternative high school placement papers. I never expected him to die!" Ellie sobbed. Mitzy reached over to comfort her.

Eric stood up and addressed Fay. "Ms. Shimmer, I suggest you secure an attorney. Ellie will need to come down to police headquarters."

"Was anyone else near the conference room after the alarm went off?" Mitzy asked.

Ellie sniffled, using her fists to wipe away tears.

"Principal Fillmore ran back into the room. Then he rushed back out carrying a folder."

"Did anyone else see Mr. Fillmore return to the conference room?"

"Maybe Mr. Ramiros, our custodian. He was around that morning. He always knows everybody's business."

"Okay," Eric said. "Thanks for confiding in us, Ellie."

With a backward glance at Ellie, Mitzy followed him to the door.

Ellie ran after them. Her aunt followed close behind.

"My diary has everything that went on. I put it all in there."

"Can I see your diary, Ellie?" Eric asked.

Mitzy's heart jumped to her throat. She would give anything to keep the detective from reading those pages. Whatever was in them, he would surely see them as damning.

"Don't you need a warrant for that, Detective?" Fay interrupted.

"I'll be back this evening with that paper in hand."

Ellie's face crumpled. "My diary's missing."

"Maybe you left it at the hospital after your last treatment," Mitzy said.

"I don't remember if I brought it with me." Ellie picked at her arm again.

"Ellie experienced temporary short-term memory loss after both ECT treatments," her aunt explained. "Honey, stop scratching your arm before it bleeds again."

"Did your housekeeper put it away for you?" Eric asked.

Let it go, Eric, Mitzy silently prayed.

Ellie kept scratching. "Anya says she hasn't seen it!"

Mitzy saw Fay avert her eyes.

"Okay, then," Eric said. "We'll talk to you soon."

Chapter 27

Mitzy stormed into the front passenger seat of Eric's black Chevy blazer. "Why'd you harass Ellie like that?"

Eric clicked the window button down, then rested his arms on the steering wheel. The stillness of the night entered the SUV. "Look, Ellie confessed to drugging her dad. It's not what you wanted to hear, but you've got to deal with it."

"She also said Principal Fillmore returned to the conference room once it had cleared out. I recall him saying he was going back to retrieve the Barge file. Talk to him."

"This is getting to sound like a witch hunt."

Mitzy stared at Eric in disbelief. "It amazes me how quick you are to discount Fillmore's actions and totally blame Ellie for Barge's death. Two antidepressant tablets can't kill a big hulk like Barge!"

"Yeah, well it amazes me how quick you are to deny the inevitable. There's no evidence Fillmore did anything but go back for a file, like you just said. And what about the infamous diary that's mysteriously gone missing?"

She crossed her arms across her chest. "How many times do I have to tell you? Those diary pages leading up to the day of her father's death were blank. I saw them myself."

"Ellie said it told the whole story."

"Maybe she filled those entries in during lucid intervals in her catatonia. Fay or Anya could have torn out those pages. Did you see how defensive the aunt got when you asked for the diary?"

Eric turned to look at her. She could see his face clearly in the moonlight that flooded the vehicle. "Why bother to tear out pages if his death was accidental?"

"Ellie did not set out to kill her father!"

"Perhaps Fay and Anya have proof to the contrary!"

"Every time I think we're on the same page, you turn traitor," Mitzy complained bitterly.

"Chill, Mitzy. We both want the truth. We're on the same team."

"That, Detective, is debatable." Mitzy yanked open the car door and jumped out.

"Where are you going?"

"What's it to you?" she called over her shoulder as she briskly walked down the dark, tree-laden path leading away from the Barge mansion.

The SUV edged along beside her. "Your expectations are way overboard, you know that? Sometimes it takes a while before the puzzle pieces fit."

Mitzy shot him the finger and continued down the winding path.

"Explode someplace else," he snapped. "There's deer out here. A ravine up ahead."

Resolutely gazing forward, she kept walking.

Eric killed the ignition and leaned out the window. "No way are you just pissed about Ellie. You've got unresolved issues all your own. You wanna talk, I'll be here."

Mitzy walked off without a glance.

"At least leave your cell phone on," Eric called after her.

~

Eric awoke to find Mitzy peering at him from outside the vehicle. "Wasn't too brilliant leaving the window all the way down while you slept," she said.

He squinted at his watch in the moonlight. Midnight. He must have dropped off waiting for her to come back. "You've been gone almost an hour. How smart is that?"

Mitzy shuffled from foot to foot, hugging herself in the damp night air. "Look, you were right. Some old memories were coloring my soul."

Eric reached across the passenger side and unlocked the door. Mitzy slipped inside. Without a word, Eric grabbed an Aztec blanket from the back seat and handed it to her.

Mitzy tucked the blanket's rough folds around her. "When I was five years old, my father was killed in a robbery gone bad. The police theorized the guy who robbed my dad's pharmacy was a drug addict. The robbery occurred late at night and there were no witnesses. After twelve hours of continuous questioning by the police, the guy confessed.

"My mom and I passed this guy on the street all the time. He was homeless. Sometimes we'd buy him a cheeseburger from McDonald's. 'What, no Big Mac?' he'd whine. With his hard-luck stories and his hand always outstretched for a windfall, Bob was a nuisance, yet he never harassed us.

"Bob went to prison, but my mom pressed on with inquiries into my father's death. Ten years later, the real culprit was found and brought to justice. A guy named John Melrose. My dad's car cut in front of his that very morning. The guy had been drinking and was plenty steamed. That night, he killed my father."

"How did the police find him?" Eric asked.

"They didn't. He confessed. Part of his alcohol rehabilitation. DNA samples proved his guilt. He was convicted and Bob set free."

"Ellie has already confessed to fatally poisoning her father," Eric said softly.

"How many times have you arrested a family member who's willing to be the fall guy?"

"Now you're reaching."

Mitzy plunged ahead. "My gut tells me someone else was the actual culprit. What about Ellie's other teachers?

They certainly had motive. Barge terrorized them. They all hated him."

"And they all took antidepressants, right?"

"I don't know, Eric. You're supposed to find that out. Have you even tried to interview them yet?"

"Everybody's got an alibi."

"Did you even explore my theory of Barge's self-destruction?"

"Ah, yes, your theory."

Eric's voice was neutral; she couldn't tell if he thought she was on to something, or was patronizing her. "Just promise me you won't stop until you've connected all the dots."

The quiet was deafening. Mitzy watched Eric's face for some sign of emotion. There was none. Minutes drifted by. Finally, he sighed. "I'll research the email and diary connection again, and have a second go at the principal, the custodian, and the teachers. And yes, I'll consider the possibility of Barge offing himself. But you gotta quit second-guessing me. I don't need a monkey on my shoulder."

Mitzy giggled. "That's 'back.'"

Eric frowned.

"Understood," she said.

"My chief's hounding me about all the time I'm devoting to this case when I've got four other files to investigate, so I don't need any more grief from you."

"I get it, Eric. You want my promise in blood or what?"

He started the ignition. "I'm taking you home."

Mitzy rolled her eyes. What a control freak!

~

"Ms. Maven."

Classroom key in hand and a stack of grammar packets balanced in the crook of one arm, Mitzy turned towards the familiar voice. "Good morning, Mr. Fillmore."

"And a good morning to you, too, on this sparkling

spring day," the principal answered cheerily. "Your kids counting down to summer vacation?"

"We all are."

"I was scanning the Houghton Mifflin textbook orders and noticed yours was missing. It needs to be turned in this afternoon by three o'clock, along with any other purchases you're requesting for next year."

"No problem," Mitzy said, opening the door to her room. She shifted the packets and flipped on the lights. "Writing end-of-the-year reports and updating IEPs, the book order kind of slipped my mind."

"Don't worry. By this time next year, you'll have the routine down pat," he said as he leaned against the door moulding.

The grammar packets fell from Mitzy's hands, smacking the worktable with a thud. "Wait. You're definitely asking me back for next year?"

Fillmore frowned. "You were in my office a few months back when Roz indicated that was the plan."

"I never got a written contract."

"Obviously you didn't receive the email sent to all new teaching staff first week of May. The school board voted to rehire all three of you non-tenured teachers for the next school term. Come in after school to sign your new teaching contract."

His statement made her remember her second thoughts about this job. "I'm not sure that will work."

"Tomorrow morning after eight o'clock, then."

"That won't work either."

"That's fine. Just make sure it's signed by Friday." Glancing at his watch, Mr. Fillmore turned to go.

Mitzy took a deep breath. "I'm not sure I'm going to be staying."

"What?"

"I might be going back to the newspaper."

He looked perplexed. "We're lucky to have a creative young teacher who's dedicated to ensuring each of her special ed students actually meets their IEP goals. We don't want to lose you."

Mitzy choked up, and grabbed a tissue from her desk. "This is so embarrassing. I never cry."

"You worked so hard to get your teaching certificate. And now you want to quit?"

"I'm debating whether I can be more effective for these kids through the written word. Here, it's only one student at a time."

"Mitzy, you've been blessed with the ability to change the lives of these kids. The ability to bring laughter and joy to learning; two ingredients sorely missing in our curriculum. I sincerely hope you'll make the right decision and stay." He smiled. "Next year we might even be able to give you your own classroom."

"My own classroom? That does put things in a different perspective," Mitzy joked, dabbing her eyes.

"If we can retain a new teacher with your potential, it's worth it."

"Wouldn't that be a waste of space, since I spend most of my day doing inclusion?" Mitzy asked more seriously as she extracted a hand-held mirror from her briefcase. Black mascara had formed wet pools beneath her eyes.

"When I was young, my grandfather was principal of an elementary school in Skokie. He'd complain there were two schools within his building, and never the twain met. Students with special needs were segregated in self-contained classrooms and resource rooms, only allowed to mingle with the other kids during art, gym, and music."

"So inclusion solved the problem?" Mitzy asked.

Principal Fillmore shook his head. "Eight class periods a day in a general ed classroom are too fast-paced for some kids. Too many distractions. These students learn best in a resource room setting for at least fifty percent of their school day. Roz was ecstatic when the school board gave their approval to hire you as a full-time resource teacher."

Mitzy swiped at the new tears that were forming. "I am honored that you and Roz put so much trust in me." Taking a deep calming breath, she gathered up the grammar packets and began distributing them to the empty desks. "By the way, where is Roz? I haven't seen her around lately."

"She's been busy battling the 'Big C.'"

Mitzy's jaw dropped. "Cancer? She never said a word!"

"As warm and outgoing as Roz is, she's really a very private person. She took early retirement to spend what little time she has left with her children and grandchildren."

How horrible, thought Mitzy. "I'll pay her a visit."

"I'd advise you to call first. I visited her recently. The chemotherapy really takes a toll."

The high-pitched ring of the bell reverberated through the room. "Let me know ASAP regarding your plans for next year," Fillmore said as he headed out the door. Then he poked his head back into the room. "By the way, any updates on Ellie?"

Mitzy flushed. She certainly wasn't going to tell him about Ellie's confession. "The second ECT treatment brought Ellie out of her catatonic state."

He nodded. "Please give Ellie and her aunt my regards when you see her next."

Mitzy froze. She didn't know he was aware of her home visits. Hadn't even bothered to ask if a teacher was allowed to do that. "Will do," she said meekly.

"Nothing's been in the newspaper lately concerning suspects in her father's death," Fillmore said, drumming his fingers on the oak doorframe.

The inquisitive note in his voice made her cautious. "Ellie's aunt is hush-hush about the investigation. She says the police are still looking into it."

"Detective Whelan was back again last Friday, interviewing teachers he missed on his initial go-around. He get to you?"

"He interviewed me when he was here the first time." A small smile crept across Mitzy's lips. The principal was clueless about her ongoing relationship with Eric. Plus, Eric had taken her passionate plea into account. Oh, the possibilities.

"Hey, Mr. Fillmore." Tremayne strolled into the

classroom and threw his Bulls backpack onto his desk. "What'd you think about yesterday's game?"

"The Bulls really knocked 'em dead," Fillmore said, giving the dark-haired boy a high-five. "Have a good day, son."

As Mitzy observed the brief interaction between the affable principal and the feisty student, she dismissed any faint suspicions she'd had about him.

Chapter 28

"Mr. Ramiros?"

"*Sí?*" The custodian briefly glanced up, then continued moving student desks from circular formation back into rows.

Eric eyed the clock on the wall. 3:56 p.m. He flashed his badge. "I wonder if I could have another word with you?"

"I already tell you everything I know, *señor.*"

"May I see your driver's license or green card again, sir?"

The custodian stopped to wipe his face with a rag. Then he fished in his trouser pocket and pulled out a driver's license. "What this about?"

Eric copied down his license number and handed him back the card. "You know a student named Ellie Barge?"

"*Sí.*"

"You get along with her?"

Ramiros shrugged.

"Word is she can get pretty nasty. Did Ellie ever get nasty around you?"

"It not her fault. Parents not teach her right."

"Ellie's father came to school a lot. Did you ever meet

him?"

The custodian ran the buffer across the floor. "*Sí.*"

"What did you think of him?"

Ramiros stopped what he was doing. "He very angry man. Pound on classroom doors, scare students."

"Was Mr. Barge nasty to you, too?"

Ramiros hesitated, then shook his head.

"Did you ever hear any of the teachers or the principal say bad things about Mr. Barge?"

Ramiros laughed bitterly. "That list is very long, *señor.*"

"How about Ellie? Did she ever tell you she wanted to hurt her father?"

Ramiros shook his head. "I pretend I no speak English so she not know how bad her words make me feel."

"Any of Ellie's friends want to hurt her father because they feel sorry for her?"

The custodian looked away. "This girl have no friends. Always alone or doing bad things."

"Like dunking a student's head in the toilet?"

Ramiros stared at Eric, then turned and lugged his cleaning supplies to the door.

"Was Sammy Cooper the boy you saw pull the fire alarm?"

"I no can talk anymore."

Eric's heartbeat quickened. "Do you think Sammy Cooper was responsible for Mr. Barge's death?"

"I need this job for my family, *señor.*" With that, the custodian flicked the light switch, leaving Eric in the dark.

~

"Did you notice your marigolds need watering?" Mitzy called over her shoulder as she lugged a five-gallon pot of purple pansies to the far end of the balcony.

"I underwent hip surgery, not the removal of my corneas," her mother said, pushing an iron plant stand into a sunny spot.

"Let me move that for you," Mitzy said. "Dr. Katz said

you're supposed to take it easy for one more week."

"Dr. Katz doesn't care. He's living it up in Miami with a girl less than half his age."

"That girl's his oldest daughter, the one who just graduated from Miami State."

"She's less than half his age, isn't she?" her mother asked innocently.

Mitzy laughed. "You are incorrigible!" She stood on tiptoes to spread extra potting soil into a hanging geranium.

Shirley Maven plopped down on a footstool and methodically started pouring soil into a row of six-inch pots.

"A brisk wind's going to knock those over," Mitzy said.

"Thanks for sharing," her mother replied grumpily.

"So how's the wedding plans coming along?"

"Finally she remembers to ask."

"I can't believe you waited until this week to send out invitations."

"The wedding's a month off yet. What's the rush?"

Mitzy paused from hanging philodendrons. "Most people send their wedding invitations out at least ten weeks before the big day when it's a summer wedding."

Her mother shrugged and continued potting. "The less people who show up, the less money Harry has to dole out."

Mitzy gave her an incredulous look.

"Kidding! I told everybody in April."

"How 'bout the people coming in from Arizona and California?" Mitzy said, swiping at her sweaty brow.

"They purchased their plane tickets a couple of months ago. More importantly, how are your dance lessons coming along?"

"This week's our last class," Mitzy said as she picked up a heavy brass planter full of ivy and searched for a spot to hang it.

"Maybe you and Eric can give Harry and I some pointers."

"You guys go ballroom dancing once a month."

Her mother looked around to make sure the bluejays and robins weren't listening, then she confided, "Harry's a lousy dance partner."

"What?"

"After all these years, he's still inept at leading the rhumba and fox trot. Forget about the swing! Now those gorgeous young Europeans, they really got what it takes! When they glide their partners across the dance floor, it's like poetry in motion."

Mitzy rolled her eyes. Her mother did love her clichés!

Her mother's pleading words brought her back to earth with a thump. "Don't tell Harry I said he's lousy at leading. It'll break his heart."

"My lips are sealed."

"Invite Eric to stop by so you can teach us some of the moves you guys learned."

"That's not going to happen."

"Again you don't want to help your mother? I labored with you in my stomach for twenty-six hours. Nursed you 'til you were three years old. I still got the bite marks to prove it." Shirley started to remove her shirt.

Mitzy sat down on a tattered rug, shielding her eyes. "I'll get back to you."

Her mother stuck her arm back into the sleeve. "Good. I can cross off 'dance lesson' from my To Do list. Now I gotta contact Abe and make sure he can come to the wedding."

"I thought you said you contacted everybody back in the spring."

"Abe's a new neighbor. He draws caricatures."

"Wait. You're hiring a caricature artist to draw your wedding guests?"

"You got it." Her mother sounded pleased with herself.

"A klezmer band's weird enough. Now this?"

"You got to be willing to try new things, Mitzy, or your life will shrivel up right before your eyes," Shirley said, her eyes dull with disappointment.

"Nobody's ever accused me of being a conformist, Mom."

"It's my special day. I should be able to choose my entertainment without any backlash from you."

Silence hung between them.

Mitzy plucked a wooden splinter from her tush. "You know, you could really use a new rug to go with these colorful flowers. Maybe one that looks like a stained glass window."

"So will you and Eric come by for the lesson?" Shirley begged.

Mitzy concentrated on dislodged a second splinter. "Give it a rest, Mom."

"Okay. What happened?"

"He ordered me to stay out of the Barge investigation."

"You're angry about that?" her mother asked, sounding incredulous.

"I'm not the one who's got the anger management problem."

"Did you put your nose where it doesn't belong?"

Mitzy shrugged.

"Correct me if I'm wrong, but wouldn't you be livid if Eric started messing around with your lesson plans, spouting his ideas like raspberry seltzer water?"

"Probably."

"Who're you kidding? You'd be on his case like that lion who clawed Siegfried."

"Oh my gosh, you don't let up."

"Forget this petty bickering and invite the guy over. Do it for your mother."

"I'll run it by him, okay? By the way, I almost forgot to tell you. I got hired back at Lake Forest for next year."

Shirley smiled. "*Mazel tov*! You really earned it, working with those *meshugana* kids."

Mitzy eyed her mother suspiciously. "Thought you wanted me to go back to the newspaper."

"I was just testing you, honey. Wanted to see where your heart was at. Your heart is with those kids."

Mitzy bristled. "I'm sick and tired of these tests you throw at me! I don't need you to examine my choices and find them wanting. From now on, I trust my own decisions. Got it?"

To her surprise, Shirley was beaming. "*Mazel tov.*
You've finally come of age. Let's say the *Shecheyanu*
together, thanking G-d for this special day."

A sweet feeling of vindication spread through Mitzy.
Who knew it would be this easy to demand that her mother
take a step back in their relationship? "I already said it to
myself when the principal told me," she mumbled.

"So I can't have some nachos, too? You know, I said that
prayer aloud in the delivery room right after I gave birth to
you, and you've brought me joy ever since."

"Okay, okay."

Her mother put her arm around Mitzy and drew her
close. Together they chanted the prayer of thanks. "That
wasn't so bad, was it?" her mother said, smiling.

"How 'bout we spend the next half-hour planting in
silence?" Mitzy asked.

"Sounds good." Shirley gave her a quick squeeze. "I
almost forgot to tell you."

"Mom, give your vocal chords a rest."

"Forget it. No big *gefairlach*."

"If it's a big deal to you, it's a big deal to me," Mitzy
said, exasperated.

"On Sunday, June eighth, Marion Diamond's daughter
Allie is graduating from the University of Illinois in
Champaign. You know Harry's a lot older than me."

"Five years?" Mitzy volunteered.

Shirley pointed upward.

"Ten years?"

"Something like that. And his eyesight's not so good."

"You want me to drive you guys to Champaign?"

"Weren't you her camp counselor at Chi one summer?"

Mitzy groaned. "She was the kid with the freckles and
braids who stuck gigantic wads of gum to the bottom of each
camper's luggage on the last day of camp. The bus had to
wait an extra hour while we scraped it off."

"You became a special ed teacher to help all the Allies of
the world," her mother said solemnly.

"Now you're stretching it."

"So will you drive us or not?" her mother asked impatiently.

"I'll check my daily planner."

"Great. Put your mother on hold."

"Did I ever mention that Lake Forest's eighth grade English teacher and school principal are both from the U. of I.?" Mitzy said, trying to steer her mother from the question at hand.

"So?" her mother asked curtly.

"I didn't say I wouldn't drive, Mom. I just need to check it out first."

Her mother tossed her a spray bottle filled with Miracle-Gro. "Can we finish potting these plants in this decade?"

"Definitely," Mitzy said, smiling.

Chapter 29

Eight-thirty a.m. The last day of school. Excited chatter radiated through the halls as students clad in shorts and spaghetti-strapped tops shared summer visions of overnight camp, whitewater rafting, and visits to foreign countries. Those willowy-minded pushers of the pen embarked on that last hour of structured learning with the waning gusto of an automobile engine sucked dry.

In fact, the last hour was hardly structured at all. Final attendance was taken. Envelopes sealed nine months before with furtively jotted academic and social goals for the upcoming school year were finally returned to their owners. Hundreds of inquisitive fingers tore open their envelopes of hopes and dreams. Then they silently compared projections with reality. The majority of regular ed students broke into high-five smiles, along with a dozen or so special ed kids. The rest of the group pretended nonchalance about their personal failings.

Eighth grade graduation had come and gone, the end of childhood like biting into a lemon. Tears and hugs flowed freely on this last morning of middle school as students ferreted out teachers and peers whose well-wishes had yet to be recorded on the inside covers of their yearbooks. Strangely enough, Mr. Fillmore was absent on this special day. Home with the flu but he wishes you all the best, the attendance lady said. The students' faces fell. Their principal's handsome, smiling face had greeted them each morning as they entered the school building. He'd enthusiastically applauded their every band recital, play rehearsal, cheerleading competition, and basketball game. Especially the basketball games, for he had been one of the Five Fighting Illini, attested to by the ring he wore on his pinkie finger.

At the eighth-grade dance, Mr. Fillmore had stood behind the beverage table for hours, pouring rainbow sherbet punch. Proudly, he'd handed out diplomas on graduation day, shaking hands and delivering a few whispered words of encouragement to even the biggest troublemakers as they walked across the stage. So integral had he been to their final year of childhood accomplishments that a wave of sadness swept through the hearts of the students.

As the final bell chimed, the new graduates tearfully clung to each other, promising to stay in touch over the long summer hiatus. Then they shuffled out of the school building, some arm in arm, others with hands in pockets, and disappeared into a myriad of minivans and SUVs.

~

Mitzy rubber-banded posters of athletes and entertainers who'd once upon a time been special ed students themselves. Luckily, she'd toted boxes of books and personal belongings home earlier in the week. This box would be her final cargo.

As she rolled the posters, she thought about her best friend in college. Becky had been an untreated dyslexic who could neither sound words out phonetically nor read; a brilliant girl who bullshitted her way through school by memorizing the spelling of thousands of words, dictating essays into the computer, and listening to books on tape. Once she hit college, she could no longer keep pace with the amount of information she needed to absorb in each class. To dim the shame, Becky had turned to cocaine. Six months later, Mitzy had pitched a handful of dirt into her open grave as Becky was laid to rest.

The athletes and entertainers on these posters had been more fortunate than her friend. Sharing their academic vulnerabilities with those who could help, these children had grown into successful young adults who learned to cope with their disabilities.

Mitzy secured the posters beneath her armpit, then reached for her last carton of personal materials. Wednesday had been her last "student" day of the school year. During the final week, general ed teachers required all their students to complete end-of-the-year tasks, and so speech pathologist, social worker, and special education support services had been terminated.

This morning, a group of Mitzy's eighth graders had rushed into her room for last-minute yearbook signings, and she'd received some sweet gifts. A gift certificate to a local nails and spa boutique. Dinner for two at the Lake Forest Country Club. And two tickets to the upcoming Paul McCartney concert. Harry and her mother might appreciate those tickets as an encore wedding gift.

When Mitzy was growing up, old Beatles music permeated the one-bedroom apartment she and her mom had shared. But the famous rock musician her mom adored was getting on in years, his wife dying of cancer a handful of years ago. It was depressing to realize that someone as gorgeous as Paul was in his youth had reached the age of extreme appearance changes.

Yet Paul was still an incredible musician, and he'd recently married a beautiful girl named Heather. True, his fairytale marriage was already in the divorce courts, but that wouldn't happen to Shirley and Harry. After fourteen years of dating—her mother could be exasperatingly slow—those two would finally sprint into the wilderness of marriage to explore their remaining years together. Mitzy sighed. Hopefully she would track her own soul mate down at least one day before the end of time.

After giving her resource classroom a quick once-over, Mitzy locked the door and trudged down the hall, carton in tow. It had been a tremendous first year. "You really got what it takes," she heard her father's voice say, the words he would have said had he still been alive. "Not everybody has the chutzpah to switch jobs midstream." *I'm my mother's daughter*, she answered him silently. *Chutzpah is my middle name.*

It had taken months for Mitzy to view herself as a real teacher, rather than an impostor walking down these hallowed halls of education. She'd obsessed about being a lame disciplinarian. Yet when called upon to provide a safety net for her students' self-esteem, she'd repeatedly risen to the occasion.

Her thoughts turned to Ellie, who had been allowed to attend her graduation ceremony, but not to reenter the school building pending closure on her father's cause of death. She wondered if Eric had dug up any new evidence pointing to a culprit other than Ellie. Eventually, Mitzy would have to email him regarding the quickie dance lesson at her mother's, but she was still incensed over their previous encounter. Here she was, trying to help, and Eric was treating her like some run-of-the-mill busybody. Infuriating!

Mitzy dragged the heavy cardboard box to the side door, then peered outside. Only one other staff member's car still flanked the parking lot. Hoisting the cardboard box and posters, she backslid her way out the side door exit and slipped off the single step.

"Here. Let me help you up," came a soft voice from behind.

Mitzy looked up, then scowled when she saw who it was. "I'm good."

Eric turned to walk back to his unmarked Chevy. "Just thought you'd want to know we found Barge's killer," he said, tossing the words nonchalantly over his shoulder.

Her heart jumped into her throat. "Wait!" she called. In the staff parking lot, a teacher she didn't recognize turned her way. As Mitzy raised her arm to wave her off, the heavy box slipped from her grasp and landed with a thud, the posters rolling down the sidewalk. Swearing under her breath, Mitzy kneeled down to gather the scattered items. Her gaze on the ground, she sensed Eric's kneeling presence before she saw him.

She jumped to her feet and dusted off her pants. "I'm sorry I was a jerk just now. Tell me."

Eric handed her the posters. Then he lifted the box and headed towards her car. "You're not sorry, you're just plying me for information. Read about it in tomorrow's news."

"You were an asshole the other night in the woods."

Eric turned to face her. "I apologize. You were getting a little too close, that's all."

"Professionally or personally?" she asked.

His face reddened. "Both."

"Obviously you have issues," Mitzy said, mimicking the statement he'd made about her.

He placed the box beside her car. "I'm outta here."

She laid a hand on his arm. "Let's start over. Hi, Eric. What information about Joseph Barge's death do you wish to share with me?"

Her heart skipped a beat as Eric stared at her with his piercing blue eyes, obviously trying to decide whether or not he could trust her. Finally he pulled an envelope from his shirt pocket and handed it to her. She opened it, took out the single sheet of paper inside, and read:

> *To the Parents, Students, and Teaching*
> *Staff of White Oaks Middle School,*
> *I apologize for allowing rumor to take*
> *hold regarding the death of Joseph Barge on*
> *April 15 of this year. Speculation about the*
> *presence of environmental pollution in the*
> *school is entirely unfounded. Since that date,*
> *not one member of White Oaks Middle School*
> *has submitted a valid complaint of any*
> *respiratory or other health-related ailment.*

Joseph Barge was a parent who felt no compunction about harassing the members of our eighth-grade teaching staff while classes were in session. His actions frightened our students and disrupted the learning process. While most WOMS students enjoy an affluent, crime-free community, their home lives do not always provide the nurturing environment needed to emotionally thrive. Children, our most precious commodity, are being forced to grow up under the care of nannies or their own devices, all for the sake of power and money.

On April 15, I sought to restore harmony by performing a single spontaneous act during a frantic moment when the conference room had cleared. I had in my suit jacket two anti-anxiety capsules prescribed for my grandfather, who suffers from Alzheimer's. Praying that my grandfather's meds would produce a relaxed, attentive parent who would do right by his daughter and sign off on her alternative placement papers, I placed both capsules in Joseph Barge's coffee. I was stunned when Mr. Barge instead keeled over dead!

Yet, I admit to feeling relieved that this raging bull will no longer terrorize our teachers and students. To that end, my goals have been achieved. Let it be known to all teaching staff and students that there was at least one brave warrior who fought for their right to learn in a fear-free environment.
Sincerely,
Jerry Fillmore, M.A.
Principal, White Oaks Middle School

Mitzy frowned. "How did you get this?"

"Belinda Riggs, your school secretary, phoned the police department this morning, saying there was a sealed envelope on her desk addressed to Detective Eric Whelan, Lake Forest Police Department, from White Oaks Middle School principal Jerry Fillmore. He also left a voice mail message saying he was home sick with stomach flu. The secretary says she phoned his home at nine-fifteen to check on his condition, but no one answered. Anyhow, Fillmore's grandfather does have Alzheimer's; he's at Glen Tree nursing home."

"I know," Mitzy said. She unlocked her car trunk and hoisted the box and posters inside. "Jerry was visiting him the day I went there to visit my ex-boss. Neil Grant; he was there for rehab after a hip replacement."

"Here's something I wager you didn't know."

Mitzy slammed the trunk. "I'm game." Then she remembered the promise she'd made to her mother. "If you lose, you and I teach my mom and Harry some cool dance moves."

"Deal." Eric shook her hand. "Fillmore's grand-dad was taking anti-anxiety drugs for severe mood swings. Nurse said he would tongue the meds because they made him sluggish."

"Ew! Fillmore put saliva-packed meds in Barge's coffee!"

"Knew it," Eric said. "You had no clue!"

Mitzy put her hands on her hips. "And you have no clue what I do or do not know, Detective."

Eric's eyes twinkled. "My guys are rummaging through Fillmore's office as we speak. They've already been to his house in Riverwoods."

"So Jerry was home."

"Nope. Got some uniforms looking for him." Eric handed Mitzy a second note. "He left this on his kitchen table."

"For a sports guy, he sure likes to write a lot," she said, reaching for the note. She read aloud:

I've done my moral duty by confessing to

the killing of Joseph Barge, thereby releasing his daughter Ellie from any further suspicion. But I am not about to spend my remaining years in jail, cowering from rapists and serial killers.

Please tell the students and staff at Lake Forest they will remain forever in my thoughts. I wish them joy and success in their lives. Though I know not what my future holds, I will not contact you again.

Sincerely,
Jerry Fillmore

Mitzy chortled.

"What's with you?" Eric asked, obviously shocked by her reaction.

"If those letters were a stage performance, my hands would be raw. Jerry didn't talk like that, and he certainly didn't write like that. Heck, he was on the Fighting Illini."

"I wondered about that," Eric said.

She gave him a confused look. "About Jerry's college basketball career?"

"About the letters," he said, with a touch of impatience. "Fillmore could've written them—just because he played college ball doesn't mean he can't write a sentence—but I've talked to him a few times now. You're right, there's no similarity. Something's off."

"'Off' is right. There's a big difference between writing a grammatically correct sentence and putting one's ideas on paper in that particular way."

"Like what?"

"Word choices. Sentence structure. 'I know not what my future holds'? That's extremely formal English, like something from the late eighteen-hundreds. Not the kind of letters a thirty-something guy is going to pen." She frowned at him, puzzled. "Why did you tell me you'd found Barge's killer if you weren't sure Jerry wrote these?"

"Got your attention, didn't it?" Then he sobered.

"Actually, I wanted your take. You work here, with Fillmore and everyone else. If Jerry Fillmore didn't write those letters, who did?"

"Somebody well versed in English, or maybe the dramatic arts." She paused as a thought struck her. "Come to think of it, Lynette LaFleur wasn't at school today either."

He frowned. "You told me she took anti-anxiety meds. The coroner's report said Barge had those in his system along with antidepressants."

Mitzy nodded. "Lynette took the most abuse from Barge. Just last week she said her panic attacks have disappeared since his death."

Eric pulled out his cell phone, then stepped away and made a quick call. He mumbled too low for her to hear what he said. Then he turned back to her. "It's worth checking out."

"Maybe Jerry and Lynette are both in on Barge's death," Mitzy said.

Eric gave her a puzzled look. "A couple of days ago, you were sure Ellie's aunt and nanny were the culprits."

Mitzy coolly stared at him. "What made me a good investigative reporter was that I matched new evidence to a theory, not the other way around."

"If the teacher and principal are guilty, why confess? All bets were on Ellie."

"They're educators, not bogeymen. They couldn't let an innocent child take the rap for his death. Maybe they even felt noble, standing up for teachers and students Joseph Barge had victimized."

Eric gave her a disgusted look.

"Okay, maybe that example was farfetched," Mitzy conceded.

"Like twelve ball parks from Wrigley Field farfetched."

She smiled. "I love your analogy."

A grin flickered across Eric's face. Then he went back to serious cop mode. "Did Fillmore and the English teacher have a personal relationship going on?"

Mitzy shook her head. "That kind of news would have

fanned through the halls like wildfire."

"How about family or significant others?"

"Roz said Jerry's grandpa was his only living family member. Lynette never talked about family."

Eric shook his head. "Looks like both their lives centered around this school."

"Well, whatever happens in this part of the investigation, I'm staying out of it," Mitzy said.

Eric looked taken aback. "You're not itching to tag along to the LaFleur residence?"

"Nope."

"I bet you'd feel a hell of a lot differently if Joseph Barge was someone you'd never met."

"No way do I want to watch you arrest two dedicated educators whose nemesis suffered a fatal reaction."

"Maybe at their hands," Eric said.

"Whoever did it should have kept his or her pen capped."

"You're playing with me again, right?"

She folded her arms. "Nobody killed Barge on purpose."

"We don't know that."

"Don't you get it? Even if Jerry and Lynette are found innocent, they'll never be able to work in education again."

"Maybe they could get a job with your former boss."

"Now you're getting mean."

"Better yet, a tabloid newspaper." Eric framed his eyes. "I can see it now: The Deadly Duo."

"Hey, I could be all wrong about them," Mitzy said.

"You sounded damn sure a few minutes ago."

"That's ridiculous."

"You drive me nuts, know that?" Eric said angrily.

"I wager nobody drives you anywhere you don't want to go," she said.

"One minute you're insightful, the next a pain in the ass!"

Mitzy's voice rose. "Enough, Eric!"

He stared at her stonily, then pulled a key from his coat pocket and headed towards his car. "Enough is right."

Instantly she regretted her combative tone. She sprinted

after him. "Can we please stop arguing? You find Jerry and Lynette. I'll give Ellie and her aunt the good news."

"What good news?" he grunted. "All we have are loose ends."

She smiled up at him. "I'm sure Fay Shimmer will be relieved to know Ellie is no longer considered a suspect."

"I never said that," he said gruffly.

"But you are turning those accusatory eyes of yours elsewhere, aren't you?"

Eric unlocked the Chevy. "Just covering all the bases. Nothing more."

"By the way, when are you free to show my mom and Uncle Harry some of our dance moves?"

"I didn't lose!"

"I wouldn't be so sure about that," she said delicately.

Eric glared at her, then climbed into his car without a word and sped off.

"Don't worry. You can let me know," Mitzy shouted after the retreating vehicle.

Chapter 30

Mitzy paused to catch her breath in the shallow end of
the athletic club's Olympic-sized pool. She marveled at
Maggie hurling herself through the water without coming up
for air. Her friend's swimming technique mimicked the
barracuda determination she brought even to her most
complex homicide cases. Never in Mitzy's wildest
imagination would she have predicted they'd become friends
after Maggie fatally shot her attacker on that long-ago
Christmas Eve.

As a young reporter, Mitzy had cringed at Maggie
O'Connor's blunt communication style, similar to the rough
language used by the City Hall heavyweights Mitzy often
interviewed. She'd been even more surprised when Maggie
confided she'd been a psych major at Northwestern
University, Mitzy's own alma mater. As Lynette LaFleur had
said last week, looks were deceiving. If Lynette was the
person responsible for fatally poisoning Joseph Barge, then
Eric had been right. She had been blindsided. Just not by
Ellie.

Mitzy glanced at her water-proof watch, then at Maggie,
whose pace had switched from aggressive barracuda to

languid swan. It was an hour from the Lake Shore Athletic Club to the Barge home in Lake Forest, and Mitzy wanted to arrive there before dark.

They got out of the pool and headed for the locker room, where they showered the chlorine off their skins. "You pooped out fast," Maggie said, as she toweled off. "Thought you were on the swim team in high school."

"Stomach cramps," Mitzy lied. "Think I'm getting my period." She headed for the nearest hair dryer.

Maggie followed. "Need me to tag along to Lake Forest? I'm not on shift tonight."

"That's really sweet, but I'm driving up there to tell Ellie and her aunt the good news, then heading straight home to bed."

"Speaking of bed, how's it going with Eric?" Maggie yelled over the competing roar of their hair blowers.

Mitzy held up a hand in a "wait" gesture. Maggie nodded. With her hair dry and both blowers off, Mitzy quickly glanced down each locker room aisle. "You are so lucky there's nobody else in here!"

"Touchy, touchy. So what's the scoop?"

"I don't know where you get the idea my relationship with Eric is anything but professional."

"That's not how Eric sees it."

Mitzy blushed. "What did you say to him, Maggie?"

"Nada. I called to ask how the Barge investigation was progressing. Then I asked if you'd been a help or a hindrance. What do you think he said?"

Mitzy shrugged, staring into the mirror as she straightened her short hair. "I need to get some highlights. Brassy red or auburn?"

"He said you were a real pain in the ass."

Mitzy whirled so fast, the cord of her hair straightener flew out of its plug. "He said what?"

"Shit, Mitzy! You need anger management."

"So now you're on my mother's side."

"Huh?"

"She always says I can't control my anger."

"Maybe you should consider therapy," Maggie said. "Just don't use the same shrink that girl's father used."

"Very funny," Mitzy said, attempting to plug in the hair straightener. "Ouch!" she screeched as a spark of white light zapped her fingers.

"See?" Maggie chuckled, spreading mousse through her curly hair. "Anger doesn't pay."

Mitzy massaged her hand. "That ungrateful bastard."

Maggie put her hand to her heart in a theatrical gesture. "You must really have it bad for Romeo. You're even using profanity!"

"Here I am, imparting my knowledge of the Barge family, accompanying him to their house, brainstorming possible suspects."

"Helping him out with his dance lessons," Maggie added.

Mitzy gave her a look. "He told you that?"

"Well, yeah."

"He mention the woods, too?"

Maggie smirked.

"So this is how he repays me!"

"You really slam-dunked him in the school parking lot the other day."

"Now you're his confidante," Mitzy said, miffed.

"Slow down, *compadre*. You haven't exactly been talking much yourself lately."

Mitzy looked away. "I just didn't think you'd be interested."

"What? Not interested in hearing about your fiery romance?"

Mitzy laughed. "Dream on. It was the last day of school. Eric had some new information to share." She told Maggie about Fillmore's supposed confession notes and her own suspicions about who might have authored them. "I mentioned it was unfortunate Jerry Fillmore and Lynette LaFleur will be bounced from the field of education, whether they're guilty of killing Joseph Barge or not. He got pissed off. End of story."

"You think the English teacher is linked to the case?"

Maggie asked.

"I think Barge's death was caused by a combination of meds."

"If Eric is still investigating, it's premature for you to be telling Ellie's aunt about the confession notes."

"You're probably right," Mitzy said. "I just want to bring some joy back into the lives of that

"You're way too invested in the outcome family."

She felt her friend's pitying gaze. "Looks like Eric was on target about you, after all."

"What's that supposed to mean?"

of this case. You need to step away."

"Meaning?"

"No further contact with Ellie and her aunt 'til the case is resolved. They'll see what they need to on the news."

"Ellie will feel abandoned."

"The family hire an attorney?"

Mitzy nodded.

"She's got her aunt, her nanny, and an expensive lawyer on her side. Odds are he wouldn't allow you to see the girl, anyway."

"Fine," Mitzy said. She felt despondent as she pulled on her shoes.

"Come on. You need to get your mind off this case and have some fun. Let's hit the karaoke bar downtown."

"It's a school night. And my stomach's hurting."

"Yet you were willing to traipse back up to Lake Forest tonight."

"Fine. Only for an hour."

Arm in arm, they headed out to the parking lot. "We'll get you some seltzer water. Did you invite Eric to your mom's wedding yet?" Maggie asked.

"I was going to, but he's been such a jerk."

"You really should give him a chance. He's a decent guy."

"I'm tired of everybody, Eric included, telling me, 'Mitzy, you're too intense.' Live with it, damn it!"

Maggie applauded. "You go, girl!"

They reached Mitzy's Celica, and she unlocked the door. "All this holier-than-thou crap makes me want to puke."

"Don't stop now, you're on a roll."

Usually it took a couple of drinks for Mitzy to spout off on her philosophy of life, but she was incensed at Eric turning his back on her. "Why can't we all accept each other's quirks and fantasies and move on?"

"Did you say fantasies?"

Mitzy blushed. "That word just popped out."

"Does Eric know about Juron?"

"No! And you better not tell him."

Her friend looked at her innocently. "My jaw is glued shut."

"Not funny. Eric definitely is drop-dead gorgeous, but he's quirky as heck."

Maggie snickered.

"What?"

"In one breath, you advocate a kinder, gentler world of acceptance. In the next, you take your marbles and go home because Eric's too prim and proper for you."

"We're always butting heads. He thinks his way is the only way."

"It all boils down to if this guy has potential in the love department."

Mitzy slid into the driver's seat, then rolled down the window. "It's only been eight months since Juron moved out."

"So you'd have no problem with me making a move on Eric."

Mitzy gave her a searing look. "Bitch!"

Maggie chuckled. "That's what I thought. He invite you to his sister's wedding yet?"

Mitzy shook her head. "That's still three months away."

"Unless you've secretly applied to appear on *The Bachelorette*, you better get your ass in gear and invite that guy to your mom's wedding."

Mitzy peered through the windshield. "Don't look now, but I think there's a guy watching us from behind that bush."

"Where?" Maggie turned away, reaching for her gun.

"Toodles," Mitzy called as she sped off. *No karaoke tonight.*

Chapter 31

"I've attempted to answer all your questions," Jerry Fillmore said wearily. "Can we get this over with so I can go home and get some—"Abruptly, he got up and bolted from the room.

Eric raised his eyebrows. "Fourth time he's done that in the past hour."

Phil Flanagan pushed away from the conference table, his chair rolling back on its coasters. "This is unbelievable. My client should be back in the hospital."

"We could have interviewed him there. It was his choice to have us bring him in to the station."

"Nothing he says here will hold up in a court of law."

"If he comes clean about the confession notes, Mr. Flanagan, he won't have to worry about going to court."

"He already told you he did not write those confession letters."

Eric knew that. But there was no harm in trying to rattle Fillmore so he'd spill any details about he and Lynette acting in concert. If they had. "Why should I believe him?"

The attorney looked at him solemnly. "My client is an integral part of the community, respected by parents, students, and teachers alike."

"Your client couldn't stop Joseph Barge from verbally abusing his teachers and frightening students. In the end, the only way he could save face was to permanently rid his school of the problem."

"A person can write that he wishes to rid the world of terrorists. Desire does not equal reality."

"Tell me about it," Eric mumbled, thinking of his tumultuous relationship with Mitzy Maven. Irritated, he pushed the thought of her away. He had a job to do.

The attorney leaned his arms on the table. "What more do you need to know, Detective?"

"Yes, what more do you need to know?" a pale Jerry Fillmore asked, tucking his shirt in as he reentered the conference room.

"Your first confession note."

"How many times do I have to tell you, Detective? I did not write those notes!"

Eric ignored him. "First note says you put anti-anxiety tablets in Mr. Barge's coffee so he'd calm down long enough to sign his daughter's alternative high school placement papers."

"I may have thought it, but I'd never act on it."

"Ellie Barge saw you enter the meeting room immediately following the fire alarm, then reemerge carrying a manila folder."

Fillmore nodded. "I retrieved the Barge file. Is that a crime?"

Eric stared at him in exasperation. "You had motive, opportunity, and means."

"Detective, I must ask you to stop harassing my client," Flanagan said. "He told you he went back to retrieve a folder."

"And minutes later, Joseph Barge was dead."

"The teaching staff and students were standing outside the school building for at least fifteen minutes before firefighters signaled we could reenter the school," Fillmore said, wiping his sweaty brow.

"Which gave you plenty of time to place the drugs in Barge's coffee."

"I believe my client is suggesting someone else had an opportunity to commit the crime," Flanagan said.

"Can we quit this sparring? My stomach's going to explode again any second."

Eric's voice softened. "Any juror would understand you didn't mean to kill the victim."

"For the last time, Detective Whelan, I did not drug Joseph Barge!" Fillmore yelled. He abruptly covered his mouth and ran from the room.

Flanagan grabbed his briefcase. "This despicable show is over!" he snapped, then ran after his client.

Slumped in his seat, Eric made a half-hearted attempt to balance a pencil on his palm. Deep in his gut, he knew Fillmore was telling the truth. Mitzy had told him as much, confirming his doubts about the letters. Yet she had her own motives, hoping to protect her student. Could he trust her? He grasped the pencil and felt its sharp point pierce his skin. Great. Now he'd get blood poisoning and die.

After carefully extracting the pencil from his palm, he headed for the coat closet. He removed a first aid kit from the top shelf and cleaned the blood off his hand with an antiseptic wipe. This wasn't the first time he'd allowed an intelligent, good-looking woman to get under his skin. His ex-girlfriend, Vanessa, had been quite a looker, with her long blonde hair and green eyes, and was a belly dancer in bed. I'll never leave you, she'd murmur in his ear, night after steamy summer night.

One fall morning, he awoke to find her side of the king-sized bed empty, no scent of her pear perfume remaining, the bedroom closet stripped of women's wear. She'd flown to New York, her sights set on becoming America's Next Top Model.

Vanessa had never contacted him to apologize. Nor had she responded to his sister's wedding invitation, which was a good thing in case he decided to bring Mitzy. He shook himself, remembering that she, too, was now out of the picture.

The one-carat diamond he'd planned to give Vanessa that fateful September morning was buried in his socks drawer, probably forever. Because you just couldn't trust them, these women with their lofty aspirations and loyalties to things he didn't understand.

Mitzy had probably led him astray on the English teacher, too. He'd interview Lynette LaFleur again as a matter of course, but it occurred to him that Ellie Barge could have written those confession notes. Mitzy said the girl loved to write and liked Shakespeare. From Ellie's own confession just days ago, she'd shown a dramatic flair.

~

Mitzy yawned as she sat in front of the computer screen playing Pipes. At 5:30 a.m., her fingers clumsily attempted to assemble the colored pipes within the allotted seconds. One week into summer vacation and she was still on school time. Plus, the game was addictive.

The IM screen popped up. Mitzy sucked her lower lip as she read the message from the email user:

tcooper: *This is Theresa Cooper. A belated thanx for helping Sammy this year.*

*She got up at 5:30 a.m. to say tha*t? Mitzy blinked drowsiness from her eyes and typed back.

actionlady: *No prob. He'll be great in general ed. classes this fall. What's the big guy doing this summer?*

tcooper: *Starting chess camp on Mon. You?*

actionlady: *Taking grad course on classroom discipline + attending mom's wedding. She's getting remarried. Have good summer!*

Mitzy was about to sign off when new words appeared:

tcooper: *Sammy wanted me to tell you that on morn girl's father died, he saw a woman reenter the conference room a few minutes after everyone cleared out. She was carrying a briefcase.*

Mitzy felt a jolt of adrenalin shoot through her body. She

typed quickly:

actionlady: *How'd he see if he was outside?*

tcooper: *He was in line. Their class was heading outside.*

actionlady: Was it a teacher?

tcooper: Sammy couldn't tell.

actionlady: *Did he report what he saw?*

tcooper: *He was scared. Didn't even tell me until last night.*

actionlady: *Suggest you contact Detective Whelan.*

tcooper: *Would appreciate if you tell him yourself.*

Mitzy let the space following her user name go blank. How could she contact Eric when they were at a stand-off?

tcooper: *Ms. Maven??*

Reining in her normally impulsive response, Mitzy typed back.

actionlady: *Will contact u soon with answer.*

This one she definitely couldn't answer on six hours' worth of sleep. She shut down the Pipes game and logged off the computer, then retreated to her bedroom with a glass of grape juice and *People Magazine*.

~

His knuckles sore from rapping, Eric shuffled down the three flights of threadbare stairs and was heading into the outer vestibule when he heard a female voice call down the stairwell. "Who eess it?"

"Ms. LaFleur?" he called up the winding staircase. This was one hell of a strange neighborhood for a classy English teacher at a school in the northern suburbs, he thought.

A stocky, dark-skinned young woman flanked by three young children stared back at him. "She no live here, *señor*." Tossing her long black hair over her shoulder, the woman turned back to her apartment.

Eric frowned. That made no sense, unless the school's files were out of date. "*Un momento, por favor, señora*," he called, holding his detective's badge out for her to see as he

climbed the stairs. The young woman stared down at him.
When he reached her, he took Lynette LaFleur's picture
from his jacket pocket and held it out. *"Quien una joven?"*
The woman shrugged, then entered her apartment and
shut the door. He heard the lock click shut.

Once outside, Eric tucked the picture away, then dug out
a Post-it and compared the numbers on the front door with
the address he'd scribbled down. The two addresses
matched: 2000 W. Division. He scanned the neighborhood.
Rehabbing had yet to begin in this area, cluttered by barred
pawnshops and liquor stores and an occasional homeless
person carting an assortment of plastic bags filled with
personal belongings. *Must be an investment property, and
something went wrong.*

He had been toying with the idea of buying a "fixer
upper" himself and renting it out. He could do his own
carpentry work; people always said he was a chip off the old
block. As a little kid growing up in the Austin area, he got to
keep all the leftover wooden toys his dad carved but couldn't
sell. Later, when Martin Whelan's carvings had progressed
to exquisitely fashioned tables and chairs, their family
moved into the more desirable Park Ridge.

Eric admired how his dad was always there for him and
his sister, even as they grew more affluent. Dad attended
every one of his ball games, cheered Eric's sister through
numerous gymnastics competitions and violin concerts, and
sat by them during night after night of endless homework.
He knew his dad was looking down at him from above,
proud of his son, the detective.

He shook himself. He was getting as bad as Mitzy, going
off track. He frowned. Even now he was thinking of her.
*Has she called your cell phone? Sent you any emails or
instant messages? Let it go*, he told himself brusquely.

~

A half-hour later, Eric pulled up to the address he'd
found in the white pages. He stepped out of the car and

looked around. This was more like the place a teacher in an upscale school district would live. A hundred yards to his right, foamy waves rolled in off Lake Michigan. To his left, rehabbed apartment buildings sported "Luxury Two and Three Bedroom Apartments Available" signs.

Shielding his eyes from the sun, Eric peered at the shoreline. The sandy beach seemed smaller than it used to, but size could play tricks with your memory. The last time he'd been to Pratt Beach was fifteen years ago, as a high school sophomore visiting his older sister in her dorm at Loyola University.

Knowing how much he enjoyed playing volleyball, Susie had dragged him along to a beach game. As he helped set up the net a safe distance from Frisbee-throwers, families barbecuing, and sunbathing couples, Eric realized his sister's boyfriend was the only other guy in their group. Eric played tentatively at first, but quickly adjusted when the ball banged his forehead, recognizing these girls with laughing eyes and teasing serves were taking no prisoners.

On and on they played into the dusk, then afterwards, with lanterns and lightning bugs illuminating the jet-black sky. He'd loved the feeling of community along the beach as laughter and talking surrendered to the sound of thunderous waves crashing against the shore. By the time they'd all lined up at the ice cream truck, his legs were ready to buckle.

Sweet memories. Eric turned back to the six-flat apartment building where Lynette LaFleur lived. He'd never forgotten how his sister had included him, the sense of camaraderie he'd felt with her friends. Hard to believe Susie was getting married in two months, to the same boyfriend who played volleyball with them that night.

He walked up to the building's front door and eyed the list of names next to their respective apartment numbers. Lynette LaFleur's name was conspicuously absent. What the hell was going on with this lady? Puzzled, he pressed the building manager's buzzer.

A few minutes later, a thirty-something Brad Pitt look-a-like turned up. After Eric showed his badge through the glass door, the pseudo-Brad buzzed him in and led him through a mirrored hallway into a well-appointed office. "What can I do for you?" the man asked.

"I'm looking for Lynette LaFleur," Eric said. She lives in Apartment 2A."

The building manager checked his roster. "Sorry. There's no one in this building by that name."

"That a list for renters and owners?"

"Uh-huh."

Eric took out the teacher's picture again. "Recognize this woman?"

"I'm sorry, sir. I don't," the manager said. "Maybe she lived here prior to the condo conversion, when this building was strictly rental apartments."

"When did the conversion take place?"

"Four months ago."

"What about the folks who lived here before?"

"Each apartment dweller received a letter describing purchase or higher rental price options."

"Was Ms. LaFleur a renter?"

The manager shrugged. "There's no way to tell. When our management company took over this property at the end of January, we created a list of former residents who opted to stay, then discarded the old files."

"Anyone still work here from the previous management company?"

"Just the night janitor, but he's in Jamaica this week visiting a sick family member. He should be back on Monday unless his grandmother gets worse."

Eric laid his card on the desk. "When he comes back, contact me."

The manager picked it up. "Will do."

~

"Hey. It's me," Eric said into his cell phone.
"What do you want?"
He willed himself to ignore her sarcastic tone.

"Wondering if you happen to have Lynette LaFleur's address?"

"Try the White Pages." She sounded ready to hang up.

"Wait."

"Wait? So you can tell me to butt out of your business, ridicule me for protecting a student, and disappear into the sunset when I ask you to demonstrate a dance step to my mom? I don't think so." She slammed the receiver down so hard, the sound made his head vibrate. He'd give his seventh row Bulls tickets to not have to click redial.

He did it anyway, and braced himself. "Hello?"

"I'm not allowed to give out contact information of school personnel. Good bye."

"Mitzy, don't hang up. Just give me Lynette's phone number and address and I promise I'll get over to your mom's house tonight."

"Isn't blackmail against the law, Detective? Or do you just pick and choose the laws to follow?"

"Actually, that concept refers to threatening someone with a particular consequence. Holding something over their head."

"I want to hold something over your head, and it's not pretty. Stop calling me."

Bang went the telephone once again. Now Eric's other ear felt deaf. He clicked redial one last time.

"Hello?"

"Please don't hang up again," he pleaded. "My ears can't take it."

"What part of 'stop bothering me' don't you understand?"

"Listen, I need to interview the English teacher. I've been to two addresses, neither of which is hers. Will you help me?"

Brief silence from Mitzy. He hoped that was a good sign. "On one condition," she said.

"What's that?"

"I go with you."

"No way. She might harbor a weapon."

"Now who's talking nuts?"

Eric stopped short of telling Mitzy he'd read her colleague's personnel files and learned the real reason for her leaving Cawley Day School. It had taken him some digging to find all the pieces and put them together, but he'd managed it. Why make this harder than it had to be? "Let's just say I don't want to put your life at risk."

"And you're making that choice for me. Okay, good luck."

"All right! You win. You can come along, but let me do the talking."

"Toodles, Eric."

"Let me do most of the talking."

"Fine. Be there at 4:05 p.m." Eric heard her smile into the phone. She gave him the address. "And Eric?"

"Yeah?" he grumbled.

"Got some new information you might want to hear."

"Spill it."

"Later. When I see you." The phone line went dead.

Damn it, he thought. She'd hooked him again.

Chapter 32

"You're a difficult person to locate," Eric said, wiping his brow as he sipped iced tea.

"I'm sorry you had so much trouble finding me." Lynette LaFleur set a fruit bowl on the checkered tablecloth in the dining room of her small apartment.

"You really ought to get this window fan replaced," Eric said. "This week's supposed to be the hottest in ten years, more like late August than first week of June."

"The building engineer's got a big stack of work orders before mine." Lynette topped off her glass of iced tea and eased herself into a folding chair. "Sit down and join us, Mitzy."

"In a second," Mitzy's voice rang out from the living room. Floor-to-ceiling bookcase. Charles Dickens, F. Scott Fitzgerald, Ernest Hemingway, Ayn Rand, J.D.Salinger, John Steinbeck. "You've got quite a collection here."

"It's a pain hauling all these books around every time I move, but I can't forsake them."

"If I were you, I'd ditch the Hemingway and Salinger," Mitzy said.

The English teacher chuckled. "You're lucky my English

professor can't hear you spouting such heresy."

"How long have you lived here?" Eric asked.

"Only a couple of months. That's why the place looks so barren. Except for my books, of course."

"So you move around a lot?"

Lynette nodded. "I get bored fast."

"That apartment on West Division looked pretty run down."

"Investment property. I planned to rehab, but my finances changed. The tenants pleaded with me to leave the building in its current condition, so I sold the building as is."

"Why would they do that?" Eric asked.

"They were scared their rent would skyrocket and they'd have no place to live."

"Then you moved into a studio down by the lake?"

Lynette nodded.

"Nice building," Eric said. "Why'd you leave?"

"New management came on board and rehabbed the apartments, then turned them into condos. I bailed when they told me my studio was selling for $250,000, plus $300 a month for association fees."

"Prices are getting ridiculous," Mitzy said, thumbing through a book.

"So what brings you guys down to my neck of the woods?" Lynette asked.

Mitzy glanced over. "Detective Whelan had some questions about the death of Ellie's dad. I came along to monitor his every word and make sure he didn't treat you too harshly."

The detective gave Mitzy the evil eye. She mouthed the word *sorry*, picked up her iced tea from the table and turned to peruse a second bookcase.

"You interviewed me right after Mr. Barge passed away."

"We only had a couple of minutes to talk. You were rushing off to a doctor's appointment."

"That's right," Lynette said. "I totally forgot."

"And you were absent from school on Tuesday, when I

did my second round of interviews."

"Please. Ask me anything you like," Lynette said pleasantly.

Eric leaned across the table. "You read about Ellie's confession in the newspaper?"

Lynette nodded. "So sad."

"The medical examiner doesn't buy her story," the detective lied.

"Oh?"

"Were you friendly with Jerry Fillmore?" he asked, switching gears.

She shrugged. "Sure. He was my school principal."

"Did you see him outside of school?"

She shook her head. "We're both single, but he's not my type."

"You had a couple of things in common, right?"

Lynette nodded. "We both played for U. of I."

"And you both hated Joseph Barge."

She gave him a puzzled look. "I guess."

"Bet you had a hell of a time reassuring your students that everything was all right following one of Barge's raids."

She scowled, then sipped her tea. "The guy was a terrorist in a gabardine suit."

"Mitzy said you had panic attacks."

Lynette nodded. "My psychiatrist put me on an anti-anxiety drug."

"Was it an SSRI or an MAO inhibitor?"

She looked at him quizzically. "Most people don't know the difference."

"MAO inhibitors are stronger, right?"

"Those were the ones I was taking. Just a couple per day."

"How did your principal deal with Barge?"

"Jerry told Ellie's father he'd be forcibly removed unless he followed the rules concerning appropriate parent-teacher communications. Police were called in when Barge refused to abide by the rules."

"Did that work?"

"Eventually."

"You and the principal must be relieved to have Ellie's dad out of your lives."

"Lynette, there's three baby cardinals in your birdhouse," Mitzy called. "How cute!"

The English teacher paid her no heed. "Euphoric! Not that Ellie's dad died, of course, but that he was permanently de-commissioned."

"That's an unusual choice of words," Eric said.

"I take pleasure in employing the most effective word choices when communicating."

"Does that go for written communications as well?"

"Of course."

Lynette stood again and headed for the kitchen. Once she was out of view, he switched their drinking glasses.

Lynette returned with a platter of Caramel Delites just as Mitzy drifted back inside. "Yum. I love Girl Scout cookies," Mitzy said. She grabbed a handful and then headed back to the patio.

He sat back. "When we initially spoke, you said you taught at Cawley Day School. You mentioned you weren't hired back because of a change in administration. Can you elaborate on that?"

"It was really more of a difference in mission statement."

"Meaning?"

"The new administrator's focus was on test scores, a perfect prelude to No Child Left Behind. But most of the students at that school were high achievers. I agreed with Bradley Boker, the former administrator, that affording those students an innovative, challenging curriculum was where Cawley Day School excelled."

"Were you friends with Mr. Boker?"

"Brad was my mentor. He'd been an administrator in the private school system for twenty-five years and really knew how to get things accomplished."

"He died of food poisoning at summer barbecue he hosted for his teachers, right?"

Eric watched her flinch. She covered it with a smile, but not fast enough. "Let me make some fresh iced tea." She exited for the kitchen.

"I love your wind chimes," Mitzy called from the outside patio. "Gotta buy some for my mom's back porch."

Moments later, Lynette refilled the detective's glass. "I squeezed a whole lemon in here, so it's pretty tart."

Eric made no move to taste his drink. "The police brought you in for questioning concerning Boker's death."

"They interviewed a lot of people that night," she answered warily.

"Was Bradley Boker your lover, Ms. LaFleur?"

She stiffened. "That's ludicrous."

"Brad resigned from Cawley to accept an administrator position at a school in Hyde Park. You followed suit after he promised you a teaching position. That final barbecue was a big shindig. All the teachers were there. You were excited because this night your lover was going to ask his wife for a divorce, and the two of you would ride off into the sunset together. Except real life got in the way, didn't it, Ms. LaFleur?"

Lynette toyed with the lemonade pitcher. "You have a vigorous imagination, detective."

"No, no. It's all in the police files."

Her jaw dropped. "Those files are closed! Nothing was ever proved."

"Just prior to the barbecue, Carolyn Boker confronts her husband about the affair. The mortgage and all the bank accounts are solely in her name. If he leaves her, she will financially destroy him. She demands he break it off with you. After all the guests have been fed, you join Brad at the grill as he prepares a salmon steak for himself. Your lover attempts to let you down easy; divorce is out of the question. And hiring you on at the new school? Bad idea. Your sobbing is drowned out by the background music."

Lynette's brittle façade dissolved. "It was a very difficult moment for me. I wasted three years of my life waiting around for that bastard," she said, her voice suddenly forlorn.

"Only difficult, Ms. LaFleur? Out in the cold without your lover, and no teaching job?"

Lynette swiped at her eyes. "I was devastated, all right? Humiliated and devastated!"

"Now's your chance for payback time. Embarrassed at your outburst, your lover disappears into the house to take a piss. You dig out a mini bottle of nail polish remover from your purse and pour it over the salmon. Then you dash out the backyard gate."

Lynette smirked. "Nail polish remover can't kill you."

"Unless that bottle contained a totally different liquid. Something poisonous, yet undetectable."

Mitzy eavesdropped from the library. Man, he was good. Lynette's face paled. "That's ridiculous!"

"Brad returns to find you've left the barbecue. He downs one too many glasses of pinot grigio and fails to notice the bitter taste of your culinary handiwork until it's too late."

"The police never proved it was me," she said. Now she acted cool and calm, like she was talking about the weather.

"Carolyn Boker suspected, though. You told her to keep silent or you'd plaster her husband's infidelity all over the Internet."

Lynette's eyes turned cold. "I would have had a field day."

"If the case is reopened, you just might get your chance. Then there's the issue of Joseph Barge's death." Eric whipped the folded confession letters from his shirt pocket and threw them on the table. "I believe these are yours."

~

Detective Whelan watched the teacher pretend to read the words for the very first time. "You give me too much credit, detective. How would I know Jerry's grandfather had Alzheimer's, and routinely refused his medication?" she said. "Those aren't topics discussed in the teacher's lounge."

"Mitzy told you about her chance meeting with the principal at Glen Tree Nursing Home. It's common knowledge that Alzheimer patients often refuse their meds because they think they're being poisoned."

"Nice work, Detective." Lynette swung her crossed legs beneath her and picked up her iced tea. "Just one problem. The confession note is signed Jerry Fillmore, not Lynette LaFleur. And there were no witnesses."

"Not true." Mitzy was back; Eric hadn't heard her come in. *Well done*, she mouthed at him. A smile played on his lips. So she'd heard everything.

The former investigative reporter plopped into a chair facing Lynette. "Those eloquently worded confession notes are the perfect witnesses. More befitting of the talents of an English teacher surrounded by literary classics than a basketball star turned school principal."

Lynette pursed her lips. "I had no idea you were into perpetuating stereotypes."

"So you deny you authored the confession notes?" Mitzy said.

Eric shot her a warning glance, but she was busy staring down Lynette LaFleur.

Lynette's gaze didn't waver from Mitzy's face. "All you need to know is I took no part in facilitating Joseph Barge's demise."

"Sammy Cooper's mom emailed me early this morning. Sammy saw a woman with a briefcase go back into that conference room minutes after Ellie exited."

"Oh? Maybe it was the school social worker. She was at the meeting. Or it might have been the nurse."

Mitzy leaned back in her chair. "We all know who that person was, don't we, Lynette?"

Lynette abruptly stood. "Did Sammy identify me?"

Mitzy turned to Eric. "He was too far away to make a positive ID."

The English teacher visibly relaxed. "Well there you go."

Eric pulled out a notepad. "Did you reenter the conference room after the fire alarm was pulled, Ms. LaFleur?"

Lynette glanced at Eric. "Jerry hasn't denied he wrote those letters, has he?"

"Actually he did, in between puking his guts out," Eric said.

Lynette's mask of indifference fell away. She looked pleadingly at Mitzy. "You know what a jerk Barge was. He had the whole school terrorized."

Mitzy gave her a cold stare. "When you heard Jerry was home with the flu, you wrote those letters and put them on the secretary's desk."

Lynette looked away. "Ellie confessed. I lifted the burden from her shoulders."

"Lake County coroner believes a second person was involved," Eric said.

Lynette grabbed the iced-tea pitcher. Suddenly she looked wild-eyed. "I wrote those letters. But I didn't kill Ellie's father!"

The detective stepped towards her. "Enough of this masquerade, Ms. LaFleur."

"I thought I could do it, but I lost my nerve!" Lynette flung the pitcher across the card table at Eric.

With a two-handed thrust, he sent it flying back at her. It toppled over, spilling liquid and ice everywhere. "Guess all those years of volleyball paid off," he said.

"I didn't go to jail for Bradley, I'm not going now!" Lynette jumped up and ran for the door.

Mitzy jingled a set of keys. "Looks like your Lexus and your house keys are on here."

Eric pulled a set of handcuffs from his back pocket. Then he approached the teacher. "You have the right to remain silent. Anything you say can and will be used against you in a court of law."

Lynette turned and ran toward the bathroom. "You've got the wrong person, I tell you!"

"The bathroom window sticks, hon. I checked when I was outside."

"Bastards!" screamed Lynette.

"You have a right to an attorney. If you cannot afford an attorney, one will be provided for you."

Mitzy grabbed the handcuffs from Eric and moved slowly towards the English teacher. "Lynette, if you're innocent, we'll do our best to protect you from the fallout."

"No!" Lynette dashed around them into the foyer. Eric followed, Mitzy a step behind. A loud crash filled the air. "This is my final answer," Lynette screamed as she waved a six-inch bloody shard of glass at them. Near her on the wall was a shattered mirror, the jagged remnants of it clinging to the wooden frame.

"Drop the shard and let us get you to emergency," Eric said.

"Get out of my way!" Lynette shouted. Blood dripped from her fingers.

"You thought you were ridding the world of a monster," Mitzy said, continuing to advance toward her. "People will understand. We all make mistakes."

"Some mistakes are worse than others." Lynette ripped the shard down her bare arms, leaving bloody trails behind. Then she fell to the floor.

"Lynette, no!" Mitzy screamed, running to her side.

Eric pulled out his cell phone. "Civilian down," he said tersely into it. "6424 North Damen. Apt. 3."

Chapter 33

"This thing's got me all shook up," Mitzy said, half-heartedly smacking the tennis ball across the net.

"I can tell," Maggie said, slamming the ball back. "Your backhand is way off today."

Mitzy curved her racket in an underhand thrust. "I respected Lynette's commitment to the kids."

"Misplaced respect can prove fatal," Maggie said, with another hard whack at the ball.

Mitzy ran to retrieve the ball from the far right-hand corner. "I'm really grief-stricken here," she said, breathing hard. "Besides killing Ellie's dad, she attempts to frame an innocent man."

"You saw a hell of a lot worse when you worked as a reporter in Chicago," Maggie said.

"As a teacher, I thought I'd be safe in my cocoon."

"And then life happened," Maggie said sympathetically.

"I figured people who helped children would restore my trust in the world. Lynette destroyed that vision."

"Converts make the most ardent believers."

Mitzy paused. Her mother had voiced similar sentiments about Eric. "I guess I did want to convert. From the darkness of political intrigue to the light of a child's innocent smile."

"Face it. You sabotaged yourself. No person, no profession, will ever meet your pristine expectations."

Mitzy jumped to her feet. Once again, adrenaline surged through her. "I know, I know. Teachers are going to rise and fall just like the rest of society."

Maggie smirked. "That 'rest of society' include Eric?"

"Hey, I'm giving you the stars," Mitzy said. "Don't ask me to pattern them into constellations, too."

Maggie whipped out her cell phone. "Call him."

"Isn't it enough he and I took Lynette down together?"

"You haven't spoken to Eric since last Sunday?"

"He called a few days ago to tell me Jerry was cleared by the police. And Lynette resigned from WOMS after the media got wind of the circumstances surrounding her former employer."

"Did Eric say what's next?"

"The Bradley Boker cold case is being reopened. And Lynette is being held at Cook County Jail until sentencing for the death of Ellie's father. Her attorney's offering a plea bargain."

Maggie rolled her eyes. "Who's she attempting to implicate now? The kid who pulled the alarm?"

Mitzy shrugged.

"Odds are, Ellie will get community service." Maggie handed her cell phone to Mitzy. "Okay, girl. Time to make amends."

"Fine," Mitzy said. She resolutely punched in the familiar numbers.

~

Mitzy pulled up to a two-story brick home flanking the train station. She'd visualized the northern suburbs as mile upon mile of strip mall shopping centers, but Deerfield appeared to be a quaint little village flanked by just enough stores to do it justice. A Borders bookstore loomed at the corner of Waukegan and Lake Cook, and a nursing home that looked like a country club ran along Waukegan Road.

As she rapped on the maroon door, Mitzy admired the variety of flowers springing forth in colors of the rainbow. She leaned back on her heels, envisioning her LD supervisor's visible relief when she learned Ellie was slated for community service, not the juvenile penal system. She didn't expect the sight that met her eyes when the door opened.

A feeble-looking woman in a housedress, barely recognizable as Roz Cohen, poked her head out the door and sniffed the pansies and carnations. "Thank God I can still smell!" Then she reached for Mitzy. "Come in! Come in!"

Could a person change this much in six weeks, wondered Mitzy as she leaned into Roz's embrace.

Roz adjusted her brown wig, which sat askew. "Not what you were expecting, huh?"

Mitzy attempted to hide her embarrassment. "No. I mean, yes."

Roz ushered her into the living room. "Come sit down. Can I get you a diet soda? Bottle of water?"

Mitzy felt suddenly shy. "I'm good."

Roz shuffled over to a steel gray couch and patted the seat beside her. "So how was graduation? I was so sorry to miss it."

Still that same *joi de vivre*, Mitzy noted, yet her breathing sounded labored.

"Nobody tripped over their robes on stage. Ellie Barge wasn't allowed to attend the eighth grade party, but she did get to walk across the stage and receive her diploma."

"Good for her."

"She was catatonic for weeks, then a breakthrough occurred. She became lucid once again."

"I pray that such a breakthrough will occur for her mother."

"I'm pretty sure they don't use electroshock therapy on comatose patients," Mitzy giggled. "Like, *bing!*" She acted out a mummy coming to life.

Roz gave her a funny look.

"Sorry. Sometimes these pictures in my mind jump right out at me."

"That's what makes you a great special ed teacher. Did you renew your contract for next year?"

Mitzy nodded. "Mr. Fillmore promised me my own resource room so I won't have to teach in the library when Norman's working with his kids."

"Lovely."

"I knew you'd been absent for a while, but I was surprised when the principal mentioned you opted for early retirement."

"Working with special needs students pales in comparison to the battle I'm waging." A wave of sadness flitted over Roz's face. "Unfortunately the outcome of this battle is already signed, sealed, and delivered."

Listening to her mentor describe her fate was unbearable. "With all the new treatments available, cancer patients can stay in remission for years. I once did an article for the—"

Roz cut her off. "Brain cancer is an insidious breed unto itself. The side effects are miserable. The neighbors are rooting for me to die."

Mitzy stared at her in horror. "Surely not!"

"My prognosis is measured in months, not years," Roz said, a sad smile on her lips.

Ever the problem solver, Mitzy plummeted forth. "I researched it. Brain cancer is no longer a death sentence. Proton therapy is the wave of the future."

Roz's eyes turned frosty. "My decisions are my own, Ms. Maven. I need not explain my reasons to you or anyone else."

Mitzy's last name dripped like an icicle from Roz's lips. Her heart hung there, open and vulnerable for the older woman to see. "I'm an idiot. Please forgive me."

Roz's countenance cleared. "Apology accepted."

"Whew!"

"Let's talk about something more colorful than my health problems, shall we?"

Mitzy nodded.

"Jerry visited me a few weeks ago, but he refused to discuss Joseph Barge's death."

"We had no definitive answers as to the culprit until day before yesterday."

Roz leaned forward on the couch. "Do tell."

"It initially appeared that Barge had overdosed. Drugs plus his alcohol and untreated hypertension killed him."

"Yes, yes. I recall reading about that in the newspaper."

"Then Ellie confessed she'd popped her own Nardil capsules into her dad's coffee after the fire alarm cleared us out of the conference room."

"I'm aware of that development."

"Turns out Sammy Cooper was the student who actually pulled the alarm."

"Bravo!"

The older woman's reaction bordered on hysteria. Nonplussed, Mitzy shifted to the far end of the couch. "The police retrieved two confession notes that pointed to Jerry Fillmore."

"He certainly did hate Ellie's father."

"But the signatures on the notes were forged. Jerry was cleared."

"Go on."

"Detective Whelan confronted Ellie's English teacher at her apartment. Lynette LaFleur confessed to writing the notes, but insisted she had nothing to do with Joseph Barge's demise."

The woman's eyes sparkled. "Quite a quandary."

"When the police failed to believe her, Lynette, unable to flee the apartment, sliced her arm with a shard of mirror. She was taken to the ER and is still recuperating."

A frigid silence permeated the room.

"You were at her apartment during the interrogation?"

Apprehension struck Mitzy's soul. "Yes."

Roz was wheezing now. The room suddenly felt like an empty helium balloon. "Lynette LaFleur was your trusted colleague. You used that friendship to frame her for Joseph

Barge's death!"

This woman could die any moment, thought Mitzy, and she'd be the cause. "Lynette left her previous school under suspicious circumstances."

Roz gave her a vacant look. "Lynette couldn't be the one."

Mitzy realized she'd been holding her breath. "Why not?"

Roz fell back on the cushion. "It's strange, but I feel like I had something to do with it."

Mitzy's heart was racing. "That's ridiculous. You acted totally professional with the man during numerous conferences."

"Looks are deceiving."

"That's what Lynette said."

"Since I've been ill, my memory plugs in and out of its socket."

No way could her LD supervisor be involved. "Maybe you had a nightmare about Ellie's father and awoke to believe it true."

Roz sat bolt upright, her face flushed. "I'm telling you I know I did something!"

"Educated people don't go around offing people they dislike!"

Roz banged the glass cocktail table with her fist. "Barge was a brutish lout who harassed the teachers without mercy and shattered a safe learning environment for Ellie and her classmates."

"The police handled it, Roz. WOMS issued a restraining order against him, remember?"

Roz gave her a glassy stare. "Police were called to his home on numerous occasions, but the big shot only got a slap on the wrist."

Mitzy knew she should text Eric. He'd say she'd been blindsided, just not by Ellie. Then again, brain cancer could produce strange bedfellows, including paranoia, sudden verbal or violent explosiveness, and memory loss.

"Motive and accessibility evens the playing field," Roz continued in a monotone.

Surely there was a logical explanation. "Let me call your doctor for you," pleaded Mitzy. "Improper doses of certain meds can cause hallucinations."

Roz banged her forehead with both fists. "Oh my God! It's coming back to me now! When I first got sick, the doctor put me on anti-anxiety drugs before I went in for radiation treatment, but I still had some pills left. I dropped two anti-depressant drugs in Barge's coffee to relax him enough to sign off on Ellie's alternative placement."

Mitzy grabbed her supervisor's fists. "It was an accident!"

Roz whipped a prescription bottle from her housedress pocket. "Maybe it wasn't! Fortunately, I won't have to watch my reputation be smeared all over the Internet." With that, she tossed her head back and dumped the contents down her throat.

Mitzy knocked the bottle from her hand. "No!"

Roz fell back on the couch.

Mitzy felt for a pulse, then put her fists together and pumped the woman's stomach. Swiping tears from her face, she broke away to punch in 911.

~

"Rocky road and vanilla, right?" Mitzy asked, shifting away from the ice cream counter to distribute the last two waffle cones to Ellie and Sammy.

"This was so sweet of you to do," Mrs. Cooper said, daintily licking her lemon ice.

"Pistachio nut's my favorite," Fay Shimmer said, biting into her own cold treat.

"Matches your hair color," Ellie teased.

Fay scrunched her nose at her niece. "Only the highlights."

"I hope you like these, too," Mitzy said, doling out four items from her Prada bag.

Ellie read the words on her blue-green wristband. "'Nothing is impossible.'"

"I got the same one," Sammy said, stretching the wristband over his hand.

"So did we," Fay said, eyeing the band on Mrs. Cooper's wrist.

"I've never seen these bands before," Mrs. Cooper said, running her fingers over the indented lettering.

"They came out after 911, starting with the yellow LIVE STRONG band," Mitzy said.

"The wristbands were supposed to be a fundraiser gimmick, but the whole concept took hold," Fay said. "Ellie's got a whole collection of bands, each with a different saying."

Sammy held his up. "Before she got sick, Ms. Cohen gave me a blue one that says 'Believe'"

"'Nothing's impossible' and 'Believe' pretty much sum up the future I see for you and Ellie," Mitzy said, her tone more serious now. If only Roz had survived to rejoice in this day of reconciliation between their students.

"Huh?" Sammy asked.

"She means we can be whatever we want to be as long as we believe in ourselves, dummy," Ellie said.

"Ellie," Fay warned.

"Sorry." Ellie gave Sammy a friendly look.

"Sticks and stones," Mrs. Cooper whispered to her son.

"Cut it out, Mom," Sammy said. "You're embarrassing me."

Mitzy willed herself to focus on Ellie and her aunt. "Have you guys been downtown to visit your new high school yet?"

Ellie nodded. "The school's pretty cool."

"Einstein High School is housed in a historic old building that used to be a theater," Fay said.

"Maybe there'll be ghosts of famous actresses and actors there," Ellie said.

"That's highly unlikely," her aunt said. "The building's been totally renovated inside. But you can take drama as an elective during your second semester."

"I'll probably be at Lake Forest High School by then," Ellie said airily.

Mitzy and Fay exchanged glances. "The best thing for you to do, sweetie, is to take each day as it comes," Mitzy advised. "Learn to control your behavior."

"I'll keep a lid on it."

"If you keep a lid on a can of boiling soup, it still spills over," Sammy said.

Mitzy smiled. "Great analogy, Sammy."

"Besides fulfilling her academic caseload, Ellie will receive psychotherapy on a daily basis, which should help her deal with a variety of issues," Fay said. "And she'll need to perform four hours of community service per week, per the judge's order."

"It's not going to be that hard, you guys," Ellie said. "I'm going to be serving dinner two nights a week at a homeless shelter. But if I don't like it there, I can switch to a different project second semester."

"The program director says you have to prove you're a responsible volunteer at the shelter before you can be considered for another position," her aunt reminded her.

"I think I'd rather work with kids," Ellie said.

"Just follow the program, sweetie," Mitzy advised. "If something upsets you, write it down in your journal instead of getting in someone's face."

"Okay, okay," Ellie said, then crunched the last of her waffle cone.

"Ever find the yellow-flowered journal I gave you?"

Ellie nodded. "One morning I woke up and it was back on my computer desk."

Mitzy saw Fay hide a smile behind her napkin. "Okay, then. I'll look forward to getting your emails, Ellie. And I'll see Mr. Sammy in the fall."

"You're coming back to school?" Sammy asked.

Mitzy nodded.

Sammy grinned. "Oh, yeah!"

"Thanks again for being so supportive of my son," Mrs. Cooper said.

"My pleasure," Mitzy said. She waved goodbye as she moved toward the door of the ice-cream parlor. "Ms. Shimmer, could I see you for a sec?"

Ellie's aunt followed her to the door, a quizzical expression on her face.

Mitzy looked at her suspiciously. "Do you know who hid that yellow journal?"

"Anya did," Fay said. "We thought there'd be incriminating evidence against Ellie in there."

"And was there?"

Fay returned her gaze. "The two days preceding Joe's death were blank."

"And the week before?"

"Nothing about plotting to kill her father, if that's what you're getting at."

Let it go, Mitzy told herself as she shook Fay's hand. "You've got a long road ahead. If there's anything I can do to help, contact me."

Fay smiled. "It's reassuring just knowing you'll be there for Ellie if she ever needs you."

"What's going to happen to the home in Lake Forest?" Mitzy asked.

"As long as Lani is still hanging on, we'll keep the house going. Joe's life insurance should cover expenses. Hopefully Einstein High School will instill in Ellie the self-discipline she needs to become a productive member of society."

"Who knows?" Mitzy said. "Maybe two years from now, Ellie will be walking the halls of Lake Forest High School."

"I pray that will happen."

"My prayers are with both of you. Take care," Mitzy said, giving Ellie's aunt a quick hug.

Chapter 34

Mitzy and her mom were the only patrons at the discount wedding boutique, yet they'd been waiting fifteen minutes when an almond-skinned sales girl who looked barely out of her teens finally reappeared at the counter holding a plastic-covered full-length dress. "Here it is."

Shirley Maven raised the plastic for a better look beneath the fluorescent ceiling lights. Then she chuckled. "Purple sequins in a size four? Definitely not. "

"I told you we should have gone to David's Bridals, Mom," Mitzy said, impatience dripping from each syllable.

"You mentioned sequins," the girl said, popping gum as she gazed back at them.

"White sequins on a square-necked white dress falling just below the knee," Mitzy's mother said for the second time.

"There's nothing like that in the stock room," the girl said.

"We want to speak to the manager," Mitzy said.

"She's off today."

"Calm down," Shirley said to Mitzy, and smiled up at the clerk. "Lucinda's doing just fine, aren't you, dear?"

The sales girl shrugged.

"Now I'm going to scoot over to the racks and find myself another dress in a size fourteen while you contact your supervisor and get me a nice fat discount."

"The dresses are priced as marked," the girl said, snapping her gum.

"It's two weeks until my mother's wedding," Mitzy said. "Do it!"

The clerk's mouth fell open. Then she skittered away.

"As I always say, why pay full price if you can get it on sale?" Shirley said, nonchalantly picking through the dresses on the rack. She pulled out a pink organdy number. "Wouldn't this look adorable on Jessie?"

"What's a kid's dress doing on the adult racks?" Mitzy asked, her voice grouchy.

"I'm the one who's getting married and you're the one who's having *shpilkes*."

"I have to get over to House of Brides and pick my dress up, too, you know."

"It's only three o'clock. You got plenty of time. Concentrate on me for once, will you?"

The sales girl returned to Shirley's side. "Your dress has been misplaced."

Mitzy rolled her eyes. "We figured that out twenty minutes ago."

"My manager said we can give you twenty percent off on another dress," the girl said.

"Tell your manager to make that fifty percent and you've got yourselves a deal, dear," Shirley said.

"We can't do that."

"You might mention that my daughter here works for the newspaper."

Mitzy nudged her mom. Shirley elbowed her in the ribs. "I'm sure your manager wouldn't want this store written up in an article about poor customer service. Your name would be in there, too."

The girl's face blanched and she once again scooted off.

"This takes the meaning of 'discount' to a whole other level," Mitzy hissed.

"Quit complaining and help me find another dress that doesn't make me look too matronly," her mother said.

Together they fanned through rows of turquoises, pinks, and yellows. Mitzy pulled out a sea green, three-quarter length satin number with sequins around the neck. "How's this?"

Shirley looked at the dress, her eyes twinkling. "This one's got my name on it."

Mitzy giggled. "Don't you want to pick out some others, just in case this doesn't fit?"

"It'll fit," Shirley said, her voice dancing as they headed to the back of the store.

The clerk intercepted them. "My manager said thirty percent off is the best she can do."

"Well done, dear," Shirley said. "It's a miracle what the right dress will do for one's morale, don't you think?"

"Uh, right," the girl said.

Mitzy gave the girl a thumbs-up, then hurried after her mother.

~

"Eric holds Mitzy's hand as gently as a rose petal, Harry," Shirley Maven said as they watched the young couple twirl around their brightly lit living room.

"Hey, you guys hear the one about the medical student doing a rotation in toxicology at the poison control center?" Harry called out from the sofa. "This woman calls in, frantic 'cause she caught her little daughter eating ants…"

Shirley popped her hand over Harry's mouth. Harry raised his hands in defeat.

Shirley removed her palm. "Look at the way Eric's arm is crooked at the elbow and held away from his body."

"Hmph. I don't need dance lessons, Shirl," Harry complained.

"Technique. Watch how his other arm clasps Mitzy's back at armpit level."

"Did she even ask him yet?"

"She'll ask him when she asks him. Meantime, quit acting like a seventy-year-old man," Shirley fumed, her hands on her hips.

"The medical student reassures mama that ants are not harmful, so she doesn't need to bring her daughter into emergency," Harry continues. "After a brief pause, the mother says, 'Even if I fed her ant poison to kill the ants?'" He smiles triumphantly.

Eric moved to turn off the boom box. "Did you say something?"

Shirley smiled at the young couple and shook her head. "They didn't even hear you," she shouted into Harry's ear.

"But you did," Harry said, a pleased smile on his face.

"Hmph," Shirley grumbled.

Harry got up from the La-Z-Boy. "Thanks for the lesson, kids," he shouted over the music. "Keep dancing. I'll go watch the game in the bedroom."

"Harry, we didn't even get a chance to practice," Shirley complained.

"You've just got wedding bell jitters," Harry reassured her from the hallway.

"That man drives me crazy," Shirley said, dramatically placing her hand on her forehead.

Eric lowered the volume on the boom box. "Did you want to practice awhile, Mrs. Maven?"

Shirley smiled. "Why Eric, I'd love to." The CD player was spinning, "Heaven, I'm in heaven—"

"Time to change partners," Shirley commanded as the song ended. She handed Eric off to Mitzy. "Thanks for giving an old lady some joy, Eric" she said. "I'm gonna join Harry."

When they were alone, Eric looked into Mitzy's half-closed eyes. "I know it's late but there's something I want to ask you."

"And me, you," Mitzy said dreamily as they glided around the living room. Her mother's favorite oldie but goodie was playing: The Carpenters, "We've Only Just Begun".

Eric cleared his throat. "Would you accompany me to my sister's wedding?"

Mitzy looked up at him, then planted a big juicy kiss on his lips. She closed her eyes as he returned her kiss with equal enthusiasm. *This one's a keeper.*

THE END

PROFESSIONAL ACKNOWLEDGEMENTS

Adolescent catatonia is so uncommon that finding a psychiatrist with first-hand knowledge regarding current treatment procedure was impossible! My dilemma was solved upon reading *Catatonia; a Clinician's Guide to Diagnosis and Treatment*, written by Max Fink, M.D. Professor of Psychiatry and Neurology Emeritus at Albert Einstein College of Medicine, New York and Michael Alan Taylor, M.D., Professor of Psychiatry, Finch University of Health Sciences in North Chicago and published by Cambridge University Press in Jan. 2003.

Selective mutism in children and adolescents was explored through Nathan J. Blum, M.D. et. al.'s article entitled Case Study: Audio Feedforward Treatment of Selective Mutism in the *Journal of the American Academy of Child and Adolescent Psychiatry* (Jan. 1998). Also helpful were Julie E. Lafferty, M.D. and John N. Constantino, M.D. from the Departments of Psychiatry and Pediatrics, Washington University School of Medicine in St. Louis, Missouri for exploring in an open study the effects of fluvoxamine on a young child exhibiting selective mutism and obsessive compulsive disorder.

DRUGDEX DRUG EVALUATIONS, through Microdex® Healthcare Series, listed the various types of prescription anti-anxiety and depression drugs, along with patient symptoms, drug interactions, and adverse side effects.

Thank you Susan M. Irvin for your *AORN Journal* article (March 1997) on treatment of depression with outpatient electroconvulsive therapy, and Deborah A. Banazak for your *American Family Physician Journal* article (Jan. 1996) entitled Electroconvuslive Therapy; a guide for family physicians.

Information for Oppositional Defiant Disorder and Post-Traumatic Stress Disorder was acquired through FOCUS ADOLESCENT Services. The CENTER FOR EFFECTIVE COLLABORATION AND PRACTICES provided valuable information on improving services for children with emotional problems. The CHICAGO BOARD OF EDUCATION'S POLICY STATEMENT offered a discipline procedural guide for dealing with students with disabilities.

BOOK DISCUSSION QUESTIONS

1. Why did Mitzy choose to leave her career as a newspaper reporter? Did her decision seem valid? Why/why not?

2. What job-related skills did Mitzy transfer into her new career as a special education teacher? How did these skills benefit her?

3. Describe Mitzy's relationship with her mother. How does their relationship change over time, if at all?

4. How does Harry's entrance into their lives affect Mitzy and her mother?

5. Compare and contrast the relationship between Ellie and her parents with that of Mitzy and her parents.

6. Hypothesize how the car accident and resulting comatose state of Ellie's mother psychologically impacted the daughter.

7. Discuss how Mitzy's attention deficit disorder affects her relationship with her students, friends, and family. How is her ADD a positive/negative in her life?

8. Compare and contrast the academic and psychological strengths and weaknesses of Sammy and Ellie. How do those tensions play out in their relationship?

9. Discuss the personality traits of Joseph Barge which led to his death. Were you surprised at learning who "did him in"? Was it an accidental or purposeful act? What was the motive?

10. Describe the belief system shared by the English teacher and the special education supervisor. To what lengths did they go to achieve their mutual goal? How did you feel about the choices they made?

11. How did Mitzy's caustic style affect her relationship with Eric? What hopes, if any, do you have for their relationship in the next book?

12. What impact, if any, did the interjection of Jewish traditions serve in the novel?

RESOURCES

CH.A.D.D.
(Children and Adults with Attention Deficit Disorder
www.chadd.org

CEC
(Council for Exceptional Children)
www.cec.sped.org

IDA
International Dyslexia Association
(Founded in memory of Samuel T. Orton)
Email: info@interdys.org
Web Site: http://www.interdys.org

Instrumental Enrichment
Skylight Training and Publishing
www.iriskylight.com

Optometrists Network
www.optometrists.org

Rush NeuroBehavioral Center
Rush Children's Hospital
www.RNBC.org

MORE

Jennie Spallone

Please turn this page
for
bonus excerpts from
Award-Winning
Deadly Choices
and from
Window of Guilt

www.jenniespallone.com
www.amazon.com
Autographed copies at
spalloneauthor@aol.com

ISBN for Deadly Choices:
1-932695-06-0

ISBN for Window of Guilt:
1-4637-6849-4

Deadly Choices

Chapter 1

Warning lights unlit, siren silent, Ambulance #60 careened down fog-drenched streets in the pre-dawn autumn darkness. Some unseen radar directed the drier as she deftly maneuvered the ghost-like rig down West Madison Street through a maze of shattered liquor bottles and discarded syringes. The ambulance soundlessly streamed past derelicts pasted on a backdrop of scarred buildings.

Replenishing supplies in the back of the rig, paramedic Beth Riley stole a glance at the driver. She grimaced as her paramedic officer pulled a sandwich bag from her jacket. Angie often relied on that white stuff in her baggie to anesthetize herself against an avalanche of shootings, beatings, and vehicle collisions.

After five years as a nurse in Viet Nam, followed by 22 years as a paramedic with the Chicago Fire Department, Angie Ropella seemed to delight in all forms of human trauma. Knuckled in-between 24-hour stints of stabbings, multi-vehicle collisions, and assaults was an assembly line of little old ladies forgetting their insulin, yuppies jogging into cardiac arrest, and winos urinating in the doorways.

Beth quickly averted her glance as Angie smirked at her through the rearview mirror. Her face still felt hot with shame at the tongue-lashing she'd received tonight. She had efficiently resuscitated a drug addict lying half-dead on his bungalow porch as neighborhood kids hopped over his unconscious form in a midnight game of tag.

But the last fiasco had completely unnerved her. A scrawny seventeen-year-old kid in an oversized leather biker jacket had been weaving his motorcycle back and forth across four clear lanes of traffic when his luck was stolen by a black Toyota traveling southbound down Lake Shore Drive.

"Where's the body?" Beth, the former librarian, had asked.

"The kid must have been a human slingshot. Probably hit a tree and bounced into an oncoming lane of traffic. Let's check out the median strip," Angie said, grabbing a backboard. "Don't forget your gloves."

Extracting a pair of gloves from her pants pocket, Beth scurried to match Angie's long strides. Six weeks into her job, she had no intention of contracting AIDS.

About fifty feet north, a tree lay broken in half. The limp body of a kid in a motorcycle helmet sprawled across the adjoining median strip. Carefully, the paramedics lifted the broken body onto the backboard and velcroed on a cervical collar. Upon applying a tourniquet to halt the bleeding from his leg and splinting several broken bones, they gently placed the boy on a stretcher and boosted the gurney into the ambulance.

"Oh, man," Angie said, groaning. "Check out this bone sticking through the kid's thigh. As if he won't have enough grief with a fractured pelvis, severe neck and back injuries, and a fractured skull."

After one look at the mangled body, Beth vomited all over the back seat. Angie just grinned. "You gonna be a medic, Riley? You can't keep having these little accidents. Clean it up. Then keep the kid company back here. I'll drive."

Up front, Angie picked up the radio. "This is Ambulance #60. We've got a trauma bypass and are en-route to Masonic."

The early morning weekday scramble had already kicked in as Angie switched on her illegal boom box to some old Led Zeppelin. Flipping on the siren and lights, she expertly weaved the red and white rig through a maze of congested traffic. She zigzagged around buses that suddenly jutted out in front of her onto Halsted and Clark. Cab drivers leaned on their horns while joggers sprinted off to work and the unencumbered meandered home from all-night bars.

Lights and sirens still whirring, Ambulance #60 finally pulled up the ramp to Illinois Masonic Hospital. Angie jumped out and ran around to the back of the ambulance, yanked open the doors, and wheeled the gurney into the ER where the trauma team waited.

~

Beth was wiping down the back of the ambulance with peroxide when Angie poked her shoulder. "Listen, I got to take a pee and get some supplies. Why don't you jump start the paperwork, then we'll split for tacos?"

"Sure. Meet you back on the ambulance. I mean the rig." Pushing the empty gurney out through the double doors, Beth considered confiding in her best friend Sue Dotson about yet another of Angie's cocaine breaks. Nix that plan. Sue's familiar refrain was "The woman has sinned against her body and should be reported."

After fourteen years as a medical librarian for the University of Chicago, Beth could spout drug statistics in her sleep, but she'd already memorized the fire academy's unwritten code; never pimp on your partner.

Whenever she felt guilty about not squealing, Beth reminded herself that Angie was a dedicated professional whose performance was always top notch. Her uncanny ability to accurately diagnose a patient's physical condition with little more than a glance and a few physical probes was firehouse legend. Probably the reason no one had ever reported the veteran paramedic's coke habit.

Unfortunately, Angie's sarcasm was also legendary. It took all of Beth's emotional strength to not disintegrate when Angie would zap her with a searing retort coupled with a disgusted shake of the head and rolling eyes. Many nights she would climb into bed feeling as though her soul had been ripped from her body. Yet she somehow continued to endure, feeling blessed to inhale even one daily air bubble of knowledge from the former Vietnam nurse whose heroic performance in saving lives could fill a textbook. So, she remained silent.

~

Once in the hospital laboratory, Angie allowed herself a whiff of congratulations from the white stuff in her Baggie. Only two years from retirement, adrenaline still rushed through her every pore. What a high it had been to save that kid's life! Amazing he'd survived at all, considering the damage done to his kidney and spleen. Angie grinned as she grabbed another backboard and more peroxide from the ER supply cabinet and then headed back to the rig.

Firing the ignition, Angie glanced into the rearview mirror; Beth the Barfer was straightening supplies. In compliance with the Equal Opportunity Act, the fire department had to hire female trainees, but hiring this wimp was really taking it out-of-bounds. Being a paramedic meant quick reflexes, a strong stomach, and the ability to instantaneously analyze a life or death situation. Pretty similar to the emergency nursing she'd done in Viet Nam. Yet there was so much to learn. As a trainee, she had devoured every tidbit of information her paramedic officer would share regarding procedure, medical conditions, and firehouse protocol; Totally different scenario with Riley.

The former medical librarian was as silent as a turtle, her reflexes not much faster. Riley acted spooky, always at her elbow, watching her every move. But what really blew her mind was that even though Riley was textbook knowledgeable about some of the medical emergencies they encountered, she shied away from actually working on a patient; and the constant barfing! Definitely not paramedic material. She'd do her best to make sure this wuss didn't become a firehouse fixture. Confident with her decision, Angie was sailing high when her rig slam-banged into something, nailing her against the wheel.

Chapter 2

Beth was straightening supplies in the back of the ambulance when she felt a thud. What had they hit? Stomach churning, the paramedic trainee struggled into a sterile set of rubber gloves and leaped off the ambulance.

A young woman, about eighteen or nineteen years old, lay sprawled out in a pool of blood, which also oozed from her ears. Attempting to still her panic at the sight of so much blood, Beth focused on clamping the pressure cuff onto the patient's arm. Noting the dangerously low blood pressure, she flipped back the girl's eyelids; unconscious, seizing, bloated belly. Palpitating her patient's abdomen, a sudden gush of fluids spurted out. Lifting the girl's dress, Beth gasped as a tiny head emerged through the girl's vagina.

Tentatively rubbing her ribs, Angie jumped from the ambulance and squinted through the fog. "What the hell's going on? Did we hit a pothole? A dog?"

Beth ran back to the ambulance and grabbed her OB kit. "We hit a young mother whose baby is crowning!"

"Oh, my God," shrieked Angie. Running toward the patient, she was at the young woman's side, checking her vitals.

"What do we do now?" Beth asked nervously, peering over Angie's shoulder. Her head felt as though it was gripped in a vise and that nauseous feeling was threatening to overcome her.

"Check for ID."

Beth felt around the girl. No purse, no wallet. "Nothing."

"Probably a runaway." Angie paced, pounding her fist into her hand, trying to erase the vision of Vietnamese women and children being blown to smithereens as they tried to outrun the bombs. Countless lives lost which she couldn't out back together. Now, thanks to her own recklessness, this new mother would die, too.

Beth knelt to check the girl's blood pressure again. "She's fading. Should we radio the hospital?"

Shaking her head, Angie briskly stepped toward the rig. She was too close to retirement. No way could she get called down on this accident.

Beth ran to catch up. "Angie, I need your help! She's unconscious."

"Well, that makes it all the easier. She's not going to move on you."

Frantically, Beth tugged at the paramedic officer's sleeve. "We can anonymously call 911 from the all-night diner!"

Slapping Beth's hand away, Angie climbed onto the rig. "And risk being recognized? You've been on the job for six weeks. You know what to do."

Beth's insides fluttered with a powerful urge to flee, yet her feet seemed glued to the concrete. "I can't work on the mother and deliver the baby at the same time!"

"Look, the girl's hemorrhaging through the ears. She's gonna croak any minute. You want my advice? Save the baby."

A thin, steady rain framed each step as Angie hurried back to the ambulance, then climbed aboard.

Window of Guilt

Chapter 1

The lanky youth stumbled on blistered feet through the pebbled landscape. Neither dog walker nor bicycle enthusiast dotted his path.

As the stranger dizzily traversed the sandy trail, he fingered a crumpled Greyhound ticket receipt and a worn paper napkin containing two addresses printed in kindergarten script.

An energetic lake breeze failed to muzzle the sun's high-noon intensity. Sweat zigzagged down the young man's back like a football player breaking for a touchdown. Wincing, the stranger stopped to shake tiny gray stones from his dusty sandals.

Nearing his destination, the vagrant eyed the hodgepodge of houses to his left. Some were English Tudor, others modern monstrosities with floor-to-ceiling windows stripping away the illusion of privacy so coveted by the upper class.

Strips of modest-sized homes flanked by withered grass sat sandwiched between structural giants. Through glassy eyes, he confirmed the top address on his napkin matched the country mailbox of a simple white frame house set back on a corner lot. Like the other summer homes in its midst, the corner property sat naked of fence and gate.

The youth unscrewed the cap of his army canteen and thirstily ran his tongue around its circumference. Not a drop of liquid remained. He fumbled through his pants pocket for a mint. A lone peanut salvaged from the dusty road was his jaw's only solace.

In a frenetic burst of energy, he sprinted toward the corner lot. A fluffy white dog the size of a bed pillow yapped at the far end of the yard. Shielding his eyes from the blazing sun, he gazed at the tiny white house, dwarfed by its scorched acreage.

Head down, the diminutive white dog slunk towards him. Its warning growl tweaked the silence. The young man tossed the nut shell past the dog's head.

As the miniature creature raced towards the perceived treat, the youth dashed across the treeless yard. Suddenly, he grabbed his throat. Panic engulfed his facial features.

The curtained kitchen window sat in full view as the young man futilely gasped his last breath. Before losing consciousness, his eyes locked upon the small white animal lounging on a grassy area a few feet away, the nut shell stuck to his whiskers.

~

Laurie Atkins burrowed her hoe into the garden bed, and then swiped at her perspiring brow. She'd been working outside in the blistering sun since Ryan had high-tailed it off to the lake three hours ago. It was crazy, her being outside for such an extended period while the air-conditioner fans droned her name in the distance. But this morning's argument with her husband had so incensed her that she needed to work off the fuel that burned deep within.

Swiping at the sweat running down the bridge of her nose, Laurie surveyed the drooping tomato plants that, despite the town's ban on watering, she'd so diligently attempted to resuscitate. Even though gardening was definitely absent from her DNA strand, she was committed to giving it a run for the money.

In recent years, Laurie and her husband had continued her parents' tradition of driving up to Oconomowoc's lakeside community in an effort to escape Chicago's most sweltering month of the year. This summer, she'd vowed to plant a single fruit tree in the back yard of their summer home to commemorate her father's recent passing. Wisconsin's record high August temperatures had scorched that vow.

With a sigh, Laurie visualized the flowered landscape that might have been had her renters bothered to water the garden throughout the year. But by the end of May, Shakia and her roommate had graduated college and returned home to the Chicago area, abandoning Laurie's plants and flowers to nature's capricious design.

Lightheaded, the thirsty gardener clicked the hose for a drink. Not even a trickle of water emerged. She glanced at the two water bottles that had kept her company through the morning hours. Nary a drop of liquid remained. Her throat felt like sandpaper.

Peering up at the sky, she noticed the sun directly overhead. Even an urban cowgirl like her knew when it was time to fold up and walk away. Besides, no yogurt had passed her lips this morning and she was starting to feel lightheaded.

Laurie was collecting her gardening tools when the sound of her dog's sharp barks drew her attention to the front yard.

"Hold on, Rocky. Mommy's coming," Laurie shouted, wiping her brow as she ambled across the rotted acreage. Her Bichon was circling in a frenzy. "If you found a dead squirrel, don't go near it!"

The sight she came upon confounded her. Rocky was licking the face of an emaciated-looking young man in a sweat-soaked yellow jersey and blue jeans. The young man lay prone on the withered grass, his head to one side.

Laurie's eyes darted toward the road flanking Lac La Belle. Who was this unexpected visitor napping on her property? The landscapers often took their siestas on Laurie's front lawn during their weekly visit, but their truck had already been out this week.

She tentatively nudged him with her foot. "Hey." She jumped back at the rank smell emanating from his body.

Where was Ryan when she needed him? Earlier this morning, she'd been studying for the third retake of her real estate exam when he'd picked a money argument with her. One in a cascade of similar arguments since his heart attack.

Soon after, he'd stalked off to the lake.

The seagulls' screeches pierced the stillness. Laurie held Rocky under one arm and warily poked the horizontal figure's yellow jersey. "I'm talking to you." The young man refused to acknowledge her presence. Perhaps he was a vagrant, or a college kid selling magazine subscriptions. Privacy was rapidly becoming a rare commodity in this neck of the woods.

Holding her nose, she knelt beside the man and lightly pressed his wrist. Shit! Her heart pounding like a classic rock singer on acid, she moved her hand to the stranger's neck. "This isn't happening." Laurie felt in her shorts pocket. She'd left her cell phone inside the house.

"Stay," she ordered Rocky, placing him by her side. Praying the young man didn't have a communicable disease, Laura pinched his nose and breathed three quick breaths into his mouth. Then she started CPR. Thrust. Thrust. Thrust. Breath. Breath. Breath.

Outside, the hot, sticky air clung to her like a cloak. Her heart pounding like a furnace, she willed herself to stay on task. Thrust. Thrust. Thrust. Breath. Breath. Breath. After five minutes without progress, a wave of nausea hit. He was dead.

Laurie jumped to her feet. "Fire!" she screeched. That word, alone, should produce an immediate response. Then she laughed giddily. Up here, their nearest neighbors were a half acre away.

Laurie's breathing came fast and shallow now. Heat exhaustion coupled with shock at finding a young person dead on her front lawn jumbled her depleted brain cells. Check for water. Her fingers clumsily unscrewed the young man's canteen. Empty. Feverishly, she observed her dog licking the young man's hand.

Back in Chicago, another mom, nanny, or passerby would have heard her scream, and this lone figure would have a chance to survive. Scratch "might". They lived near De Paul University, where the police and fire departments responded without donning bulletproof vests.

Call nine-one-one. Like a drunk swaggering home from

Jennie Spallone

an all-night party, Laurie weaved across the yard and laboriously climbed the porch stairs. Rocky nipped at her shorts. She slammed the screen door on him.

Once inside the house, Laurie collapsed on the cool kitchen floor. Refusing to acknowledge her dehydration, she scanned the kitchen for a telephone. Neither her cell phone nor the cordless were in clear view. She crawled across the white tiled floor.

Laurie eyed the wall unit parallel to the pantry door. The one in a million times she'd actually replaced the cordless receiver in its holder. Dizzily, she reached up to knock the phone from the wall. The telephone unit crashed to the floor, grazing her right temple on its descent. Her eyes closed. Rocky's whimpering echoed through her ears. Darkness.